MY LIFE AS EMPEROR

MY LIFE AS EMPEROR

SU TONG

Translated by Howard Goldblatt

HYPERION EAST

NEW YORK

The translator is grateful to the National Endowment for the Arts for supporting this project and to Li-chun for her careful reading and superb suggestions.

Library of Congress Cataloging-in-Publication Data

Su, Tong
    [Wo de di wang sheng ya. English]
    My life as emperor / Su Tong ; translated by Howard Goldblatt.
       p. cm.
    ISBN 1-4013-6666-X
    1. Su, Tong—Translations into English.   I. Goldblatt, Howard.
  II. Title.

    PL2904.T86W6213   2005
    895.1'352—dc22

                         2004047484

FIRST EDITION

10 9 8 7 6 5 4 3 2 1

AUTHOR'S PREFACE

FOR YEARS I HAVE DREAMED of becoming a prolific writer and have devoted all my energies toward realizing that dream.

My Life as Emperor could be considered a pleasure cruise through my inner world. It has long been my wish to penetrate the millennia of China's history, to transform myself into an old customer at some teahouse on an ancient street in the midst of a kaleidoscopic world with its teeming masses, and soak up the passage of time with my eyes. I am fascinated by classical times; fascinated by palaces, concubines, and traditional music; fascinated by the lives of popular entertainers who roamed all over the landscape to perform for the people; fascinated by the intermingling of suffering and pleasure. I sigh over the turbulence, the ups and downs of life, and have come to feel that the perfect life is nothing more than the organic unity of fire and water, of venom and honey. This may be a naïve and illogical way to look at life, but it has been, without doubt, the stimulus for *My Life as Emperor*.

I hope my readers do not approach *My Life as Emperor* with the idea that it is historical fiction; that is why I have set the novel in no particular time. Identifying allusions and determining the accuracy of events places too great a burden on you and on me. The world of women and the palace intrigues that you will encounter in this novel are but a scary dream on a rainy night; the suffering and slaughter reflect my worries and fears for all the people in all worlds, and nothing more.

I have said that my writing and my life both emerge from a dream world. *My Life as Emperor* is a dream within that dream world.

MY LIFE AS EMPEROR

ONE

ONE

THE SUN, LIKE A BROKEN EGG YOLK, hung suspended behind the summit of Brass Rule Mountain on the frost-laden morning the Imperial Father passed away. I was reciting my morning lessons in front of Mountainside Hall at the time, and saw a flock of white herons sweep in low from the black tallow tree forest. They circled the vermilion corridors and black-tiled roof of Mountainside Hall for a moment, leaving in their wake cries of anguish and a fluttering of feathers. I saw that my wrist, the stone table, and my books were covered with gray, watery heron droppings.

Those are bird droppings, my young attendant said as he cleaned my wrist with a silk handkerchief. Autumn is deepening, and the Prince should return to the palace to study.

Autumn is deepening, and calamity will soon befall the Xie Empire, I said.

At that moment, palace attendants entered Mountainside Hall to report the Imperial demise. They carried the Black Panther banner of the Xie Empire and were dressed in white mourning clothes, their bereavement headbands fluttering slowly in the wind. Four attendants behind them entered with an empty palanquin, and I knew it was there to take me back to the palace, where I would stand with people I revered and others I despised to pay my last respects to the Imperial Father.

I despised the dead man, even though he was my father and had ruled the Xie Empire for thirty years. His bier now rested in Received Virtues Hall, surrounded by thousands of golden yellow daisies. Sentries ringing the casket looked like cypress trees in a graveyard. I stood on the top step of Received Virtues Hall, where my grandmother, Madame Huangfu, had led me by the hand. I did not want to be there, did not want to be so close to the bier. The sons of my stepmother stood behind me, and when I turned to look at them, I was confronted by what seemed to be looks of hostility. Why were they always looking at me like that? I did not like them. What I did like was the sight of the Imperial Father's bronze alchemy cauldron. It was what now filled my eyes. I saw it standing in solitude against the palace wall, a fire still burning beneath it, the elixir inside sending a shroud of steam into the air. A servant was feeding kindling into the pile of ashes. I knew it was Sun Xin, the aged attendant who often went up into the mountains behind Mountainside Hall to cut firewood. Tears rolled down his cheeks when he saw me, and he went down on one knee, pointing off toward the Xie Empire beyond the palace with his kindling knife. Autumn is deepening, and calamity will soon befall the Xie Empire, he said, as he had said so many times before.

Someone struck the large bell hanging in the vestibule, and the people in front of Received Virtues Hall fell as one to their knees. Sensing I should kneel along with them, I did. I heard the aged yet still robust voice of the Funerian break the stillness: The late Emperor has a testamentary edict. The Emperor has a testamentary edict. A testamentary edict. An edict.

When my grandmother, Madame Huangfu, knelt beside me, I saw a jade *ruyi*, the symbol of power, hanging from her girdle. Carved in the shape of a panther, it touched the step no more than a foot from me, and was a powerful distraction. Furtively I reached out and grabbed the *ruyi*, wanting to snap the strap from which it hung. But Madame Huangfu, aware of what I was doing, pushed away my hand and whispered somberly, Duanbai, listen to the edict.

Suddenly I heard the Funerian speak my name, the gravity of his voice deepening: Fifth son, Duanbai, succeeds to the throne as Emperor of Xie. A buzz erupted in front of Received Virtues Hall, and when I turned to look, I saw an expression of joyful satisfaction on the face of my mother, Madame Meng. The faces of the royal concubines varied: some were impassive, others wore looks of anger or despair. My four half brothers' faces paled. Duanxuan bit his lip, while Duanming muttered something and Duanwu showed the whites of his eyes. Duanwen alone pretended to be unaffected, but I knew that he felt worse than all the others, for his heart was set on ascending the throne, and he likely had never dreamed that the Imperial Father would hand it to me. Nor had I. Never in my life had I thought that one day I would suddenly find myself Emperor of Xie. The aged attendant in charge of alchemy, Sun Xin, had said, Autumn is deepening, and calamity will soon befall the Xie Empire. But what had been written in the Emperor's final edict? I was summoned up to the Imperial Father's gilded throne. I did not know what all of this meant. Still a child at fourteen, I could not figure out why I had been chosen to continue the Imperial line.

My grandmother, Madame Huangfu, motioned for me to go up and receive the edict, but I had barely taken a step when the aged Funerian walked up holding my father's Black Panther Imperial Crown in his hands. He walked so unsteadily, with a thin stream of sticky drool sliding down his chin, that I grew anxious for him. Rising slightly on my toes and stretching my neck, I waited for the Black Panther Imperial Crown to press down on my head. Bashful and embarrassed, I cast yet another glance at the alchemy cauldron up against the west palace wall, where Sun Xin sat dozing. The Imperial Father had no more use for elixirs, and yet a fire continued to burn beneath the cauldron. Why is it still burning? I asked, but no one heard me. The Black Panther Imperial Crown settled slowly yet heavily onto my head. My scalp felt cold.

All of a sudden, a chilling shout exploded from the crowd in front of Received Virtues Hall: Not him, he is not the new

Emperor of Xie. A woman burst from the line of imperial concubines. It was Madame Yang, the mother of Duanwen and
Duanwu. I watched as she threaded her way through the dumbstruck throng, mounted the steps, and made her way up to me,
where, like a crazed woman, she removed the Black Panther
Imperial Crown from my head and held it to her bosom. Listen to me, all of you, Madame Yang shrieked. The new Xie
Emperor is Duanwen, the eldest prince, not the fifth prince,
Duanbai. She drew a sheet of rice paper out from her clothing. I
have here a testamentary edict stamped with the late Emperor's
personal seal, she said. In it the Emperor bequeaths the throne
to Duanwen as the new Xie ruler. The edict naming Duanbai is
a forgery.

Another roar erupted in front of Received Virtues Hall. As I
watched Madame Yang clutch the Black Panther Imperial Crown
to her body, I said, Take it if you want it so badly. I certainly never
wanted it. In the turmoil I tried to slip away, but my grandmother,
Madame Huangfu, blocked my escape route. By then, sentries
had seized the crazed Madame Yang, one of them gagging her
with a funeral sash. I saw them carry her down the steps and bundle her out of the tumultuous Received Virtues Hall.

I was stunned, wondering why all this had happened.

On the sixth day of my reign, the Imperial Father's casket
was moved out of the palace. The vast funeral cortege surged to
the southern foot of Brass Rule Mountain, where the tombs of
generations of Xie rulers were located, as well as the grave of

my younger brother, Duanxian, who had died in infancy. It was during that procession that I laid eyes on the face of the Imperial Father for the last time. A ruler who had once held sway over heaven and earth, a proud and gallant, carefree and dashing Emperor, now lay in his camphor casket like a shrunken, decomposing log. The thought of death horrified me. I had always assumed that the Imperial Father would live forever, but there was no denying that he was dead now. I saw there with him in the casket a variety of funerary objects— some made of gold, others fashioned from silver, jade, and agate, and all sorts of gems. There were many that I coveted, including a short bronze sword with inlaid rubies, and I had to hold back from reaching in to retrieve it for myself, knowing I was forbidden from removing any of the Imperial Father's funerary objects.

The procession of chariots halted in the marshy land at the entrance to the tombs to await retainers conveying red caskets containing the imperial concubines, who were to be buried with the Imperial Father. From where I sat on horseback, I counted seven in all. I was told that the women had been ordered to hang themselves with white silk in the early morning hours. Now their red caskets were arriving, to be arrayed auspiciously around the Imperial Father's tomb, like the Big Dipper encircling the moon. I was also told that Madame Yang had been commanded to commit suicide along with the others, but had refused, running barefoot through the palace, only to be caught by three retainers, who had looped a piece of white silk around her neck and throttled her.

After the seven red caskets were in place, a thumping sound emerged from inside one of them, causing everyone within earshot to go pale with fear. I watched as the lid slowly rose and Madame Yang sat up in her casket. Her disheveled hair was flecked with sawdust and red sand, her face white as paper. Sapped of energy, she could no longer shout as she had done only days before, and I watched as, for the last time, she waved the edict with the imperial seal to the crowd assembled around her. Retainers rushed up and filled the casket with dirt before nailing the lid shut. I counted: They drove nineteen long nails into the lid.

Everything I knew about the Xie Empire I learned from the Buddhist monk Juekong, whose name meant Enlightened Void. Chosen by the Imperial Father as my mentor, Juekong was a man of profound learning, a master of the martial arts, and an adept at music, chess, calligraphy, and painting. During my days of exhausting study in the cold confines of Mountainside Hall, Juekong never strayed far from my side, always ready to instruct me in the two-hundred-year history and nine-hundred-li territory of the Xie Empire, and to relate incidents in the lives of rulers and of generals who had died in battle. He chronicled the totality of mountains and rivers within our borders, and told me that our subjects spent their days planting millet, hunting game, and fishing.

Once when I was eight, I was accosted by little white demons. Whenever the lamps were lit, they hopped onto my desk, even onto the squares of my chessboard, and leaped about, scaring me out of my wits. Juekong ran over as soon as he heard my cries, drew his sword, and drove them away. And so, from my eighth year on, I revered Juekong, my mentor.

I summoned Juekong to the palace from Mountainside Hall. As he knelt before me, looking wretched and desolate, a dog-eared copy of *The Analects* in his hand, I noticed that there were holes in his cassock and that his straw sandals were coated with dark mud.

Why has the mentor entered my presence with a copy of *The Analects*? I asked.

Your Majesty has not finished studying it. I made a mark where we left off and have brought it with me so that he can finish it, Juekong said.

I am now the Xie Emperor. Why burden me with more study?

If the Xie Emperor does not continue his studies, this poor monk must return to a life of meditation in Bitter Bamboo Monastery.

You may not return, I shouted abruptly as I took *The Analects* from Juekong's hand and flung it onto the imperial bed. I will not permit you to leave me, I said. If you go, who will drive away the demons? Those little white demons have grown up, and they will squirm inside my bed curtain.

I spotted two little serving girls stifling giggles with their hands over their mouths. Incensed that they were laughing at my fear, I pulled a lit candle out of a candelabra and flung it into the face of one of them. Stop that laughing, I shrieked. I'll send the next one who laughs to the Imperial Tombs to be buried alive.

. . .

Chrysanthemums in the Imperial Garden bloomed riotously in the autumn breezes, and everywhere I looked my eyes were filled with a yellow that emitted the repellent smell of death. I had given an order for the gardeners to root out every last chrysanthemum in the Imperial Garden, which they had fawningly agreed to do. But then they had gone behind my back and reported to my grandmother, Madame Huangfu. I later learned that it was she who had ordered the planting of chrysanthemums everywhere in the Imperial Garden. They were her favorite flower, in part because she insisted that their unique fragrance had a soothing effect on her chronic light-headedness. My mother, Madame Meng, once told me privately that in the autumn, Madame Huangfu feasted on chrysanthemums, ordering the imperial chefs to prepare them both as a cold dish and a hot soup, closely guarded recipes to keep her healthy and prolong her life. But I was not won over. Chrysanthemums never failed to remind me of cold, stiff corpses, and swallowing the petals of chrysanthemums was virtually the same as eating the flesh of the dead, a nauseating thought.

The tower bell rang out when I held an audience with my chief ministers and officials to hand down opinions on imperial memorials. My grandmother, Madame Huangfu, and the Empress Dowager, Madame Meng, sat on either side of the throne. My opinions always derived from them, either by a veiled look or a whispered comment. That is how I preferred it. Even though I was of sufficient age and knowledge to excuse the two women from administering state affairs from behind the scenes, I chose not to so that I could avoid having to watch my every word and overtax my brain.

I sat there holding a cricket jar on my knee. The black-winged cricket inside would, from time to time, shatter the suffocating decorum by calling out crisply. I loved crickets, but I was growing anxious as autumn chills deepened, afraid that palace servants would find it increasingly difficult to catch any of the ferocious, black-winged crickets on the mountain.

I did not like my ministers or officials, who approached the vermilion steps to the throne on trembling legs to report on the status of provisions for our frontier armies or to offer ideas on land distribution south of the mountains. Not until they stopped talking and Madame Huangfu raised her purple sandalwood longevity cane was I free to bring the audience to an end. However impatient I grew, I was stuck. The monk Juekong once told me that the life of an emperor is spent amid gossip, complaints, and rumors.

In the presence of the ministers, Madame Huangfu and Madame Meng maintained a dignified and genteel demeanor. The two women appeared perfectly matched and were politically shrewd, but after the audiences ended, they were invariably embroiled in heated arguments with each other, lips on the attack, tongues rapier-sharp. On one occasion, the ministers had barely left Abundant Hearts Hall, my throne room, when Madame Huangfu slapped Madame Meng. I was aghast, and could only watch as Madame Meng held her cheek and ran behind the curtain, where she broke down and cried. I followed and heard her say between sobs, Damn that old crone, the sooner she dies the better.

I stood there gazing at a face twisted by humiliation and loathing, a beautiful face despite the gnashing of teeth. From my earliest memory, that singular look was a permanent, unchanging expression on my mother's face. Always a suspicious, apprehensive woman, she was sure that her son, my brother Duanxian, had been poisoned, and that the likely suspect was the late Emperor's favorite concubine, Dainiang, who subsequently paid for her alleged cruel deed with the loss of all ten fingers. After that she was thrown into the filthy Cold Palace, where, I well knew, concubines who had fallen out of favor lived out their days in misery.

I once sneaked over to the Cold Palace to see what Dainiang's fingerless hands looked like. Located at the rear of the palace grounds, the area was threateningly cold; all sides of the courtyard were overgrown with moss and draped with cobwebs. Peeking through a window, I spotted Dainiang, who lay in a lethargic sleep on a bed of straw, next to which stood a cracked chamber pot, from which rose a sour stench that hung in the air. I watched as Dainiang rolled over, exposing one of her hands to me; it hung limply over the side of the straw bed, caught in a beam of sunlight that filtered in through the window. Resembling a blackened flat cake coated with putrid dried blood, it had attracted a swarm of flies, which perched fearlessly on the crippled limb.

I could not see Dainiang's face, and since palace women were as plentiful as the clouds, I did not even know which concubine she was. Someone told me that she had played the balloon guitar like a dream. But the thought occurred to me that no one, however talented, could ever again strum a balloon guitar without fingers. I wondered if, on the holidays and special occasions that followed, some other lovely concubine would ever stroll through the gardens with a balloon guitar, playing beautiful music, as if inspired by immortals. I did not doubt for a moment that Dainiang had plotted with one of the imperial chefs to place arsenic in the sweetened porridge of my brother, Duanxian. And yet I had my suspicions as to why her fingers had been cut off. So I asked my mother, Madame Meng, who sighed before saying, I hated those hands of hers. But even that answer did not satisfy me, so I took my question to my mentor, Juekong, who said, That is easy to answer. Dainiang's fingers could produce beautiful music on the balloon guitar, and Madame Meng's cannot.

Up to the time I ascended the throne, eleven discarded concubines had been confined to the Cold Palace in the grove of parasol trees. At night, the sound of their weeping floated over to swirl around my ears. That late-night weeping annoyed me terribly, but there was no way to still it, since the inhabitants, women with strange temperaments, were beyond caring about life or death. During the days, they covered their heads and slept, but after nightfall, they came to life and kept the residents of the palace awake with their heartrending weeps and wails. It drove me mad, but I couldn't stop the noise by having servants stuff rags in their mouths, since the Cold Palace was off-limits to just about everyone. My mentor, Juekong, advised me to accept the women's weeping as one of the palace night sounds. In his view, the weeping was no different from the clang of the night watchman's brass gong as he made his rounds outside the palace walls. The watchman's duty was to announce the passage of time through the night with his gong, while the discarded concubines in the Cold Palace greeted the arrival of dawn with their weeping. You are the Xie Emperor, the monk Juekong said to me. You must learn to be tolerant.

I found Juekong's counsel incomprehensible. I was the Xie Emperor, why must *I* learn to be tolerant? In fact, quite the opposite: I possessed the power to obliterate anything that annoyed me, including sounds of weeping that came in the night from the grove of parasol trees. So one day I summoned the Imperial Executioner and asked if there were some way to keep those women from crying. Only if you cut out their tongues, he said. I asked if they would die from having their tongues cut out. Not if it's done properly, he replied. Then do it. I don't ever want to hear those demonic wails and wolfish howls again.

My command was carried out in utmost secrecy; no one but the Imperial Executioner and I knew of it. Afterward, he brought a bloody paper packet to me. Their days of weeping are over, he said as he slowly unwrapped the packet. I looked down to see what it held. The tongues from those weepy concubines looked like salted pigs' tongues, which were quite a delicacy. As I rewarded the executioner with pieces of silver, I ordered him not to tell Madame Huangfu under any circumstances what he'd done. If she asked, he was to say they had carelessly bitten their own tongues off.

I was restless all that night. No sounds emerged from the Cold Palace, as promised. In fact, throughout the palace, only the soughing of autumn winds, the rustling of falling leaves, and the occasional clang of the night watchman's gong broke the deathly silence of night. But I tossed and turned on the imperial bed, visited by thoughts of the tongues I'd ordered the executioner to take from those pitiful women, and I grew afraid. No longer were there any sounds to disturb my rest, and yet I could not sleep. The serving girls at the foot of my bed, sensing my restlessness, asked, Does Your Majesty wish to relieve himself? I shook my head and gazed out the window at the flickering lantern light and the royal blue sky, images of the sad women in the Cold Palace who could no longer cry running through my mind. Why is it so quiet? I asked the serving girls. It's so quiet I can't sleep. Bring me my cricket jar.

One of the serving girls returned with my darling little cricket cage, and for many nights after that I fell asleep listening to the crisp cries of black-winged crickets. But threads of melancholy were always present, for once autumn had passed and the first snow of winter fell, my pet crickets would die off. How would I pass the long nights when that happened?

I began to grow anxious and fearful over the evil I'd had the Imperial Executioner commit in my name. I detected no sign that either Madame Huangfu or the chief ministers were aware of what had happened, so one day, following the imperial audience, I asked Madame Huangfu if she had been to the Cold Palace recently, and then divulged to her that all the women confined there had bitten off their tongues. She gazed long and lovingly at me before saying with a sigh, No wonder it's been so deathly quiet the past few nights. I haven't been able to sleep a wink. Did you enjoy hearing those women weep late at night, Grandmother? I asked. With an ambiguous smile she said, Their tongues have been cut out, and that is the end of it. But under no circumstances are you to let word of that travel beyond the palace walls. I have already warned that anyone who leaks word of this will lose *his* tongue.

In that instant the stone in my heart fell away. My grandmother would have inflicted the same form of punishment as I, and that knowledge brought me comfort tinged with uncertainty. Apparently, I had done nothing wrong. In the eyes of Madame Huangfu, it was all right to cut out the tongues of the eleven women confined to the Cold Palace.

The bronze alchemy cauldron in which immortality pills were refined remained standing in a corner of the hall. Though the cinders beneath it were now cold, the bronze, which had changed color from the touch of human fingers, was still hot. The late Emperor had taken the pills the year round, after spending a great deal of gold to bring an alchemist from the distant fairy isle of Penglai. And yet, the Penglai elixir had lacked the power to prolong the fragile and dissolute life of the late Emperor. The alchemist bolted from the palace the night before the late Emperor expired, proof that the elixir, touted as a panacea for all ills and a guarantee of immortality, was mere quackery.

The palace attendant who tended the fire, Sun Xin, was a graying old man. I watched him pace in front of the alchemy cauldron as autumn winds swept past, and then stop to pick up splinters of kindling and cold cinders. Each time I passed by, he crawled up on his knees, holding ashes in the palms of his hands, and said, The fire is out, and calamity will soon befall the Xie Empire.

Like everyone else, I knew that old Sun Xin was a madman. Others wanted to drive him out of the palace, but I stopped them. For not only was I fond of the man, I was equally fond of repeating his inauspicious incantation. I stared at the refining ashes in his hands for a long time. Then I said, The fire is out, and calamity will soon befall the Xie Empire.

Any time I was surrounded by palace officials and civil servants, fawning, smiling creatures all of them, I thought of Sun Xin, with his sad, teary face, and would say to those around me, What is the meaning of all those idiotic smiles? The fire is out, and calamity will soon befall the Xie Empire.

In the autumn, our hunting grounds turned deserted and desolate; underbrush and wild grasses grew knee-high. Fires set to drive the game down the mountain toward us drifted in and out of view. The valley below Brass Rule Mountain reeked with the smell of burned forest, and as jackrabbits, roe deer, and mountain harts ran for their lives through the smoky valley, I heard the hum of hunters' arrows and whoops of delight rise and fall.

I loved the annual encirclement hunts. Nearly all the men in the imperial family took part in that year's hunt, forming vast ranks of riders spurring on their horses, bows and arrows at the ready. My half brothers followed closely behind my roan-colored pony. When I turned to look at Third Prince Duanwu, and his brother, First Prince Duanwen, I saw what might have been gloomy looks but could have been swaggering smirks. I also saw the frail Second Prince, Duanxuan, and the slow-witted Fourth Prince, Duanming, following like tagalongs. Included in the entourage were my mentor, the monk Juekong, and a formation of Imperial Guards in purple uniforms.

The first attempt on my life as Emperor occurred during that hunt. I recall seeing a brown mountain hart cross in front of me, its beautiful coat glistening in the underbrush. As I spurred my pony ahead, I heard Juekong call out from behind, Watch out—behind you—assassin's arrow. I spun around just in time to see a poison-tipped arrow coming at me. It barely missed my white-plumed helmet, and in that split second, everyone around me broke out in a cold sweat.

I was as frightened as anyone. Spurring his horse on, Juekong galloped up and swept me off my mount onto his. Still trembling with fear, I removed my helmet and discovered that the arrow had snapped the snowy white goose feather in two. Who shot that arrow? I asked Juekong. Who wants to see me dead? Rather than answer immediately, he scanned the tree-lined mountainside. Your enemy, he said at last. Who is my enemy? I asked. With a smile, he said, See for yourself. Whoever is hiding farthest from you is your enemy.

At that moment I realized that my four half brothers were nowhere to be seen, and I knew they had taken cover behind a stand of trees somewhere. First Prince Duanwen was the likely suspect, since among the five brothers he was the most accomplished archer, and only a sinister individual like him was capable of hatching such a seamless assassination plot.

Duanwen, a roebuck slung over his shoulder, was the first to gallop back to camp after the horn was sounded to call the hunters in. Five or six wild rabbits and a string of pheasants hung over the back of his horse. His quiver was stained with the black blood of his kills. Drops of blood also spattered his white robe. The sight of his arrogant smirk as he sat proudly astride his horse had a strange effect on me. Maybe, I thought, the now dead and buried Madame Yang had spoken the truth after all. Duanwen was the spitting image of the late Imperial Father; he looked like the new Xie Emperor. With me there was no resemblance.

Did Your Majesty have a successful hunt? the still mounted, unruffled Duanwen asked coolly. Why is there no game on the back of Your Majesty's horse?

I was nearly assassinated, I said. Do you know who shot an arrow at me?

I do not. I see Your Majesty was not injured, and since I am an excellent archer, I am certain it could not have been my arrow. Duanwen bowed slightly at the waist, but the arrogant smirk remained.

Then it must have been Duanwu. I'll not spare whoever

tried to kill me, I said through clenched teeth before cracking my whip and riding off on my pony. Winds sobbed in my ears, the scrub brush snapped and crackled under the galloping hooves. Like autumnal Brass Rule Mountain itself, there was a rawness in my heart as I brooded over the assassin's arrow. Unnerved and furious, I resolved to inflict the punishment Madame Meng had used on Dainiang—I would order the Imperial Executioner to cut off the fingers of Duanwen and Duanwu, for I wanted to never again witness their displays of prowess in archery.

The incident during the hunt caused an uproar at the palace. My mother, Madame Meng, wept openly at the next day's morning audience and pleaded with Madame Huangfu and the assembled ministers to uphold justice by punishing Duanwen and Duanwu. Madame Huangfu, with her vast experience and accumulated knowledge, maintained stately airs as she counseled Madame Meng, I have seen such things happen before, and there is no cause for alarm. Do not condemn Duanwen and Duanwu on speculation alone. Leave it to me to determine the identity of the would-be assassin. There will be time to punish the culprit once the tide has ebbed and the rocks are uncovered. But Madame Meng, convinced that Madame Huangfu had always been partial to Duanwen and Duanwu, turned a deaf ear to this counsel and insisted upon having the two brothers summoned to Abundant Hearts Hall for questioning. Madame Huangfu reminded her that personal matters had no place in official court business. I watched as the official who was supposed to give the order wrestled with his dilemma in front of the vermilion steps, the fear in his eyes proof that he did not know what to do. The scene struck me as quite funny, and I had to giggle. As the stalemate dragged on, Madame Huangfu abruptly dropped her kindly demeanor and raised her purple sandalwood longevity cane as a sign for the ministers to retire. On their way out, I watched as she described an arc in the air with her cane and brought it down hard on Madame Meng's coiffure. The screech that tore from the mouth of Madame Meng was followed by a coarse, filthy, low-class epithet one heard only in the marketplace.

I was staggered. Ministers leaving the hall stopped and turned to see what had happened. Madame Huangfu was shaking with anger. She walked up to Madame Meng and poked her in the mouth with the tip of her longevity cane. What did you say? she demanded. I must have been blind to have permitted a lowly bean curd peddler's daughter to one day become Empress Dowager. A woman like you can never change. How can anyone who spews such filth have the audacity to sit in Abundant Hearts Hall?

Madame Meng began to cry as Madame Huangfu's cane moved freely all around her lips. I won't curse anymore, she said between sobs. Go ahead with your plots against Duanbai, since you won't rest until you see me dead.

Duanbai is not your son, he is the ruler of the Xie Empire, Madame Huangfu reproached her in a fearful voice. If you don't stop weeping and wailing and begin to show a little decorum, I shall send you back to that bean curd shop you came from. Making bean curd is what you're suited for, not being Empress Dowager of Xie.

The more I listened to them quarrel, the more tedious it all seemed, so I slipped away when no one was looking. But I had barely made it to a tall cassia tree when a uniformed soldier ran up to me, fell to his knees, and said, Barbarians have broken through our defenses. General Zheng on the western front has sent an urgent communiqué for Your Majesty. He held a dispatch with three feathers in his hand. I want nothing to do with it. Take it to Madame Huangfu, I said as I jumped up and snapped off a fragrant flower-laden branch of the cassia tree, with which I poked the kneeling soldier in the rear. I am not interested in your affairs, I remarked as I walked off. You give me a headache the way you're always bringing me this and that. You say the barbarians have broken through our defenses? Well, drive them back to where they came from. How hard can that be?

I strolled aimlessly around the palace, eventually stopping in front of the late Emperor's alchemy cauldron. The bronze surface glistened under the rays of the setting sun, and I thought I saw a brown pellet swirling amid the boiling liquid. I sensed a strange medicinal odor as gusts of steamy air emerged from a cauldron whose fires had long since been extinguished. My red python imperial robe was quickly drenched with sweat—the late Emperor's alchemy cauldron had always made me perspire copiously. As I lashed the surface of the spinning cauldron with the cassia branch, the aged attendant Sun Xin stepped out from behind, like a ghost, startling me by his sudden appearance. The sadness was still on his face, the madness still in his eyes. He held a broken arrow out to me.

Where did you get that? I asked, caught by surprise.

On Brass Rule Mountain. The encirclement hunt. He pointed to the northwest. His chapped lips quivered like leaves as he said, It is a poison arrow.

As I thought back to what had happened during the hunt, depression set in. The would-be assassin clearly enjoyed the protection of Madame Huangfu, my grandmother, while the poison arrow had fallen into the hands of the old madman Sun Xin. I knew neither how he had found it nor why he wanted to present it to me.

Throw that away, I said to Sun Xin. I don't want it. I know who shot it.

An assassin's arrow has been shot, and calamity will soon befall the Xie Empire. Sun Xin casually threw the broken arrow away. Once again, murky tears filled his eyes.

Sun Xin fascinated me. I found the way he worried over nearly everything fresh and interesting. I liked the old madman more than any of the other servants and slaves in the palace, an attitude over which both my grandmother, Madame Huangfu, and the Empress Dowager, Madame Meng, had voiced displeasure. But from childhood I'd forged a special bond with Sun Xin, often dragging him outside to play hopscotch.

Don't cry. I took out a handkerchief to wipe his cheeks and

took his hands in mine. Let's play hopscotch. It's been a long time since we did that.

Play hopscotch. Calamity will soon befall the Xie Empire. This he muttered as he raised his left knee and hopped through the squares—one, two, three.

I was unable to carry out my plan to punish Duanwen and Duanwu, since none of the executioners dared raise a hand against them. A few days had passed when I saw the two of them walking hand in hand past Abundant Hearts Hall, and that sight depressed me even further. I knew that my grandmother had successfully interceded on their behalf, and that made me very unhappy with her. Since her word was law, I figured, why not let her just take over the Xie throne?

Sensing that something was bothering me, Madame Huangfu summoned me to her bedside in Splendor Hall, where she silently scrutinized me. She looked terribly old and frail without her rouge and powder, and the thought occurred to me that Madame Huangfu would soon be taking her place in the Imperial Tombs at the foot of Brass Rule Mountain.

Why such a long face, Duanbai? she asked, taking my hand. Did one of your pet crickets die?

Why should I be Emperor of Xie, since I always have to do what you say? I blurted out. Not knowing what else to say, I watched as she jerked into a sitting position, a look of astonished displeasure on her face. Instinctively, I backed away.

Who told you to come here and say that? Was it Madame

Meng or was it that mentor of yours, Juekong? She bore down on me with her fearful questions as she reached for her cane beside the bed. I took another step backward, afraid she was going to hit me on the head with her cane. But she didn't. Instead, she waved it in the air for a moment before bringing it down on the head of one of the serving girls. What are you doing, hanging around here? she said. Get out.

I watched as the little girl stepped red-eyed out beyond the screen, and I couldn't keep from bursting into tears. Duanwen shot an arrow at me during the encirclement hunt, I sobbed, but you won't punish him for that. If not for Juekong's warning, they would have killed me.

I've already punished them. I hit all four of your brothers three times with my cane. Isn't that punishment enough?

No, I shouted. I want Duanwen and Duanwu's fingers cut off so they'll never be able to shoot another arrow.

You're a foolish little boy. Madame Huangfu pulled me over to sit on her bed and lightly stroked my ears. A gentle smile floated back onto the corners of her mouth. Duanbai, the first requirement of a ruler is to be merciful. One mustn't be vicious or cruel. This isn't the first time I've told you that. Why do you keep forgetting? And there's more. Duanwen and the others are descendants of the Xie imperial family, the Emperor's heirs. How could you face the spirits of your ancestors if you had their fingers cut off? Or, for that matter, face the palace officials and the rest of your subjects?

But didn't they cut off Dainiang's fingers over a poisoning? I argued.

That's different. Dainiang was a lowly menial, but Duanwen and his brothers are of imperial blood, my own cherished grandsons. They will not lose their fingers while I am alive.

Sitting on my grandmother's bed, my head bowed low, I detected the smells of musk and japonica that clung to her robes. A lovely, crystal-clear jade *ruyi* hung from her dragon and phoenix girdle, and it was all I could do to keep from taking it and sticking it in my own little pouch. If only I'd had the nerve.

Duanbai, are you aware that in the Xie court it's as easy to dethrone an emperor as it is to enthrone one? Don't ever forget that.

I had no trouble comprehending this final comment from my grandmother. I strode out of Splendor Hall and, as I passed through the chrysanthemum garden, spit savagely at the wretched flowers. Damn that old crone, the sooner she dies the better, I cursed under my breath. Something I'd learned from the Empress Dowager, Madame Meng. But not even that curse could purge my anger, so I jumped into Madame Huangfu's beloved garden and stomped on some of the yellow flowers. When I looked up, there standing beneath the eaves was the little serving girl my grandmother had hit, a look of utter bewilderment on her face. A blood blister had risen on her forehead where the longevity cane had hit her. I was reminded of Madame Huangfu's advice about being merciful, which now seemed laughable. I thought back to when I was studying in Mountainside Hall, and one of the proverbs I'd had to commit to memory: Deeds that do not match one's words constitute a human failing. As I saw it, the proof of that was found in the person of Madame Huangfu.

Just then Duanwen and Duanwu walked in through Splendor Hall's moon gate. I jumped out of the flower garden and blocked their way. The surprised looks on their faces showed that I had caught them off guard.

What are you doing here? I demanded abusively.

We're here to pay our respects to Grandmother, Duanwen said, neither haughty nor humble.

Why have you never come to pay your respects to me? I brushed their jaws with a chrysanthemum twig.

Duanwen said nothing. But Duanwu glared at me, so I shoved him, sending him stumbling backward. As soon as he caught his balance, he fixed his tiny eyes on me again in a savage glare. I reached down, plucked a chrysanthemum, and flung it in his face. If you glare at me one more time, I said, I'll have your eyes gouged out.

Duanwu turned his head, but didn't budge from the spot. He wouldn't dare keep glaring at me. Duanwen, who was standing beside me, had paled, and I saw tears glisten in his eyes. His thin, girlish lips were pinched shut, and nearly dripping red.

I didn't do anything to you, what do you have to be gloomy about? I turned and said to Duanwen provocatively. We'll see if you have the nerve to shoot another arrow at me. I'll be waiting.

Still silent, he took Duanwu by the hand and walked around me, hurrying over to Splendor Hall, where, I discovered, Madame Huangfu was standing in the corridor; she had probably witnessed the entire incident. Longevity cane in hand, she wore an indifferent, serene look, and it was impossible to tell if she approved or disapproved of my behavior. But I was too satisfied with the way I'd vented my anger to worry about that.

TWO

By the time I ascended the Xie throne, only a few eunuchs remained at court. That was because my father despised eunuchs and, over time, had driven them all away. He had then sent emissaries out among the people to search for beautiful girls, who were brought into the palace, until it became a place where feminine beauty reigned. He wallowed in carnal pleasures, giving himself over to the womanly charms he so dearly loved, forever frolicking in bed. According to my mentor, the Buddhist monk Juekong, all that dissolution was the main cause of the Emperor's early demise.

One winter, I recall, a dozen or so eunuchs lay dead at the base of the red wall in front of the palace. They had obviously died of hunger and exposure to the elements, waiting for the Emperor to summon them back inside. They had persevered there by the wall the entire winter, until a violent snowstorm had sapped their consciousness and they had died in each other's arms. For years I was baffled by the choice they had made, wondering why, instead of retiring to the countryside to plant crops or raise silkworms, they had chosen to die needlessly in front of Xie Palace. When I asked Juekong, he urged me to put those men out of my mind. They are a pathetic lot, he said, tragic figures, but loathsome men.

Juekong was the source of my deep aversion to eunuchs, and, from childhood on, I never let a single one of them wait on me. Naturally, I am talking only about the period before I ascended to the throne. So I was caught completely unawares by the epochal change wrought by Madame Huangfu one year, when she accepted three hundred young eunuchs sent from three southern districts and made plans to drive out countless frail, sickly, or disobedient palace girls. I was even more surprised to find the name of my mentor, the monk Juekong, on Madame Huangfu's list of those to be expelled.

I had not been told of Juekong's imminent expulsion. On that morning, as I sat in Abundant Hearts Hall accepting the good wishes of the newly arrived eunuchs, I looked out over the prostrated bodies of three hundred boys my age, a sea of black heads, and was struck by how comical a sight it was. But Madame Huangfu and Madame Meng were seated beside me, and I knew they would disapprove if I laughed out loud, so I covered my mouth and lowered my head. Then when I looked up, I spotted someone kneeling alone behind the rows of boys, and recognized him as my mentor, the monk Juekong. No longer dressed in his scholar's cap or sash, he was wearing a black Buddhist cassock as he knelt stiffly on the floor. I did not know what he was doing. I jumped down off of the throne, but was stopped by Madame Huangfu, who pressed the tip of her longevity cane on my foot, making it impossible for me to move.

Juekong is no longer your mentor, she said. Since he must quit the palace, he is conveying his farewell by prostrating himself before you. You may not leave your place at this moment.

Why? Why are you making him leave the palace? I demanded.

You are now fourteen years old and no longer in need of a mentor. A ruler requires a prime minister, not a bald-headed monk.

He is not a monk, he is the mentor my father engaged for me, and I want him to remain by my side. I shook my head fiercely. I don't want any of those eunuchs, I want my mentor, Juekong.

But I cannot permit him to stay here with you. He has already turned you into an eccentric boy, and is well on his way to turning you into an eccentric Xie Emperor. Madame Huangfu let up the pressure from her cane and tapped it several times on the floor. Besides, she said in a gentler tone, I am not driving him out of the palace. I went to seek his opinion, and he told me he wanted to leave the palace, that he did not want to be your mentor any longer.

No, I screamed wildly as I ran down the steps, charged past the three hundred prostrating young eunuchs—all of whom looked up at me with reverence as I went by—and threw my arms around Juekong. I cried like a baby. Those up at the front of Abundant Hearts Hall were stunned by this unexpected development. The sound of my weeping cut through the stillness all around me.

Stop crying. The Xie Emperor mustn't cry in front of his ministers or subjects. Juekong lifted up a corner of his cassock and dried my tears. The smile on his face was as serene and beatific as ever; his knees remained on the floor. I watched as he took the copy of *The Analects* out of his sleeve. You have not yet read this all the way through, he said. That is my only regret as I leave the palace.

I don't want to read anything. I want you to stay.

You are, after all, still a child. Juekong sighed softly. His gaze, like a flaming candle, settled briefly on my forehead before skimming across my Black Panther Imperial Crown. Child, he said in a melancholy voice, it is your good fortune to have become Emperor in your youth, but it is your misfortune as well. His hand shook as he handed me the book. Then he stood up and dusted off his cassock with his sleeves. I knew that he was about to leave, and that I was powerless to stop him.

Where will you go? I shouted at his retreating back.

To Bitter Bamboo Monastery. He halted, placed his palms together, and gazed up at the heavens. I barely heard his final words to me. Bitter Bamboo Monastery is in the Bitter Bamboo Forest. The Bitter Bamboo Forest is on Bitter Bamboo Mountain.

My face was awash in tears. I knew that to act as I had under such circumstances was a terrible breach of decorum, but as Emperor, I felt I could do whatever I wanted, including cry.

Who was Madame Huangfu to say I couldn't? So I turned and went back up to the front of the hall, drying my tears as I walked between the two throngs of eunuchs, still prostrate, still looking like wooden stumps, but doing their best to sneak looks at my wet face. I kicked the raised backsides of those on the end along the way, to get even with Madame Huangfu, and was rewarded by muffled moans. As I kicked my way back up to the throne, I couldn't help noticing how incredibly soft, and incredibly disgusting, those backsides were.

It rained that night, following Juekong's departure from the palace, pearls of water falling gently from the sky as I leaned against a windowsill lost in thought. Light from the palace lanterns swayed and flickered in the wet breezes, rustling dead branches and the yellowed leaves of banana trees and chrysanthemums in the courtyard. Rainy nights like that caused many wet objects to begin to rot. The sound of a page boy intoning a passage from *The Analects* drifted through the patter of rain, like a flying insect, and I plugged my ears to keep it out. I could not stop thinking about my mentor, the Buddhist monk Juekong, about his wisdom and unique conversational manner, about his thin yet transcendent face, and about the last thing he said before leaving me. I grew sadder by the minute, not knowing why they had driven my beloved Juekong away.

Where is Bitter Bamboo Monastery? I asked the page boy, interrupting his recitation.

Far away. Somewhere in the empire of Wan, amid lofty ridges and towering mountains, I think.

How far exactly? How many days on a horse-drawn cart?

I am not sure. Is Your Majesty planning to go there?

I am just curious. I would like to go everywhere, but cannot go anywhere. Madame Huangfu won't even let me step out of the palace.

I had a nightmare that rainy night. The same little white demons I'd seen when I was awake were now standing on all four sides of my bed, raising a sad wail, and while they had bodies like rag dolls, their faces were those of people in the palace. One looked like Madame Yang, who had been buried alive, another was Dainiang, who had lost first her fingers then her tongue to the knife. I awoke covered in clammy sweat, and could hear that the rain was still falling. To my horror, I also discovered drifting traces of the little white demons on the embroidered quilt, and banged the side of the bed. The serving girls sleeping on the floor next to me gathered round my bed and exchanged puzzled looks. One of them held up my chamber pot.

I don't have to pee. But get these little demons off my bed, I shouted at them as I struck out with both hands. Don't stand there like idiots. Hurry up and get rid of them.

There are no little demons, Your Majesty, one of the girls said. It is just moonbeams.

They are shadows cast by the lanterns, Your Majesty, another said.

You're all blind, blind and stupid. Can't you see those little white demons jumping up and down on my legs? I struggled off the bed. Go get Juekong for me, I said, and hurry. He'll know how to get rid of them for me.

Your Majesty, Juekong left the palace today, the girls said faintheartedly. They still could not see the demons on my bed.

All of a sudden my head cleared, and I recalled that as the rain fell, the monk Juekong was trudging along the road leading to Bitter Bamboo Monastery in the empire of Wan, and would no longer be around to drive terrifying ghosts and demons out of my life. Juekong was gone, and calamity will soon befall the Xie Empire. That strange prophecy from the mouth of the mad-man Sun Xin popped into my head, and I was overcome by grief and indignation. The sleepy, vacant looks on the faces of the serv-ing girls around my bed disgusted me, so I wrenched the chamber pot out of one of the girls' hands and flung it to the floor. The sharp crack of broken ceramic sliced cleanly through the rainy night as the girls fell to their knees in utter fright.

The chamber pot is shattered, and calamity will soon befall the Xie Empire, I announced the way the old madman Sun Xin had done it. I saw little white demons, and calamity will soon befall the Xie Empire.

In order to avoid the demons' harassment, I took the unprec-edented step of having two serving girls sleep with me, one on each side, and two more strum zithers and sing softly at the foot of the bed. Once the little white demons had slipped away, the rain stopped falling, leaving behind only the water dripping weakly off of the eaves onto the banana leaves. The fragrance of the girls lying beside me merged with the stench of rotting vege-tation and dying insects beyond the window, eternal smells in the Xie Empire. It was but one night during the early years of my life as Emperor.

. . .

My first nocturnal emission occurred during another of my bizarre dreams. The dream was about Dainiang, the onetime concubine who had been exiled to the Cold Palace. She was sitting amid a bed of chrysanthemums, strumming her balloon guitar and singing a lovely song. But all of a sudden, her fingers fell softly to the ground, like ten flower petals. She held up her now fingerless hands and glided toward me on tiny bound feet, the balloon guitar that was now strung over her back bumping gently against her snow-white naked buttocks with each airy step. A seductive smile spread across the sunny countenance of her face. Dainiang, I shouted, I forbid you from smiling like that. But that only led to an even more bewitching smile that took my breath away. I shouted again. Dainiang, don't you dare come any closer. But she reached out to me anyway, blood dripping from her stumpy hand, wanton yet tender, as it touched that sacred part of my lower body, a feeling like fingers strumming the strings of a balloon guitar. I heard music that came down from the heavens and I was wracked with spasms. I still recall how a moan of joy and shock escaped from my lips.

When morning came, I changed out of my wet underwear, and when I saw the stains, I asked the serving girls who slept by my bed if they knew what they were. They merely stared at my underwear and giggled. An older chambermaid took the garment from me and said, Congratulations, Your Majesty, those are your sons and grandsons. I watched as she turned to rush from my bedchamber carrying my underwear on a bronze platter. Not so fast, I called out. Don't wash them before I've had a chance to get a good look. She stopped. I am to report this to Madame Huangfu, she said. Those were my instructions.

This is ridiculous! Everything must be reported to Madame Huangfu, I complained. But by then, the serving girls were already entering my bedchamber with a tub of hot water sprinkled with fragrant grasses for my bath. I lay sprawled on the bed, refusing to move, trying to figure out what that dream had been about, and why Dainiang had been in it. But no answer came, so I turned to other things. I could tell by the bashful yet happy expressions on the girls' faces that something good had just happened. Maybe, I thought, some sort of reward was waiting for them in Madame Huangfu's quarters. Happy as that bunch of lowly females was, I was miserable.

Perfectly miserable.

Madame Huangfu replaced my eight serving girls with eight eunuchs to tend to my daily needs. In a voice that brooked no objection, she said, Those serving girls are no longer to stay with you in Cultivation Hall, whether you like it or not. Throughout the history of the Xie Empire, she said, once the Emperor has become a man, eunuchs, and not serving girls, have tended to his daily needs. Tradition demands it. That is what she said, and there was nothing I could do about it. So I bade a sad farewell to the eight girls in Cultivation Hall, watching heartbroken as they dissolved into tears, and wishing there were some way I could reward them for their service. Your Majesty, one of them said, since it will be all but impossible to see you after this, would you be so kind as to allow me to touch you? I nodded. You may touch me if you want, but where? She hesitated for a moment, then said, May I touch your toes? That would place me under your gracious protection for the rest of my life. I promptly slipped off my shoes and stockings and raised my feet into the air. Falling into a half kneel, she felt my toes as hot tears filled her eyes. The seven other girls quickly lined up to do the same. This unique ritual persisted for a very long time, and was highlighted by one of the girls, who bent down and kissed the top of my foot. That tickled, and I giggled. Aren't you worried that my foot might be dirty? I asked her. Your Majesty's foot cannot be dirty, she sobbed. Your Majesty's foot is far cleaner than this lowly servant's mouth.

The eight eunuchs who came to Cultivation Hall had been carefully chosen by the Empress Dowager, Madame Meng. They were pretty boys, nearly all of whom came from her hometown in Caishi County. I have already revealed my disgust with eunuchs, even as a child, which is why I returned their greeting kowtows with a scowl. As time went on, I allowed them to play games, all sorts of games, on the floor of the hall. That included hopscotch. I wanted to see if any of them stood out from the others. As expected, they stopped playing after a while, and I had to laugh at how they gasped for breath and were sweating profusely. All except one—the youngest among them—who enjoyed the game more than the others, and performed many jumps I'd never seen before. I noticed that he had the delicate features of a lovely girl and that he jumped with grace and agility, a style of jumping that belonged to the common folk and was alien to me. I summoned him up to the throne.

What is your name?

Swallow, he said, Swallow. My childhood name was Suo'er, and at school I was known as Kaiqi.

How old are you? I had to laugh at the way he rattled that off.

Twelve. I was born in the year of the ram.

I want you to sleep by my bed, I whispered in his ear as I pulled him closer by the shoulders. We can be playmates.

Swallow blushed. His eyes were clear as watery pools. The one anomaly was a red mole on the tip of one of his black, arched eyebrows. Puzzled by this flaw, I reached out to pluck the mole off his face. But I must have squeezed too hard, because he jumped up in pain. Although he didn't scream, I could tell by the look on his face that the pain was nearly unbearable. He rolled around on the floor, pressing his hand up against the mole. But only for a moment, before he sprang to his knees. Forgive this slave, Your Majesty, Swallow begged as he kowtowed. He was a fascinating boy, so I stepped down off the imperial couch, went over, and helped him to his feet. I even dabbed a bit of my saliva on his injured mole, something I had learned from the serving girls. I was just being playful, I said to Swallow. It will stop hurting with a little saliva.

Any thoughts of the serving girls who had left Cultivation Hall in a teary good-bye vanished without a trace. A great many changes among palace retainers in the Xie Empire occurred that year, with serving girls and eunuchs coming and going like a merry-go-round; my life, on the other hand, went on as normal. Liking some people and forgetting others came naturally to a fourteen-year-old Emperor.

. . .

I was so eager to see what Swallow's castrated genitals looked like that I once commanded him to show himself to me. He blanched and begged me not to expose him to such humiliation, covering his crotch with both hands. Curiosity, however, got the better of me, and I ordered him to undress. Finally, he dropped his trousers, wailing pitifully as he did so; turning his head away, he said through his tears, Please, Your Majesty, make it quick.

I examined Swallow's private parts carefully, discovering that his scar was unique, that it was dotted by several dark red marks that looked like burns. For some strange reason, I was reminded of the hands of Dainiang, who lived in the Cold Palace, and my curiosity gave way to disappointment.

You are different from the others, I said to Swallow. Who disfigured you like this?

My father, he said, no longer wailing. My father is a blacksmith. When I was eight years old, he crafted a small knife with which he castrated me. I lay near death for three days.

Why did he do that? Did you have a desire to be a court eunuch?

I do not know. My father told me to bear up under the pain, that when I entered the court in the service of Your Majesty, I would never again need to worry about having enough to eat or clothes to wear. He also said that being at court would give me the opportunity to repay my parents and bring honor to my ancestors.

Your father is an animal, I said, and if I ever meet him, I'll have him castrated too. We shall see how he bears up under the pain. All right, you may dress yourself now.

Swallow jerked his trousers up as quickly as he could and, finally, smiled at me. The red mole at the tip of his eyebrow glowed like a precious stone in light streaming in through the silk curtains.

Autumn was coming to an end. Palace servants swept the grounds clean of fallen leaves and twigs, while carpenters sealed the windows with thin slats of wood to protect against sands blowing in from the north. Several horse-drawn wagons rumbled in through one of the side gates in the rear and left loads of firewood behind in neat piles. Everywhere you looked, the Xie Palace was being readied for the coming of winter.

The last of my black-winged crickets died quietly in the eleventh month, an event that plunged me into my annual depression. I ordered a eunuch to gather up the dead crickets and lay them all together in a delicate little box, a communal casket for my beloved creatures. Their final resting place would be in the courtyard in front of Cultivation Hall.

First, I had the eunuch close the gate. Then Swallow and I dug a hole in one of the flower beds. But just as we were covering the casket with muddy soil, the face of the old madman Sun Xin appeared without warning in one of the decorative holes in the wall. Swallow shrieked in horror.

Don't be frightened, I said. He's a madman. Just ignore him. We have work to do. I don't care who sees us, so long as it isn't Madame Huangfu.

He threw a stone at me, and he won't stop glaring at me, Swallow said as he ran around behind me. I don't know him, so why does he look at me like that?

I saw the look in Sun Xin's gray eyes—it was one of anguish over the state of the universe and pity for all of mankind—so I got up and walked over to the opening. Sun Xin, I said, go away. I don't like you spying on me. As if he hadn't heard me, he began banging his head against the frame around the opening, which reverberated long and loud. Sun Xin, what do you think you're doing? I raged. Are you tired of living? That brought a stop to his laughable head banging, but he then looked up into the sky and released a tremendous sneeze, covering his hoary face with snot and tears, and I heard him utter through the opening, Now that eunuchs have gained favor, calamity will soon befall the Xie Empire.

What is he saying, Your Majesty? Swallow asked from behind me.

Don't listen to him, he's a madman. That's the only thing he knows how to say. Shall I chase him away? I am the only one he listens to.

Of course he listens to you, Your Majesty. Swallow cast a curious glance at Sun Xin. What puzzles me is why Your Majesty keeps a madman around the palace.

He wasn't always a madman. Once, years ago, he risked death to save the life of one of my ancestors in battle, for which he received the protection of five generations of Xie rulers. And so, mad though he may be, Sun Xin will always be spared punishment, whatever he does. By telling Swallow about Sun Xin, I was satisfying a desire to reveal bizarre court secrets to him. I ended my tale by asking, Don't you find him more interesting than other people?

I don't know, Swallow replied. I've always been afraid of madmen.

Well, since you're afraid, I'll send him away. I snapped a twig off of a tree and poked Sun Xin in the nose. Get away from here, I said. Go over to your pill-refining cauldron.

He did as I said, sighing over and over as he walked off. Now that eunuchs have gained favor, calamity will soon befall the Xie Empire, he again muttered.

Imperial audiences were exceptionally trying. The Heads of the Four Boards—Ceremonial Rites, Civil Service, Military, and Punishments—stood on the first row of Abundant Hearts Hall's stone steps, two on either side of Feng Ao, my prime minister. A phalanx of civilian and military officers in full dress was arrayed behind them. Once in a while, the dukes who governed each of the prefectures attended the imperial audience. They wore sashes on which a small Black Panther had been embroidered, and that told me they were of my uncles' generation, or older. But though my ancestors' blood flowed through their veins, they were not in line to ascend the Xie throne. In the Imperial Register they were listed as Northern Duke, Southern Duke, Eastern Duke, Western Duke, Northeastern Duke, Southwestern Duke, Southeastern Duke, and Northwestern Duke. Some were already gray at the temples, yet even they were required to salute me when they stepped foot in Abundant Hearts Hall. I knew this was the way it had to be. Willing or not, they had no choice.

At one of those audiences, one of the dukes released a loud fart. I tried not to laugh, but failed. The guilty party was either the Eastern Duke or the Southeastern Duke, I wasn't sure which, but I laughed so hard I nearly choked. Palace attendants ran up and began thumping me on the back. Then the embarrassed miscreant, whose face was the color of pork liver, released another fart. This time I nearly laughed myself into unconsciousness. As I rocked back and forth on the throne, I saw my grandmother raise her longevity cane and smack the Eastern Duke on his upturned rump. A stream of apologies poured from his mouth as he tugged at the back of his robe. With a noticeable stammer, he attempted to explain his indecorous behavior. I traveled all night, covering three hundred li, to attend this audience with the Emperor. The cold night air and the pig's feet I ate on the way produced a bellyful of gas. But all his explanation earned him was an even more violent caning from Madame Huangfu. No one is allowed to speak or clown around in the Imperial presence. How dare you break the silence by releasing gas!

In my experience, that was the most memorable imperial audience ever. Too bad nothing like that ever happened again. In terms of personal preference, I'd much rather have listened to the sound of dukes passing gas than be bored by discussions of land tax or military deployments among Madame Huangfu, Feng Ao, and that group.

Memorials from the congregation of officials were passed up to the Chief of the Imperial Household, a ranking eunuch who held them up to me. As far as I was concerned, they were little more than crude, tedious, useless gossip. I had no use for memorials and, I could tell, neither did Madame Huangfu. But she had the Chief Eunuch read each of them to the congregation anyway. On one occasion, the Chief Eunuch read a memorial by Li Yu, the vice head of the Military Board, reporting on bloody incursions across our western border by barbarian forces, in which many heroic defenders had shed their blood. Eleven attacks had been launched, and Li Yu requested that the Emperor set out on a western imperial tour as an encouragement to the soldiers stationed there.

That was the first memorial that actually concerned me. I sat up on the throne and looked over at Madame Huangfu. But rather than return my gaze, she paused for a long moment before turning to Feng Ao, the prime minister, and asked his opinion. Feng Ao stroked his long silver beard and rocked his head back and forth. Attacks by barbarians on our western border have been a latent danger for a long time. If our troops there can be emboldened to drive the barbarians back beyond Phoenix Pass, they will create a protective buffer along the greater half of our territory. Our armies must be brave, they cannot falter, and it seems to me that there may be a need for the Emperor to make an appearance. Feng Ao paused, as if there were more he wanted to say, but he stole a look in my direction and coughed lightly. As her brow crinkled in a frown, Madame Huangfu showed her impatience by banging her longevity cane on the floor three times. Stop beating around the bush. I asked you a question. There is no need for you to look for help elsewhere. The tone of anger in her voice was unmistakable. Continue, Feng Ao, she said. With a sigh, Feng Ao said, The Emperor is still a young man, and we are talking about an arduous five-hundred-li journey in inclement weather. I am afraid it will take its toll on the Imperial person, that unforeseen dangers may await him. At that moment, an imperceptible sneer creased the corners of Madame Huangfu's mouth. Your meaning is clear to me, she said, and I want you to know that if the Emperor decides to make a tour to the west, nothing untoward will happen to him, and there will be no intrigues to dethrone him here in the palace while he is gone. As long as these old bones remain in the palace, all of you gathered here can put your minds at rest on that score.

The true meaning of this exchange escaped me at the time, but I had the uncomfortable feeling that my views counted for nothing. So when the talk turned to the most auspicious day for me to set out, I blurted out, I'm not going. I'm not.

What is wrong with you? a surprised Madame Huangfu turned to ask me. Lighthearted quips do not emerge from the mouth of an Emperor, she said. I will abide no irresponsible talk from you.

I'm not going, just because you all want me to. I'll go only if you don't want me to, I said.

This display of defiance was met with wide-eyed, slack-jawed bewilderment. I could see I'd caused Madame Huangfu considerable embarrassment. She turned to Feng Ao. The Emperor likes to engage in youthful mischief, she said. You are not to indulge him when he has no intention of being serious.

That enraged me. An Emperor's pronouncements had always been received as golden words with the force of law, but my grandmother was treating them as a mere witticism. To others, she may have appeared affectionate, wise, and farsighted, but I knew she was just a know-nothing old woman. Tired of arguing and wanting only to leave Abundant Hearts Hall, I turned and said to an attendant behind me, Bring me the commode. I have to shit. If any of you are offended by the smell, move back. That was meant for the ears of Madame Huangfu, and it worked. She turned and glowered at me. But then I heard her sigh in exasperation and bang her cane three times on the floor. The Dragon Emperor of Xie is indisposed today, she announced. The audience is over.

Everyone in the palace was talking about the western imperial tour. My mother, Madame Meng, was especially anxious over the possibility that this was part of another conspiracy, afraid that something terrible would happen if I left the palace. They all covet the throne and are desperately looking for an opportunity to do you harm, she explained tearfully. You must be on your guard and choose only the most loyal people to accompany you on this trip. The brothers Duanwen and Duanwu cannot be among them, nor anyone you do not know well.

Once it was decided, on the orders of Madame Huangfu, I was powerless to avoid making the trip. So I decided to treat it as a grand imperial procession, contemplating many indescribable expectations. I wanted to see the scenery that covered my land for nine hundred li, and observe the world beyond the borders of the Xie Empire. So I tried to put my mother's mind at ease with words from one of the classics: The mandate of Heaven gives a ruler riches and honor. If he sacrifices his life for his nation and its citizens, his praises will be sung for a hundred generations. But she never put any store in the empty bromides of antiquity, and from that day on, whenever she spoke of my grandmother, Madame Huangfu, she used epithets normally heard in marketplaces where commoners gathered. Speaking ill of Madame Huangfu behind her back became one of my mother's true delights.

I was more restless than usual those days, and given to physically abusing my attendants for no particular reason. How could I let it be known that I was torn between anxiety and anticipation? One day I summoned the court soothsayer and asked what awaited me on the impending journey, good or ill. He laid out a pile of tallies, with which he busied himself for a very long time before concluding with a single red tally in his hand. Nothing untoward will befall the Xie Emperor on this trip, he said at last. Will there be assassination attempts? I demanded. The soothsayer responded by asking me to draw a tally. When I did, a mysterious smile spread across his face. If an arrow is fired at the Emperor, it will be snapped in two by a gust of wind from the north. Your Majesty may set out on the tour.

THREE

ⵥ

ON THE MORNING OF THE THIRD day of the twelfth lunar month, my entourage passed grandly through Luminous Virtue Gate, sent on our way by palace denizens standing high atop the fortifications waving handkerchiefs. Residents of the capital, having learned of the imperial tour, lined the street leading out of the palace—men, women, young, and old forming two human walls, all hoping to catch their first glimpse of the new Emperor's face. To their chagrin, the interior of the Imperial Carriage was blocked from view by an array of yellow silks and red satins, hiding my face from all who wished to see me. But I could hear them shout: Long live Your Majesty, Long live the Emperor of Xie, and that made me want to part the window curtain and view my subjects. I was stopped from doing so by a nervous Imperial Guardsman riding alongside the carriage. Your Majesty must not take any chances, he said. Assassins often hide in dense crowds. When I asked him when I could finally open the window, he thought for a moment. Not until we have left the capital, he said, although for Your Majesty's safety, it would be best not to open it at all. Is it then your wish to suffocate me? I snapped. If I cannot even open a window, I shall cancel the trip. The whole idea is meaningless if I cannot even lay eyes on the world outside and the people who live there. Needless to say, that final comment formed only in my mind. It would have been unthinkable to articulate such candid thoughts to a member of the Imperial Guard.

After passing through the city gate, our pace quickened and the crowds gradually thinned out. Winds blowing in from the wilderness made the flags and banners snap above my carriage. They also carried a disagreeable odor, and when I asked the guard where it came from, he told me that many of my subjects living in the countryside near the capital made their living by tanning hides, and in the early weeks of winter, they hung the bloody hides of sheep and cattle outside to dry in the sun. As it happened, we were just then passing down a road lined with the hides of many animals, wild and domesticated.

Suddenly, an old woman, intent on stopping the Dragon Carriage, materialized in the midst of the procession, having gone undetected by the horse soldiers up front and the guards arrayed on both sides of my carriage. She had been kneeling by the left side of the road for a very long time, covered by an animal hide to protect her from the elements. As we drew near, she threw off the hide and rushed up to my carriage, nearly scaring my guards out of their wits. I heard a commotion nearby, but by the time I'd pulled back the curtain, the guards were already spiriting the white-haired old woman away. She was wailing and shouting at the same time: My little Beauty, give me back my little Beauty. I beg Your Majesty to release my little Beauty from the palace.

Why is she shouting? I asked the guard. And who is little Beauty?

Your slave cannot say for certain. Perhaps she is one of the palace girls chosen from among the commoners.

Who is little Beauty? I asked a palace girl on one of the horse-drawn carriages. Do you know her? The old woman's shouts had put me on edge.

Little Beauty served the late Emperor, the girl replied with tears in her eyes. When the late Emperor passed on, she was buried with him. The girl then covered her face and managed to say before she was overcome with sobs, I feel so sorry for mother and daughter, because they cannot meet again until they are both on their way down to the Yellow Springs.

I tried my best to recall the face of this girl called little Beauty, but it was no use. One must realize that besides being graceful and beautiful, the eight hundred palace girls were remarkably similar. Quietly they came to age in the three compounds and six courtyards of the palace like buds on a flowering tree, either to blossom or to shrivel away, leaving not a trace of their passage. I could not recall the face of little Beauty, but what formed in my mind was an image of the Imperial Tombs at the foot of Brass Rule Mountain and of all the dead lying there in their coffins. A gust of cold wind came out of nowhere and, to my wonder, rushed into my nostrils, making me sneeze. My carriage felt chilled all of a sudden.

That old woman has frightened Your Majesty and should lose her head because of it, the Imperial Guardsman said.

I wasn't frightened. I was just thinking about dead people. I wrapped a peacock cape around my shoulders and cinched up my chamois waist warmer. It is much colder out here than in the palace, I said. You should find some sort of brazier to keep me warm inside my carriage.

On this trip I was treated to my first view of Xie Empire villages. They were nestled up against mountains, alongside rivers, their dome-shaped thatch rooftops scattered near ponds and on the edges of woodlands, like oversized chess pieces. The fields lay fallow as winter settled in; a few withered yellow leaves clung to mulberry trees. The sound of woodsmen chopping down trees on mountain slopes swirled in the air and merged with that of single-wheeled carts loaded down with salt creaking along a path running parallel to the public road. The passage of my procession elicited shouts from the villagers and frenzied barking from their dogs. Haggard-looking peasants, dressed in rags, crowded up to the road to watch us pass, a single glimpse of the Imperial visage enough to cause rhapsodic joy. Led by one of their elders, they prostrated themselves to perform the three kowtows and nine bows. After the Dragon Carriage had passed through a mulberry grove and we were on our way out of the village, I turned to look back and was struck by the sight of my devoted subjects continuing their obeisances. Countless sun-baked foreheads pounded the yellow earth, over and over, raising a din like thunder on a spring day.

The villages were impoverished and dirty, the peasants pitifully undernourished. That was my initial impression of the Xie countryside, not at all what I had imagined it would be like. I shall never forget a child I saw up in a tree. His sole protection against the cold wind was a thin, tattered piece of nondescript clothing as he sat in the crotch of the tree and saluted my carriage the way he saw the adults do it. Yet he never stopped digging something out of a hole in the tree with his other hand. After watching him for a while, I realized that he was foraging for white insects, which he popped into his mouth, chewed, and swallowed. I nearly vomited. Why is that little boy eating insects, I asked the guard. He's hungry. There is no more food at home, so he survives on insects. That is what many village people feed on during normal times. When natural disasters occur, after they have fought over insects, the people are forced to eat the bark of trees. Then, once that is gone, they are reduced to trudging elsewhere to beg for food. And when their hunger becomes intolerable on their way to somewhere, they dig up the clay roadway and use that to fill their bellies. That always kills them. That bone Your Majesty saw a while ago was not from a cow, it was human.

Talk of death and dying silenced me. It was not something I liked hearing about. And yet, no matter where I went, it seemed to be everyone's favorite topic of conversation. I slapped the guard as a warning to stop talking about dead people, and did

not regain my carefree mood until we were passing by Crescent
Moon Lake. In the twilight, the surface of the lake shimmered
like gold and silver, blending perfectly with the sky. Reeds bor-
dering the lake swayed with the wind as if about to fly, flinging
catkins into the air to soar with the birds and turn the sky above
into a patchwork of dark yellows and unsullied whites. But
what truly amazed and delighted me was a flock of brightly
feathered ducks that had settled on reeds near the shore. Startled
by the creaking of wooden wheels and the clatter of horse
hooves, they rose into the air and headed straight for the Dragon
Carriage. I called out to the coachman to stop, snatched up my
bow, and jumped out of the carriage. One white-headed duck
plummeted to the ground while the twang from my bowstring
still hung in the air. I shrieked in delight. Swallow spotted the
fallen bird and sped to fetch it, then ran back to me, holding it
high over his head. It's a female, Your Majesty. I told him to
keep it under his waistcoat. When we stop for the night at the
excursion palace, I said, we'll roast and eat it together. Swallow
did as I said, stuffing the wounded bird under his waistcoat, and
I watched as the yellow silk turned red from the duck's blood.

My excitement peaked when we reached the shore and I
halted the procession, so everyone could appreciate my archery
skills. Unfortunately, I was unable to hit anything else after that
first arrow. Furious, I flung my bow to the ground and thought
back to my days at Mountainside Hall, when I had read a poem
that fondly recalled the scenery around Crescent Moon Lake.
But try as I might, I could not recall the lines of the poem itself,
and so I made up two of my own: The sun sets on the shore of

Crescent Moon Lake/The Emperor of Xie takes a duck with a single arrow. To my surprise, my little creation earned applause and shouts of praise from my retainers. Wang Gao, the resident scholar, suggested that we go to a nearby wayside pavilion to honor the ancients by reading the carvings they had left behind. That's a good idea, I told him. But when we reached the pavilion, we saw that nothing remained of the lettering etched into stone, and that the lines the ancients had written on the posts had been worn away by the elements. A surprise, however, awaited us: Off to the side of the pavilion, in a grove of mottled bamboo, a little hut beckoned to us. Officials who had traveled to Crescent Moon Lake in the past said there was something strange about that hut, so one of them went up and pushed open the wicker gate. The hut is empty, he reported. But then, when he raised his lantern for a closer look, he shouted out in surprise, There is something written on the wall, Your Majesty. Come see for yourself.

I led the way into the hut and, by the light of a pine-oil lantern, read the peculiar writing on the wall: The Emperor of Xie's study. The familiar calligraphy told me at once that it had been written by the monk Juekong, and I presumed that he had left this final admonition to me on his way back to Bitter Bamboo Mountain. Thus reassured, I turned to my retinue and said casually, There is nothing to be alarmed about. This is but the scrawl of an itinerant monk.

There in that riverside hut, I imagined the scene of a black-robed monk as he trod on the dewy ground during his nightly trek. But Juekong's gaunt, pale face was already blurred in my mind's eye. I wondered if the monk, who loved books more than life itself, had managed to reach far-off Bitter Bamboo Monastery, and if so, if he was at that moment sitting by a cold window intoning passages from a dog-eared sacred text in the dim light of a solitary lantern.

We spent the night in an excursion palace at Huizhou, whose citizens were menaced by the spread of plague. So the local officials had set up a perimeter of wild mugwort torches around the palace. Choking whiffs of acrid smoke made me cough uncontrollably, while the doors and windows of the main hall, where I was to sleep, were sealed with strips of silk, stifling the atmosphere inside. Everyone said that was to keep the plague out of the palace. I resented the discomfiture, but I could do nothing about it. The prospect that I would have to spend the night in an ill-fated spot like Huizhou had not occurred to me, but my retainers assured me that we had to pass through the place to reach Phoenix Pass in the west.

So Swallow and I played cat's cradle for a while, and then I took him to bed with me. The subtle fragrance of mint on his body overwhelmed the foul air over the Huizhou excursion palace.

On the eighth day of the twelfth lunar month we crossed into Pinzhou, where we were welcomed by the holiday sounds of drums and gongs. I had been alerted that Pinzhou was one of the richest and most populous feudal states in all the empire, and that the revered Western Duke Zhaoyang was a determined and dedicated ruler. The residents were known far and wide for their fine woven silks and peerless mercantile skills. As we neared the entrance to Pinzhou, I spotted a gilded board above the gate. Pinzhou, a Blessed Place, it proclaimed. It was said that during the late Emperor's reign, he had asked his uncle, Duke Zhaoyang, for that very placard, but had received a polite refusal. So he had sent a detachment of horse soldiers who rode through the night to get here. But every one of them who tried to scale the gate received an arrow in the chest for his efforts. I was told that Zhaoyang himself stood guard at the gate to ward off the would-be thieves, who lay dead on the ground with his poisoned arrows stuck in them.

Knowing that the grudge the Western Duke held toward the Xie court had a long history, both my civil and military officials counseled caution. And to that end, they disguised the Dragon Carriage and others in the imperial procession as a caravan of merchants before entering Pinzhou. We wound our way through secluded streets and lanes until we reached the sumptuous Pinzhou excursion palace. Our arrival seemed to go undetected by Zhaoyang.

Once I was settled in the excursion palace, the holiday clamor of drums and gongs in the city disturbed my peace, so I decided to go out with Swallow in disguise to have a look around. I had no interest in investigating whether or not there were evil doings behind Zhaoyang's accomplishments, but wanted to see for myself what it was about the Twelve-Eight celebrations that so delighted the common folk, and to get a first-hand understanding of how the residents of Pinzhou lived and worked in such peace and contentment. As night was about to fall, Swallow and I changed into dark clothes and slipped out of the palace through the rear gate. He told me he had once traveled to Pinzhou with his father to peddle ironware, and knew it well enough to act as my guide.

The city seemed deserted; only the occasional hum of spinning wheels in silk mills disturbed the silence. Cobblestone streets glistened in the dying rays of the sun as Swallow led me toward the bell tower, the source of the raucous sounds of merriment. Along the way, we passed a wine shop where the red-faced proprietor was standing on a bench taking down his flag sign to close up; he waved the flag at us. Hurry, he shouted. The dancing dragon is about to pass by the bell tower.

That day in Pinzhou city, I walked a distance of two li, a first in my life. As we neared the bell tower, Swallow took my hand and led me into the crowd. By then my feet were blistered. No one took notice of us, as waves of joyful revelers flowed back and forth on the promenade. My greatest concern was that I would lose my oversized straw sandals in the confusion. I had never before been among simply dressed commoners, let alone rocked one way and then the other by holiday revelers. So I hung on to Swallow's arm for dear life, dreading the thought of being separated from him. He, on the other hand, slipped through the crowd like a silverfish, dragging me along with him. Do not worry, Your Majesty, he leaned over to whisper. Twelve-Eight brings out the crowds, that's all. I'm going to show Your Majesty all sorts of wonderful things. We will start with activities on land, then move to those on water, and from there go to things in the marketplace.

For me, that masquerade excursion was a true eye-opener. What a contrast, that between Pinzhou, with its festive airs, and gloomy Huizhou, and I was somewhat bothered by seeing how the late Emperor's bitter enemy, Western Duke Zhaoyang, governed a place that was filled with excitement and bursting with energy. With my own eyes, I drank in the sights and sounds of Pinzhou's Twelve-Eight celebration. That included: music on all sorts of instruments, clapper songs and pitch-pot games, kickball, tea spout tricks and water shows, log balancers, tightrope walkers, plate jugglers, chanting, trained birds, water puppets, magicians, sword swallowers and fire-eaters, kite flying, fireworks, and more. These were what Swallow called land activities. Next, he was going to take me to the lakeshore to see the pleasure craft and colorful little boats. That is where the real crowds are, he said, because all sorts of new and wonderful Twelve-Eight things are sold on the boats. But I was staring up at a tightrope walker, and while I was deciding whether to stay or leave, a dark-faced man stepped out from a circus tent; his eyes lit up when he saw me. You there, boy, you've got the body for it. He pinched me on the waist. That hurt. I yelped. Come with me, boy, I heard him say in a southern accent. I'll teach you how to walk a tightrope. I smiled, but Swallow turned ghostly white. Hurry, Your Majesty, he said anxiously, come with me. He grabbed my hand and dragged me off.

You scared me half to death, Swallow said after we'd gotten away. The color still hadn't returned to his face. Circus people are notorious kidnappers. If they snatched Your Majesty and took you with them, my life would be over.

So? I said firmly. Walking a tightrope is more impressive than being Emperor of Xie. Now that is a job for a true hero. I was struck by the vast differences between the tightrope walker and me. I don't want to be Emperor. I want to be a tightrope walker.

If Your Majesty becomes a tightrope walker, I'll become a log balancer, Swallow said.

Since when did you start talking like one of those clever old palace women? I pinched him on the cheek. His face turned beet red. You're blushing, I said. Why must you always act like a girl?

Swallow bit his lip, the look on his face that of a frightened fawn. I deserve nothing less than death, he said. From now on, no more blushing. I will stop being bashful. Now would Your Majesty like to take in some of the excitement elsewhere?

Let's go. Since we're here, we might as well have a really good time.

The last place Swallow and I visited was the shore of Willow Lake, in Pinzhou's western district. As promised, it was the nearest thing to a fairyland that I could imagine. Singsong girls and dancers frolicked on pleasure craft and colorful little boats, accompanied by all kinds of instruments, attracting hordes of tourists and revelers to displays of prized and unusual objects being sold by the boatmen. I saw balancing poles, opera props, flower baskets, hand-painted fans, gaudy banners, fish-shaped candies, rice cakes, seasonal flowers, clay figurines, and much more. On the shore, vendors' stalls were piled high with eye-dazzling trinkets: combs inlaid with pearls and jade, satins sprinkled with gold dust, and ivory hair ornaments. I sighed, wishing I had brought some money. Tell me what it is you'd like, Your Majesty, Swallow said mysteriously, and I can get it for you without spending a cent. I pointed to some painted clay figurines of little boys on the bow of one of the boats. Get me some of those. Swallow told me to wait there for him. So I stood beneath a tall willow tree, not completely won over by Swallow's casual promise. But hardly any time had passed when I spotted him weaving his way through the crowd in my direction, taking a clay figurine out from under his shirt as he walked. Then another, and another, four altogether, which he held in the palms of his hands and grinned.

Are they stolen? I asked as I took the figurines from him, suddenly aware of what he had done. How did you manage to steal them with so many people around?

Quick eyes, nimble hands, and fast legs, he replied with a smile as he rubbed his head. My third elder brother taught me. He can steal anything. Once he stole a whole pig right out from under a butcher's nose.

Why didn't you tell me you were such an accomplished thief? If I had known, I'd have had you steal Madame Huangfu's jade *ruyi*. Now I'd like you to steal the gilded placard above the Pinzhou city gate, I said, only half in jest. I'd rather have that than anything.

That I cannot do. It would cost me my head, and your slave is not that brave. Swallow then turned and gazed at the lakeshore. Taking hold of my sleeve, he said, We had better leave, Your Majesty. I don't want to be here when the owner of the boat sees what's missing.

We returned to the excursion palace with Swallow carrying me on his back, since I was too tired to walk. As we passed through excited crowds on the street, we heard them talking about the arrival in their city of the Xie Emperor and his entourage. I had to cover my mouth to keep from laughing. I swear that in all my fourteen years, I had never been so happy or felt so free as on that day. I later told Swallow that I intended to drive out Western Duke Zhaoyang and move the capital to Pinzhou. His laughter rose up to me when I said that. That will be wonderful, Your Majesty. That way I can bring Your Majesty clay figurines every day.

The four painted clay figurines wound up getting lost, one after the other, during my western inspection tour, and after we had passed through many towns and cities, my impression of Pinzhou and its Twelve-Eight celebrations began to fade. But on drowsy winter afternoons on bumpy country roads, I often thought back to the tightrope walker, with his red cape and black leather boots, a man whose wild nature showed in his smile and who walked through the air with consummate grace. He was like a mountain antelope as he raced across the thin steel wire high above the ground. I also thought a lot about the dark-faced man who had spoken with a southern accent. Come with me, boy, he had said. I'll teach you how to walk a tightrope.

. . .

The first auspicious snowfall of the year had just fallen in the western border region, covering the vast expanses and the nearly deserted towns with a blanket of glistening white. Year after year, this had been the scene of pitched battles, driving away all but a scant few local residents, until for miles around the barking of dogs and the crowing of roosters was but a distant memory. The area was governed by the Northwestern Duke, my uncle Dayu, who was a womanizer and a hard drinker, as I had learned early on. In his government estate I spotted more liquor vats and kegs than I could count, not to mention a huge and unimaginably deep liquor cellar. The smell of liquor in the area around the Northwestern Duke's estate was overpowering, while the puffy red face of Dayu, the duke himself, reminded me of a baboon's ass. The minute I saw him I pointed to his face and asked, Have you ever seen a baboon's ass? Well, that is what your face looks like. He had a big laugh over that and did not appear angry. Rather, he summoned dancing girls, who entertained us in the main hall with music. Among them were several barbarians with blue eyes and high noses. Dayu clapped his hands and sang along with them between drinks; leaning toward me, his alcohol-suffused face a bright red, he whispered, Is Your Majesty interested in those barbarian girls? You can take them back to the palace if you'd like. I shook my head. I noticed that all the dancing girls' exposed bellies were covered with a shiny red powder flecked with gold, adding to their seductiveness as they twisted and writhed. I burst out laughing, reminded yet again of baboon asses. See, I said, their bellies look exactly like baboon asses.

This time, I noticed, the Northwestern Duke's face fell. Rolling his eyes, he complained to his retainers softly, This dog-shit Emperor of Xie doesn't know anything, except for the asses of baboons.

Originally, I had intended to leave the next day to inspect the troops on the Phoenix Pass battlefield, but the heavy snow-fall ruined my plans, since there was a biting chill in the air. So I stayed in bed, warmed by woolen quilts, and refused to leave the Northwestern Duke's estate. I watched through the window as my retainers prepared the carriages. Then my chief of staff, Yang Song, came into my bedroom, urging me to continue the trip west as planned. Do you want me to freeze to death? I shouted angrily. I'm not leaving until the snow stops and the sun comes out. In fact, by then the snow was falling even more heavily. Yang Song returned to my bedroom after a short while to ask again when we would be setting out. This time I was so angry I drew my Imperial Panther sword, pointed it at Yang Song, and said, If you ask me one more time, you can say farewell to your head. I had no intention of getting on the road in such terrible weather. Tears glistened in Yang Song's eyes as he stood by my bed, his head bowed, and I heard his voice crack with emotion as he said softly, At this very moment, the soldiers at Phoenix Pass are holding their heads high in anticipation of laying eyes on the Emperor. Changing your mind, Your Majesty, will result in a worsening of attitude by soldiers guarding the pass, and if the Peng Empire issues the call to arms to its troops, I fear that Phoenix Pass will fall into enemy hands.

I ignored Yang Song's dire prediction. Some time later I

heard him stroking his horse out in the snow and wailing like a madman. What was there to cry about? How could changing an imperial proclamation lead to the loss of Phoenix Pass?

At lunch that day, I drank a goblet of tiger-bone liquor and feasted on venison and a variety of fruits and vegetables. Afterward, feeling warm all over, I sat down with Dayu to play a game of chess, which I won easily. Then, picking up one of the chessmen, I stuck it up his nostril. You're a fool, Uncle, I said. He responded by belching. Yes, I am, he said, not taking it as an insult. And fools are assured of a good fate. Haven't you heard people say that the descendants of the Xie founder are all fools? Most emperors throughout history have been fools, and all because of their fondness for women and drink. Not me, I refuted him. I am fond of neither, and I am no fool. Dayu burst into laughter. Your Majesty is only fourteen, he said. Slowly but surely you too will become a fool. If you fight the temptation to become one, you will have trouble holding on to the throne. Stung by his comment, I turned and left the chess table, flicking my sleeve in a show of pique. Dayu fell in behind me. Do not be offended by my drunken ramblings, Your Majesty. One more game of chess to determine the ultimate winner. I beat you already, I said, turning to look at him. I am not going to play with a fool like you anymore. Your Majesty, he called out, come with me to the liquor cellar to savor some hundred-year liquor. Get away from me, I said. I'm sick and tired of your liquor breath and alcoholic airs.

Dayu's wild game feast had raised my internal heat to an unbearable degree, which forced me to go out into the blowing snow. Now, I thought, would be a good time to set out for Phoenix Pass. What I found strange was that while my horses and carriage stood out in the snow, there were no people around. I asked Swallow, who had come out with me, Where is Yang Song, my chief of staff? His answer startled me. He has led a unit of horse soldiers to Phoenix Pass to aid the troops there. When I asked why I hadn't heard the call to battle, and when it had been sounded, he said, It was sounded while Your Majesty was playing chess with the Northwestern Duke. At this very moment, Grand Censor Liang is up in the gate watchtower with General Zou watching the battle.

Swallow opened a parasol and led me up to the watchtower, where the observers made room for me at the highest point and pointed to the northwest, where alarm smoke filled the sky. Since the snowfall had lightened up a bit, I was able to see battle flags waving above a distant valley floor, like shifting clouds, and I heard the muted blare of rams' horns and the chaotic thudding of horses' hooves. Except for that, I could see nothing. I cannot tell what is going on. How can I determine which army is winning, I asked the general who commanded the cavalry troops, Li Chong. He replied anxiously, If Your Majesty concentrates on how the battle flags for each army advance and retreat, you will know which army has the upper hand. At the moment, the Black Panther flags of the Xie Empire are beating a retreat. Things do not look good. If the Phoenix Pass is lost, the city of Jiaozhou will be indefensible, then Your Majesty should make preparations to return to the capital. But when will I visit the brave soldiers in the border areas? I asked him. A tortured smile lifted the corner of Li Chong's mouth. By the look of things, Your Majesty's western tour will have to end here. It would be too dangerous to send the Dragon Carriage into the thick of battle.

Standing there atop the watchtower, not knowing what to do, and totally unschooled in the art of war, I began to realize how a casual imperial proclamation can have serious consequences. But I quickly shifted the blame for my predicament onto the nasty weather in the empire's northwestern border. Who could have predicted a sudden deterioration in climatic conditions? As I prepared to make my way back down the watchtower, I overheard Grand Censor Liang, who was in charge of the expedition, ask the cavalry commander, General Li, how far it was to Phoenix Pass. Roughly twenty-eight li, he replied. The news threw Grand Censor Liang into a panic. With a shout, he began herding all the observers back down the watchtower. Get the horses and carriages ready to move, he said, and don't waste a minute. We are heading back at once.

Unfortunately, the accuracy of Chief of Staff Yang Song's dire prediction became apparent as dusk was falling: The first wave of beaten soldiers, after abandoning their helmets and battle armor, emerged from a grove of trees west of the city in full retreat. That occurred just as the imperial procession was setting out from the Northwestern Duke's estate, amid the shouts and defeatist talk of the fleeing soldiers. Dayu's entourage followed mine, and I heard the pitiful wails of Dayu's concubines in their carriage, with all its feminine decorations. Dayu himself sat astride a red horse with black mane and tail and bellowed at his retainers, Load my liquor vats onto a cart! To emphasize his point to the confused retainers, he brought his whip down on their heads. Now get back there and load those liquor vats onto a cart! Not for nothing was Dayu, the Northwestern Duke, known for his fondness for women and drink, I was thinking.

We occasionally came upon the body of an abandoned soldier in a wheat field alongside the road. They had died during the retreat and were tossed off covered wagons carrying the wounded as soon as they breathed their last to lighten the load for the horses. The corpses looked like wooden logs lying in the snow-covered wheat fields, though the rank smell of blood hovered above them. Seeing them reminded me of the concubines and serving girls buried in the Imperial Tombs at Brass Rule Mountain; at least they had the good fortune of lying in red coffins. As I passed in the Dragon Carriage, I counted thirty-seven corpses in all. But I screamed when I got to number thirty-eight, for I saw him straining to crawl in the snow where he lay. With difficulty, the man raised a hand, as if he wanted to shout out. But if he did, I didn't hear it. His face was a bloody mess, his red war robe sliced into strips of red cloth that fluttered in the air. He was holding his other hand over his exposed belly, and I quickly discovered that he was trying to keep a length of purple intestine from spilling out, gut that had been sliced through by a razor-sharp sword.

I'm going to vomit, I said to Swallow as I clapped my hand over my mouth. He cupped his hands. Do it in here, Your Majesty. Wracked by heaves, I buried my face in Swallow's hands. Then I heard the weeping of one of my Imperial Guards, muffled by the helmet covering his face. That surprised me. Why are you crying? He stifled his sobs, pointed to the dying man in the field whose belly had been slit open, and said, Your Majesty, that man is Yang Song, your chief of staff. I beg Your Majesty to show him the kindness of taking him back to the palace. I took another look through my window at the man, and saw that it indeed was my chief of staff, Yang Song, who had led the cavalry charge on Phoenix Pass. By now he was standing up in the snow, rocking back and forth, his intestines oozing through the gaps between his fingers, the snow beneath his boots stained red. His eyes peered out through the caked blood on his face, filled with sadness and hopelessness. His lips quivered, but no sound seemed to emerge from his mouth. Whether he was trying to shout or was just moaning, I couldn't tell. I also couldn't tell if what I felt at that moment was amazement or terror. Whichever it was, I shrank back into the carriage and shouted a single command to the guard, one that seemingly defied all reason:

Kill him.

The guard quaked, his face paled, and he looked at me with questioning eyes. Kill him, I repeated, patting the quiver of arrows on his back. I watched as the guard steadied his bow on the window of my carriage, but he held back from letting the arrow fly. Do it, I demanded. If you are thinking of disobeying my command, I'll have you killed along with him. He turned to me and said, his voice breaking, The carriage is bumping around too much for me to get a good shot. I grabbed the bow and arrow out of his hands. You're worthless, all of you, I said. I guess I'll have to do it myself. And that is what I did. Propping myself against the window, I shot three arrows at the dying chief of staff, one of which caught him square in the chest. As Yang Song fell to the snowy ground, I heard a chorus of startled shouts from up ahead and behind. People in the procession had likely discovered that the man covered in dark blood was Yang Song and were awaiting a command from me. The three arrows from my bow clearly threw fear into those who had held back, but for another group of people, those who did not fight wars, it was something to rejoice over, a true relief.

I killed him, I said to Swallow, who stood there wide-eyed and slack-jawed, as I laid down the bow. When Yang Song left without permission, he earned a sentence of death. Then he became a defeated general, and he had to be killed.

Your Majesty is a wonderful archer, Swallow complimented me in a soft voice. The look on his little face was a mixture of horror and fawning. His hands were still cupped and filled with my vomit. I heard him repeat what I'd just said: A defeated general, he had to be killed.

Don't be afraid, Swallow, I whispered in his ear. I only kill people I don't like. And anyone I want killed is as good as dead. That is the best part about being Emperor. If there is anyone you want killed, just tell me. Is there anyone you want killed, Swallow?

I don't want anyone to die. He thought for a moment, then looked up at me and said, Your Majesty, let's go play cat's cradle.

My western tour had been cut short by a surprise attack by troops of the Peng Empire, and the fault probably lay mainly with me. Our helter-skelter retreat turned what was to be a grand western imperial inspection into a laughable absurdity. My civil and military officials blamed each other and raised voices of discontent while the carriage drivers raced day and night, as commanded, to take me and other members of the expedition out of danger as quickly as possible. I am sure I must have seemed dejected as I sat in the Dragon Carriage, thinking back to what the soothsayer had revealed to me before I left the palace. If an arrow is fired at the Emperor, it will be snapped in two by a gust of wind from the north, he had said. I did feel as if an assassin's arrow imperceptibly but inexorably followed me everywhere I went. But where was the wind from the north? And how would it snap the assassin's arrow in two? Maybe the soothsayer had made it all up.

At a way station in Peizhou, en route to Pinzhou, I received word that Peng troops had seized not only Phoenix Pass but thirty li of the valley belonging to the Xie Empire. Peng soldiers had torched the estate of the Northwestern Duke and smashed countless casks and vats of liquor. Dayu was inconsolable. Holding his head in his hands, he rolled around on the ground, keening and vowing to castrate Shaomian, the Emperor of Peng, and steep his testicles in liquor for the duke to enjoy. I was unmoved by Dayu's agony. The purpose of my expedition to Phoenix Pass had been pleasure, plain and simple. Now the pass had fallen into the hands of the Peng Empire, and all I wanted was to return to my palace in safety.

I thought back to all the territorial expeditions of emperors down through history, and the dangers and mishaps that had accompanied them, thoughts I found both appealing and frightening. Back in Peizhou, Swallow and I played a game behind the way station feed tent that was more fun than anything we'd done during the trip. We dressed up in one another's clothes, and I told him to ride the imperial steed around the way station. I want to find out if anyone wants to assassinate me, I said. He looked quite regal as he sat on the horse, and was obviously enjoying himself pretending to be Emperor, while I sat on a haystack watching for any suspicious activity around him. None of the retainers who were busy feeding the horses saw what we were up to, nor did they notice that the real Emperor was just then sprawled atop a haystack. Rather, they prostrated themselves on the ground when Swallow rode by.

No assassins, Your Majesty, Swallow reported after he had made a turn around the place, a strange rapturous look on his little face. Should I ride out to where the peasants live, Your Majesty?

Get down. Suddenly, I wasn't quite so happy. I dragged him down off the horse, rather ferociously, and demanded that he change out of my clothing at once, suddenly understanding their importance, and, at the same time, realizing how much I had missed wearing them, even during the short duration of our game. I find it difficult, impossible even, to describe the unease and sense of melancholy I had felt as I sat on the haystack and gazed out at Swallow riding my horse, for it dawned on me that the imperial garb of the Xie Emperor looked as suitable and as impressive on anyone else as it did on me. Dress up in the yellow clothes of a eunuch, and you become a eunuch. Put on the

Emperor's imperial robe, and you are Emperor. That was a sobering experience.

Swallow had no idea why our game had ended so abruptly, and his eyes betrayed his bewilderment as he undressed. I warned him sternly that he had better get out of them quickly. If Madame Huangfu knew what was going on, I said, that will be the end of it for you.

Frightened, he began to cry, and I later discovered that he'd wet his pants. Fortunately, that was after he'd handed back the imperial robe. I hate to think what might have happened if he'd pissed on *it*.

After only one day in Peizhou I grew feverish, caused perhaps by the clothes-changing game I'd played with Swallow. We'd swapped clothes behind a haystack, where my fragile constitution had suffered in the chilled wind. But I told no one what we'd been up to. The Imperial Physician gave me a pill, promising that I'd be fully recovered the next day. The pill had a horrible gamey taste, and I wondered if he had made it with animal or human blood. I managed to swallow half of it, and spat out the other half. Then, the next day, shortly after setting out, I found I didn't feel good at all, which threw the officials—civil and military—into pandemonium. They immediately brought the procession to a halt and had the Imperial Physician check my pulse to see what was wrong. He brought me another of those reddish-black pills, but I kicked it out of his hand, and in the midst of my light-headed distress, screamed, Don't you dare give me any of that blood, I won't take it. The Imperial Physician picked up the broken pill and whispered something to Grand Censor Liang. Soon thereafter, we were back on the road, traveling day and night to reach Pinzhou as soon as possible, for they had learned that the three most accomplished physicians in all the empire had taken up residence on the estate of Zhaoyang, the Western Duke.

I spent virtually the entire stop in Pinzhou in bed, slipping in and out of consciousness and unaware of the frightening events taking place as I slept. Several times Duke Zhaoyang summoned the three physicians to my bedside, but I have no recollection of what they looked like or what they might have said. Not until later, thanks to Swallow, did I learn that one of them, Yang Dong, had laced the medication he gave me with poison. Trembling fearfully, Swallow told me what had happened and revealed the subsequent attempt to conceal what had occurred. He had been warned that he was not to say a word to me about any of this, on pain of death. I recall how quiet the Western Duke's estate was that day and how weak rays of sunlight filtering in through the window landed on me as I was experiencing the first stages of recovery, pricking my tender skin like thorns. Drawing my sword from its sheath beside my pillow, I sliced a nearby flower stand in two, so frightening Swallow that he fell backward onto the floor. He begged me not to reveal his name when I meted out punishment.

I summoned Grand Censor Liang and other officials, who knew at once what was wrong by the look of rage on my face. They fell to their knees by my bed and waited to be disciplined.

Only the bearded Zhaoyang, sideburns pointed like swords, wearing a white robe and black boots, knelt on one knee in the doorway, hands behind his back as if holding something.

What are you hiding, Zhaoyang? I asked, pointing the tip of my sword at him.

It is the head of my Royal Physician, Yang Dong, he said, abruptly raising a hand in the air. That's exactly what it was, a bloody human head. The Western Duke's eyes began to tear up. I, Zhaoyang, beheaded him myself, he said, and am here to receive Your Majesty's punishment.

Did your physician try to poison me on your order? I asked, showing him my back so as not to have to look at the severed head. I feared I might vomit again. Hearing a short mocking laugh, I spun around angrily and shouted, What are you laughing at? How dare you mock me!

In your wisdom you know I would not dare to mock Your Majesty. I was sighing over Your Majesty's youth and innocence, your inability to protect yourself against the elements and human attacks, and your ineptitude in getting to the bottom of things. If I had ordered the poisoning, if I truly wanted Your Majesty dead, would I have carried out the deed on my own estate? And why would I have needed to employ my physician to that end? Wouldn't I have been better off taking advantage of Your Majesty's Twelve-Eight pleasure outing?

I was speechless. Apparently, news of my earlier pleasure outing in Pinzhou had reached the ears of Zhaoyang. I looked down at the prostrating officials at the foot of my bed and saw that they were studiously keeping their silence. I suppose they were afraid of offending the noble and esteemed Western Duke.

Why did the Royal Physician Yang Dong want to kill me? I asked, once I'd calmed down.

He who lives by the sword dies by the sword, Your Majesty. Yang Dong was the brother of Yang Song, your chief of staff. They were very close, and Yang Dong learned that at Jiaozhou Your Majesty personally buried an arrow in the chest of Yang Song, who had served the throne so well. Once again, a look of grief spread across Zhaoyang's face, and he looked at me with fire in his eyes. Although it was not sanctioned by Your Majesty, Yang Song led soldiers to Phoenix Pass to come to the aid of its defenders. But it was an act of loyalty to the throne, an honorable attempt, despite the defeat, and I, Zhaoyang, do not know why Your Majesty decided to kill him in the wheat field.

Now at last I knew the background of the Royal Physician Yang Dong. But I did not know how to respond to Zhaoyang's pointed question, especially under his penetrating gaze, which first embarrassed, then infuriated me. I threw my sword at him. Get out of here, I said. I'll kill whomever I please. You can keep your concerns to yourself.

I heard Duke Zhaoyang sigh as he looked heavenward. The Emperor is young, and very cruel, he muttered, and calamity will soon befall the Xie Empire. Still holding the head of Yang Dong in his hand, he backed out of the doorway. His mournful comment was the same as the one that had so often come from the mouth of the madman Sun Xin.

Just before we left Pinzhou, we experienced a rare winter rainfall. As my procession passed by the virtually deserted execution ground, I saw through the mist that the heads mounted on the poles had been washed clean by the falling rain, so that each of the faces looked fresh and alive. The brown skin of a human being flapped amid the five severed heads, and I was told it was the skin of the Royal Physician Yang Dong. Western Duke Zhaoyang had brought Yang Dong's head to show me and had hung up his skin to show the masses, while burying his headless, flayed remains in Pinzhou's Imperial Tombs.

To my surprise, Yang Dong's skin suddenly broke free and floated over, landing on the roof of the Dragon Carriage. Everyone who saw it, myself included, was scared witless by this fluke occurrence. I will never forget the wrathful appearance and explosive slap when it hit the roof.

I slipped into one daylight nightmare after another on my dazed return trip to the capital. I saw the Yang brothers following me, with Yang Song holding his bloody intestines and Yang Dong, waving his flayed skin, hard on his heels. Assassins, assassins, I shouted in my semiconscious state, and refused to allow the procession to stop for the night. Later on, a clutch of women appeared to join up with the Yang brothers, open mouths showing their missing tongues, or flinging their pink fingers to the ground as they ran, hair flying, clothing tattered and torn, like a horde of little white demons running madly down the road. Among them were Madame Yang and the concubine Dainiang, both of whom I had all but forgotten. They were calling out shrilly as they ran. You are not the rightful Emperor of

Xie, Madame Yang was saying. My son Duanwen is the true
Emperor. There was an aura of lustfulness about Dainiang as
she chased after me, dress billowing in the wind to expose her
soft white breasts and buttocks. Come to me, Your Majesty, she
called. I heard my response: a weak panting sound mixed with
moans. Don't come up to me, I wanted to say. I'll kill you both
if you do. But, all of a sudden, I couldn't make another sound. I
kicked the bronze brazier at my feet with all my might and
scratched the face of my bodyguard with my fingernails. No one
in the Dragon Carriage knew what to do. When it was all over,
they told me that in my semi-delirious state I had repeated one
phrase over and over:

Kill them.

FOUR

I WAS LONELY AND BORED as I lay ill in Cultivation Hall.
The sound of northern winds filled my ears throughout the
winter, which seemed especially dreary with the rustling of dead
leaves on the trees outside. My mother, Madame Meng, came to
my bedside each day, either to see if I was getting better or to
shed tears in secret. She was worried that there were people at
court who would take advantage of my illness to stage a palace
coup, and suspicious that my grandmother, Madame Huangfu,
might set some sort of conspiratorial trap. Madame Meng's endless prattling disgusted me, and sometimes she reminded me of a
caged parrot. Dancing girls gathered round the brazier to sing
and dance, while musicians remained outside to play their
instruments. But their efforts were futile in the face of my stubborn anxieties and fears. Through the dancing girls' sheer, long-

sleeved dresses and gold and silver hair ornaments, I caught glimpses of bloody intestines writhing and circling through the hall and human skins floating close to the floor amid the sounds of the musicians. Kill, kill, kill. Without warning, I leaped into the midst of the dancing girls, madly swinging my sword through the air. Grabbing their heads in a panic, they scurried off like rats. The Imperial Physician at the palace announced that I was possessed by an evil spirit, and that my illness was certain to linger for some time to come, at least until flowers began to bloom in the warmth of spring.

All court business was suspended for seven days. When my grandmother, Madame Huangfu, tried to engage me in a conversation, I spoke only the single word Kill. Greatly disappointed, she attributed the onset of my illness to carelessness by officials accompanying me on my trip and punished them all. Grand Censor Liang, who had been in charge, recognized the danger in attending court that day, choosing to stay home and commit suicide by swallowing gold. On the eighth day, Madame Huangfu discussed the situation with the prime minister, Feng Ao, the two of them concurring that I should take my place on the throne despite my illness, and devised an appalling means to keep me from ranting and raving in view of everyone. They stuffed my mouth with silk and tied my arms to the Dragon Throne. That way, officials who entered the hall could look upon my face but would hear nothing.

That despicable woman and her despicable underlings were treating me, the Great Emperor of Xie, like a common criminal.

That winter, for the first time in my life, I was subjected to utter humiliation. With my mouth stuffed with silk as I sat tied to the Dragon Throne receiving a stream of civil and military officials, tears of mortification and rage clouded my vision.

The map of the Xie Empire was redrawn by the court artist. A hundred li of territory around Phoenix Pass, including the city of Jiaozhou, were now in the hands of the resurgent Peng Empire. The artist's name was Zhang. After drawing the new map of Xie, he cut off one of his fingers and wrapped it in the map, which he sent up to the throne. The palace was abuzz with word of his deed.

I cast my eyes on the new, bloodstained map. The empire had originally taken the shape of a large bird, but during the reign of my father, the right wing had been sliced off by our neighbor to the east, the Xu Empire. Now the bird's left wing had been lost under my guardianship, and the empire looked more like a dead bird, one that would never fly again.

The sky was clear, the air warm on the day I finally began my recovery, I recall, and on the advice of the Imperial Physician, I went into the grove behind the palace to listen to birds sing. He believed that this would hasten the recovery of my ability to speak. There I spotted several swing sets hanging from the limbs of trees; golden pheasants stood on the swings like humans, casting looks from side to side. In mimicking the twittering birdcalls, I found that the state of my vocal cords improved considerably. It was a wondrous morning, one that left me with enduring interest in and an abiding love for birds of all kinds.

From beyond the dense grove of Chinese scholar trees and cypresses, somewhere in the Cold Palace, came the sound of a flute, a song of grief and misery, like a stream of icy water flowing at the base of the palace wall. I sat on one of the sets, swinging back and forth weakly to the sound of the flute before settling to the ground. I truly felt like a bird in the woods and harbored a desire to fly.

Fly, I shouted abruptly into the air. It was the second sound I had made in many days. Fly. I shouted the word over and over, echoed by the eunuchs who attended me in the grove. They were both startled and delighted.

After sitting there a while, I pulled myself up by the ropes and stood on the swing seat. Then, stretching out my arms, I began stepping back and forth, recalling the sight of the tightrope walkers I had seen perform in Pinzhou. Their unfettered, soaring artistry had made a lasting impression on me. I stepped back and forth, as they had walked the tightrope, the swing seat swaying to and fro. Yet I kept my balance as if steadied by an invisible hand, controlling my movements and the seat beneath me like a tightrope walker.

Guess what I'm doing, I said to the eunuchs standing on the ground below.

They exchanged glances, probably not knowing what I was up to, but astonished that all traces of my illness had vanished. It was Swallow who broke the silence. He looked up at me and smiled, a mysterious glow in his eyes. Your Majesty is *tightrope walking*, he said. Your Majesty is actually *tightrope walking*.

I'd had no news of my brother, Duanwen, for a long time. But on the morning following my return from the western inspection tour, he had taken his bow and quiver of arrows and the works of the classic masters to Mountainside Hall at the base of Brass Rule Mountain, accompanied only by a handful of juvenile attendants. That was where I had studied before ascending the throne, and my mother, Madame Meng, assumed that he had some evil motive in choosing that particular spot for his studies. At his age, Duanwen should have already taken a wife, but he refused to even think of marriage for the time being, for he was obsessed with his study of the martial arts, and was mesmerized by Sunzi's treatises on war. She believed that Duanwen, who had brooded all these years over the Xie throne, must be cooking up a conspiracy of some sort. Madame Huangfu, on the other hand, viewed the change differently. Her attitude toward all her grandsons, each of them a prince, was one of tolerance and affection. Let him leave the palace, she said to me one day. No mountain can be home to two tigers. You and your brothers have been at odds since the beginning, and it is far better to let one of them go than to keep him around and be involved in constant squabbles and intrigues. It will also relieve some of my worries. I said I didn't care one way or the other, that it didn't concern me whether or not Duanwen was in the palace, and that I would not interfere in anything he did so long as he refrained from plotting against me.

I honestly did not care. I had long felt that the murderous
intentions of Duanwen and his brother Duanwu were on the
order of ants trying to topple a tree, and so long as they did not
enlist the support of my grandmother, the powerful Madame
Huangfu, they were incapable of harming a single hair on my
head. I pictured Duanwen's somber, even gloomy face, and then
I pictured his heroic bearing as he sat astride his red horse with
its black mane and tail and brought down a vulture with a single
arrow; that image raised suspicions in my mind and a strange
sense of foreboding. I suspected that at some point he and I may
have been switched, and at times I suspected that what Madame
Yang said before she was sealed up in her coffin to be buried
alive was right on the mark, that I was a false Xie Emperor, and
that Duanwen was the true heir. I did not feel that I had the look
of a legitimate Xie Emperor, while Duanwen definitely did.

There was no one to whom I could reveal this anxiety. In my
heart of hearts, I knew there wasn't a soul with whom I could
discuss my feelings of inferiority, not even Swallow, who was
closer to me than anyone. But from the earliest days of my life
as Emperor, when I was afraid of my own shadow, that anxiety
was like a boulder pressing down on the imperial crown, and it
affected my state of mind. That must be how I gradually turned
into a stubborn and eccentric young ruler.

I was sensitive. I was cruel. I was devoted to having fun. In
sum, I was immature.

Madame Meng could not stop worrying about what Duanwen was doing outside the palace, so she sent a spy disguised as

a woodcutter to observe everything that happened in Mountainside Hall. The spy reported back that Duanwen studied in the mornings, practiced martial arts at noon, and slept under candlelight at night, nothing out of the ordinary. But then one day the spy ran breathlessly into Spring Welcoming Hall to break the news that Duanwen had set out on a journey to the west before dawn. Madame Meng said that's exactly what she had anticipated. She believed that he was on his way to Pinzhou to ally himself with Western Duke Zhaoyang, whose favorite concubine, also named Yang, was Duanwen's aunt. By fleeing to the west, Duanwen had revealed his dissatisfaction with the current state of affairs as well as his intent to change it.

You must stop him, Madame Meng said after describing all the dire consequences of Duanwen's alliance with the Western Duke. If you do not, you will have released a tiger into the mountains. Fire seemed to leap from her eyes as she counseled me not to let the loathsome Madame Huangfu know what I was doing, for she would certainly try to stop me.

I took my mother's advice, for a woman living deep in the palace develops a profound and unique understanding of important goings-on in its chambers. I knew that Madame Meng's power came from the throne on which I sat, and that she used half her intelligence to engage in intrigues, some secret and some not, with Madame Huangfu; the other half she employed in the enterprise of keeping the crown on my head, in part because I was her own flesh and blood, and in part because I was the supreme sovereign, the Emperor of Xie.

.   .   .

My horse soldiers raced to the ferry crossing at Willow Leaf Crossing, where they blocked Duanwen's passage. Apparently, he broke free and ran like mad to the crossing in an attempt to leap onto the ferry. Standing knee-deep in the icy water, he turned and fired three arrows at the horse soldiers, throwing such a scare into the ferryman that he rowed frantically to the middle of the river, thwarting Duanwen's plan to climb aboard. After taking a few more steps toward the boat, Duanwen turned again to look at the soldiers and at the Black Panther banner one of them held aloft. The white light of tragedy and despair showed in his eyes as he decided to drown himself in the Willow Leaf River. In less time than it takes to tell, he flung himself into the river, to the horror of the soldiers on the shore, who spurred their horses into the water, dragged the drenched figure of Duanwen out of the river and laid him across one of the horses.

Saved from drowning, Duanwen now sat astride a horse, immersed in silence. Some of the people who came out to watch the returning procession knew that the rider was Prince Duanwen, first in line for the throne, and assumed that they were witnessing the return of an army from battle. Many of them lit strings of firecrackers hanging from tree branches in celebration. As tiny explosions and loud cheers filled Duanwen's ears, tears slipped down his cheeks; his gloomy face stayed wet even after he reached Mountainside Hall at the foot of Brass Rule Mountain.

I went to see Duanwen once during his confinement in Mountainside Hall, which, except for him, was deserted. The white herons had flown off to an unknown destination over the winter, and dead branches from the ancient trees lay strewn in front of the hall. Remnants of a snowfall some days earlier lay on the stone steps. I spotted Duanwen sitting alone on a stone bench, buffeted by a cold wind, waiting for my entourage to arrive, the look on his face devoid of hatred or resentment.

Were you planning to flee to Pinzhou?

I have never planned to flee anywhere. I was going to Pinzhou to buy a new bow. You know, don't you, that Pinzhou sells the highest-quality bows and arrows?

That excuse is absurdly false. The truth is, you were planning a rebellion. I know exactly what you were thinking. You have always been convinced that the Imperial Father meant for you to be his heir to the throne. That's what you think, and what Duanwu thinks as well. Me, I have never given that a thought, not for a moment. But now I am the Xie Emperor, your lord and ruler, and I do not like the flame of melancholy in your eyes, the look of loathing that surfaces over and over, or, for that matter, your arrogance and superior airs. Do you know that there are times when all I want to do is scoop your eyes out?

I know. And not just my eyes. If there were something about my heart you didn't like, you would scoop that out as well.

You are very clever, much too clever for my liking. And what I dislike most is the way you use your cleverness in conspiring to seize the throne. I am tempted to lop off that clever head of yours and replace it with the head of a pig or a dog. Which would you rather be, a pig or a dog?

If Your Majesty is determined to put me to death, I prefer to kill myself and be spared the humiliation.

I watched as Duanwen stood up from the stone bench and went into Mountainside Hall, emerging moments later with a dagger in his hand. My bodyguards rushed forward and kept a wary eye on his movements. His face was white as the snow on the ground, but the hint of a smile crinkled the corners of his mouth. He held the dagger high over his head, its red copper blade glinting coldly in the sunlight, the sight momentarily all but making me lose consciousness. Images of the bloody scenes I had seen on the western expedition flashed through my mind: General Yang Song holding his intestines as he stood in the bushes, and the bloody head of his brother, Yang Dong, the fires of rage still burning in his eyes. An overwhelming giddiness toppled me into the arms of one of my bodyguards.

Do not let him die, I muttered. Dead people make me want to throw up.

The guards rushed Duanwen and wrenched the dagger out of his hand. He stood there like a rooted tree, gazing up at the summit of Brass Rule Mountain, bathed in the wintry rays of sunlight. He looked neither sad nor pleased, yet I saw on his brow the image of the late Emperor.

You neither let me live nor permit me to die. What does Your Majesty wish of me? Duanwen said with a sigh as he looked up into the heavens.

Not a thing. I want only for you to remain in Mountainside Hall, where you will continue to study. You are not to take more than ten steps beyond the walls of Mountainside Hall.

As I was leaving, I cut a gash on the trunk of a tall cypress. Duanwen is not to go beyond this mark. But as my glance moved up the tree, what I saw shocked me. The crusty bark of the cypress was dotted with white scars, and I knew they had been made by the tips of arrows. They were all the proof I needed of the regimen Duanwen had subjected himself to in quest of his goal.

Busybodies in the palace revealed the secret of Duanwen's confinement. My grandmother, Madame Huangfu, was furious. Only mildly critical of me, she took her anger out on Madame Meng, actually beating her on three separate occasions. This rebuke, delivered with unprecedented savagery, was such a loss of face for my mother that it nearly drove her to jump down the well behind Spring Welcoming Hall.

Duanwen's confinement led to such an uproar at court that senior ministers scattered around the city came to offer their views, most of which dealt with the disadvantages of a dispute between brothers. Prime Minister Feng Ao was the only official who put forth a practical suggestion, which was to find a wife for Duanwen as soon as possible, thus bringing relative stability to the life of someone who was forever flirting with danger. The key element in Feng Ao's memorial had to do with steps to be taken following Duanwen's marriage, specifically to appoint the prince as an enfeoffed lord. That way I could send him out of the palace to guard a strategic pass and eliminate the awkward reality of strife between brothers in the Xie ruling family. Feng Ao, whose hair had turned white as snow, still had a booming voice. Now serving his second Emperor as prime minister, he had established his authority throughout the land and had earned the trust of Madame Huangfu, who nodded her approval while he read his memorial. That told me that his suggestion would soon be implemented.

I became a mere observer, since I was unwilling to countermand Madame Huangfu's order, and would have been powerless to do so even if I had tried. Yet I was curious to see what sort of bride she would choose for Duanwen. A great many palace ladies who had served my father remained in the palace, and if I'd had my way, I'd have chosen the oldest and ugliest among them to be Duanwen's wife, even though I knew that was out of the question, given the ethical bonds between family members. Madame Meng, her heart filled with hatred, made a prediction. You wait and see, she said. That wretched she-wolf will force a girl from her own family onto Duanwen, and sooner or later the Xie court will be completely under her control.

Madame Meng's prediction came true in short order, for Duanwen was betrothed to the sixth daughter of Huangfu Bin, the head of the Civil Service Board, and was, in fact, Madame Huangfu's grandniece. I knew that the girl had dark, swarthy skin and was slightly cross-eyed. The palace was buzzing with gossip about the marriage being forced upon Duanwen, and the older retainers sighed over the fact that the once proud prince had now become a marionette whose strings were pulled by the old lady. Young palace maids and the palace eunuchs were beside themselves with delight on the day of the wedding, hiding in the corridors and stuffing themselves with sweets.

As for me, I gloated, but not without pangs of compassion for him, like a fox grieving over the death of the rabbit. It was

the first time I'd ever felt sorry for Duanwen, the first time I'd
seen weakness in him. He's marrying a cross-eyed girl, I said to
Swallow. That Huangfu girl isn't good enough to be one of my
slave girls. Poor Duanwen.

The wedding took place in Blue Phoenix Hall, one of the
palace side buildings. Duanwen was, of course, a prince of the
Xie court, and as Emperor I was barred from attending weddings
and funerals of those beneath me, in accordance with precepts
passed down by our ancestors. So I withdrew to Cultivation
Hall, where I planned to spend the day. But the celebratory
music coming from that part of the palace sparked my curiosity,
so, with Swallow at my side, I sneaked over to the building
through a garden gate. The sentries, recognizing me at once,
stood there wide-eyed and slack-jawed, clearly alarmed, as I
stood on Swallow's shoulders, rising into the air as he straightened up, until I could see through the window of Blue Phoenix
Hall, where the ceremony was in progress.

The drums boomed out a second time as light from red candles painted the participants in the wedding deep scarlet, invest-
ing the corpulent bodies of the imperial family with ghostly airs.
Together, the peaked hats and wide sashes of the officials and
the petticoats, hair ornaments, and perfumed sideburns of the
women cast an aura of fanciful gaiety. I spotted my mother,
Madame Meng, in the crowd; a forced smile undulated on her
heavily powdered face. Madame Huangfu, longevity cane in
hand, sat regally in a chair, her saggy jowls flapping from side to
side as her head swayed, a common malady among the privi-
leged classes. Her swaying head signified appreciation of the

royal wedding she had engineered. The embodiment of benevolence, the epitome of contentment.

I had arrived just in time to watch the bridegroom, Duanwen, remove the red veil. His hand hung motionless in the air
for a long moment before he jerked the cloth away from the
bride's face. The movement of that hand could not mask its
owner's disappointment and dejection. The Huangfu maiden's
downcast eyes were, as usual, focused on two separate spots on
the floor, which made a mockery of her bashfulness. From my
vantage point, I could not help laughing. That my uncontrolled
laughter rocked the people inside was immediately apparent,
since their heads swiveled in the direction of the window. I
noticed the customary look of gloom on Duanwen's ashen face,
despite the fact that it was his wedding day, and saw his lips
twitch as he spotted me through the window. I could not hear
what he said, and perhaps he said nothing at all.

I jumped down off of Swallow's shoulders and fled Blue
Phoenix Hall as fast as my legs would carry me. Countless red
celebratory lanterns hung on both sides of the path from the side
building to Phoenix Rites Hall. I pulled one down as I passed
and continued on to Cultivation Hall, still running as fast as I
could. Swallow tried to get me to slow down, fearful I might
stumble and fall. But, clutching the lantern, I kept up the fre-
netic pace, not knowing what had spooked me so badly. It could
have been a feeling that the drumbeats and cymbal clangs were
right on my heels, or maybe I was frightened by the prospect
that the terrifying ceremony itself was chasing me.

Freezing rain fell that night as I lay on the imperial bed and

pondered my own future wedding. My heart felt hollow, surrounded by a sense of sadness. Palace lanterns outside Cultivation Hall flickered in the dark, their burning wicks threatening
to succumb to the rain. As a night watchman beyond the wall
struck the third watch on his clappers, I imagined that Duanwen
had already led his bride into the bridal chamber.

Those little white demons invaded my dreams again, but this
time their features were clearly defined. They were all females,
tattered clothing covering most of their ghostly white skin as
they sang and danced beside the imperial bed. Lewd, seductive
female demons, their cool, glossy skin glistening like crystal. No
longer afraid, this time there was no need for me to summon the
monk Juekong to drive them away. Sexual desire invaded my
dreams, leading to a nocturnal emission. Awakened by the experience, I climbed out of bed and changed my underwear.

Before many days had passed, Duanwen accepted an
appointment as Guangyu Commanding General. With an army
of three thousand cavalry troops and three thousand foot soldiers, he was to leave for Jiaozhou, charged with the mission of
sealing our northern border and stopping the Peng Empire from
making further incursions into our territory. When he received
his official seal in Abundant Hearts Hall, he was also given the
Sword of Nine Pearls, left behind by the late Emperor. As he
knelt in thanks to the Emperor, I noticed the jade *ruyi* carved
with a Black Panther hanging on his belt, a gift from our grandmother, Madame Huangfu, and a treasure I had often sought

but never obtained. This discovery was a blow to my self-esteem, and while Duanwen was accepting the congratulations and Godspeed of ministers and officials, I stormed out of Abundant Hearts Hall.

Just what was Madame Huangfu up to, always shifting her stance—one hand to the clouds and the other to the rain? I despised her political maneuvering, the way she dispensed little bits of favor to her sons and grandsons. Long into her declining years, why did she insist on burning the little candle remaining in her life in an effort to control the minutiae of the Xie court and exhaust herself trying to dominate all aspects of life among its inhabitants? I began to seriously ponder the possibility that she and Duanwen were somehow in collusion.

What were they up to?

That is the question I once put to Zou Zhitong, a member of the Imperial Academy. Zou was a Confucian of considerable learning, a scholar whose writings were the envy of his peers. But he turned tongue-tied when he tried to answer my question, and I could not make sense out of what he muttered. I knew that was caused by fear of Madame Huangfu, and all I could think was: Wouldn't it be wonderful if the monk Juekong were here? Unhappily, he was in his monastery on Bitter Bamboo Mountain.

Someone was sobbing softly behind the curtain. Who's there? I asked as I pulled back the curtain. It was Swallow. His eyes were puffy from crying. The moment he saw me, he stopped, fell to his knees, and begged my forgiveness.

Why are you crying? Who has been bullying you?

Your slave does not wish to startle Your Majesty, but the pain is more than I can bear.

Where does it hurt? I'll summon the Imperial Physician for you.

Your slave dare not. The pain will go away soon enough. Your slave does not want to startle the Imperial Physician.

I asked you where it hurts. I detected something besides anguish in Swallow's expression, and I knew it was time to let the tide expose the rocks. Out with it, I said, with a threatening look on my face. If you dare try to deceive your lord and ruler, I'll summon the executioner. You'll tell me once you get a taste of his whip.

My backside. Swallow pointed to his buttocks and began to cry again.

I had no idea what he was talking about until he hemmed and hawed an explanation. Then I understood. I had heard rumors about an unsavory relationship between Prince Duanwu and an actor in town, something the academician Zou Zhitong had referred to distastefully as a cut-sleeve romance. But never had I dreamed that he would brazenly bring his repugnant activities into the palace, and worse, that he would perform his wicked deeds on Swallow, my personal favorite. This constituted yet another taunt by the two brothers.

I flew into a rage and demanded that the miscreant Duanwu be brought to Cultivation Hall at once. Swallow blanched, fell to the floor, and begged me not to make the incident public. A bit of physical discomfort for your slave counts for nothing, he said. But if word gets out, it will be my death sentence. On his knees at my feet, he banged his head in supplication as if crushing cloves of garlic. Seeing him bow and scrape like that disgusted me, which I expressed by giving him a swift kick in the buttocks. Get out of my sight, I said. I do nothing on your behalf. I have long yearned to punish Duanwu for his arrogance and overbearing attitude.

After the executioners, heeding my command, had laid out their instruments of torture at the front of the hall, the eunuch I'd sent to fetch Duanwu returned to Cultivation Hall to report, Third Prince Duanwu has bathed and is now dressing. He will arrive soon.

Duanwu made his appearance at Cultivation Hall. The court eunuchs were secretly smiling, and I watched him swagger up to the table on which the instruments of torture were laid out. He reached out and picked up a scalpel and twirled it in the air. What game are you playing today? he asked the executioner, totally unaware of what was in store for him. The executioner, who was standing beside him, responded with silence. I was about to step down off of the throne platform when Swallow screamed shrilly, His Majesty is furious, Third Prince. Hurry, run away.

Duanwu reacted to the shout with terror, and he turned to run, picking up the hem of his robe. He slipped into his leather sandals and broke through the ranks of eunuchs. Elder Empress Dowager, save me! he shouted as he fled in panic, cutting a sorry, comical figure. The eunuchs ran after him, but returned empty-handed after a few minutes to report that Duanwu had in fact run straight to the elder Empress Dowager's Splendor Hall.

My chance to punish Duanwu in secret had gone up in smoke, so I turned my anger on the victim, Swallow. How could he have sunk so low? You disgusting slave, you will take Duanwu's punishment. I commanded the executioner to give Swallow three hundred lashes as punishment for his disloyalty. But since I could not bear to watch his agony, I walked back to the throne, filled with indignation, and listened through a curtain to the cracks of the whip as it tore his flesh.

The depth of Swallow's degradation was perplexing, and I wondered if it had been passed down by his blacksmith father. Had a perverse birth produced a perverse character? The crack of the whip continued, accompanied by Swallow's moans and womanish sobs. He kept saying that a bit of physical discomfort for a slave counted for nothing, but the sacred altars of the state counted for everything, and that he, the slave, would die with no regrets if he could avoid causing a rift between Emperor and prince.

Moved by Swallow's words, I grew fearful that his delicate body would not hold up under the whipping I had ordered, so I told the executioner to stop. Swallow rolled off of the whipping bench, struggled to his knees, and kowtowed to express his gratitude. His little round face had not lost its peach-colored glow, but his cheeks were awash with hot tears.

Does it hurt?

No, not now.

You're lying. How could a hundred lashes not hurt?

Your Majesty's benevolence has allowed your slave to forget his pain.

I found Swallow's dissembling humorous. There were times when I was disgusted by his obsequious behavior, but more times when I appreciated, enjoyed it even.

The world around me was complicated and eventful during the early years of my life as Emperor. Shifting tides in the palace and beyond its walls were recorded by men of letters, amounting to many volumes, and anecdotes of the Imperial court spread throughout the empire. But it is my first winter as Emperor that is most indelibly stamped onto my memory.

I was fourteen. It snowed on the twenty-seventh day after the winter solstice, so I led a group of young palace eunuchs out to a garden pavilion, where we engaged in a raucous snow fight. The elixir-refining cauldron that had been in use during my father's reign now sat abandoned beside the pavilion, where the snow accumulation was the deepest. The toe of my boot happened to bump into something soft next to the cauldron, and when I dug down into the snow, I discovered the frozen body of an elderly court eunuch.

The frozen corpse was none other than the madman I had known so well, Sun Xin. Why, I wondered, had he chosen to remain alongside his cauldron as snow fell to earth the night before? Maybe he had slipped too far into madness to ever be brought back, or maybe he was thinking he should light one more fire for the late Emperor's longevity pill amid swirling snowflakes.

Sun Xin had died clutching an unburned piece of kindling. His face, blanketed by snow, was moist and fresh, like that of a child. His deep red lips were parted, and it almost seemed as if I could hear his raspy voice say to me, Sun Xin is dead, and calamity will soon befall the Xie Empire.

TWO

LADY HUI, WHO HAD COME from a rich merchant family in Pinzhou, was clever, intelligent, and quick-witted. She was also a woman of ethereal beauty and celestial fragrance. In my arms she was an obedient and adorable little lamb, and among my concubines she stood out as a proud and unique peacock. In my youth, I found it all but impossible to be away from Lady Hui's charming, innocent smile and the unique aroma of her skin, and I was deeply hurt by all the palace disturbances that resulted from her favored position.

I recall encountering Lady Hui one spring morning alongside the Imperial Stream; she was still a young palace girl then, recently brought into the palace. As I crossed the bridge on horseback, the clatter of hooves startled a flock of birds, sending them into the air above the river, and frightened a girl who was running beside the stream. Through a thin veil of mist I saw her mimic the motions of a bird on the wing, flapping the baggy sleeves of her dress as she ran. When the birds settled back to earth, she stopped, put her fingers to her mouth, and made a series of birdcalls. She did not spot my pony until the birds had flown away over the tops of nearby willow trees and disappeared, and I watched as she ran panicky behind one of the trees and wrapped her arms tightly around the trunk. She managed to hide her face, but her pink, trembling hands and a pair of grandma green jade bracelets were out in plain view, which I found laughable.

Come out here. Whipping my pony, I galloped over to the tree and poked the little hands with my whip, eliciting a shriek of fright from behind the tree. But she stayed hidden from view, refusing to show herself. So I poked her again, drawing another shriek from her and a hearty laugh from me. If you don't come out, I said, I'll use my whip on you.

A face of peerless beauty peeked out from behind the tree, a look of fear and trembling nestled in the radiant, nearly heart-stopping aura of the girl's twinkling eyes and glistening teeth. All but blinded by her beauty, I was utterly captivated.

Forgive me, Your Majesty, your slave girl did not know that Your Majesty had ridden up. As the girl fell to her knees, she looked up at me out of the corner of her eye to satisfy her curiosity.

So, you know who I am, do you? Why have I never seen you before? Do you work in Madame Huangfu's quarters?

Your slave girl is so new in the palace that her name has not yet been entered in the Imperial Register. She smiled softly, which I noticed as she raised her head slightly and gazed at me with a bold, mischievous look. The moment I laid eyes on Your Majesty's elegant bearing and Imperial countenance, I guessed the Imperial identity without having the fortune of encountering it before. You are the supreme and lofty Emperor of Xie.

What is your name?

I currently have no proper name, and would be honored if Your Majesty were to give me one.

I jumped off my jade hare pony and lifted the girl up off the ground. Among all the palace girls, she was the purest, most innocent, loveliest I had ever seen. And none of the others had ever dared speak to me as she had done. I took her hand in mine; it was a delicate and smooth hand, the palm of which held several crab-apple blossoms. Come ride with me. I lifted her up onto the horse, which drew a shrill cry of panic from her. I don't know how to ride. That was followed by silver bell peals of gleeful laughter. Is horseback riding fun?

Words fail me when I try to describe the joy and the excitement I felt upon meeting Lady Hui. I can, however, recall how riding with her behind me that morning signaled the end of my abhorrence of girls. The aroma of her clothing and her jet-black hair was fresh and bewitching, close to the subtle fragrance of blooming orchids. My jade hare mount trotted along the Imperial Stream on its way into the depths of the Xie Palace. Early-rising gardeners stopped trimming trees and bushes to gape at the jade hare mount and its two riders. Truth be told, for those hopelessly startled gardeners, for me, and for the flattered Lady Hui, it was a truly memorable morning.

Were you trying to fly like a bird just then? I asked Lady Hui as we sat astride the horse.

Yes. Birds have been my favorite since childhood. Does Your Majesty like them?

More than you do. I looked into the sky above the Xie Palace, which was filled with streaks of golden light from the sun as it climbed slowly above Sundial Gate. Early morning birds that normally perched on the glazed tile eaves were nowhere to be seen. The birds have flown away, I said, somewhat puzzled. Your arrival has frightened off all the palace birds.

Harmony had never existed between my grandmother, Madame Huangfu, and my mother, Madame Meng. But the attitude both women adopted toward Lady Hui was identical. They disliked her and found the way I doted on her intolerable. Madame Huangfu was disgusted by the barbarian airs she saw in Lady Hui and chastised the official in charge of selecting concubines for bringing a girl like that into the palace. As for Madame Meng, who was instinctively jealous of pretty girls, she considered Lady Hui to be the human reincarnation of a seductive fox who would one day corrupt the palace with her promiscuous deeds, ultimately affecting even the future of the empire.

In tandem, the two women blocked my attempt to elevate Hui Xian, the girl from Pinzhou, to the status of First Imperial

Concubine. I suffered through an entire spring over this unpleasant affair, trying every strategy I could concoct to prove that my love for the girl from Pinzhou was Heavenly ordained. Like me, she was a devoted bird fancier who, given the youthful innocence of her soul, perfectly complemented my solitary nature. But the two narrow-minded, stubbornly biased women treated my pleadings as delirious ravings, and, suspecting that the girl, Hui Xian, was a behind-the-scenes instigator of my desires, vented all their anger on her.

Madame Huangfu began by summoning Hui Xian to Splendor Hall, where, after a lengthy interrogation, which was long on ridicule, she warned her that she was to stop seducing the Emperor. My mother, Madame Meng, then summoned Hui Xian to the cold confines of the rear palace, where she was shown the palace women who had been crippled by all manner of punishments. With a smile, she asked Hui Xian, Is this the path you wish to take? Weeping openly, Hui Xian shook her head and said, I am guilty of nothing. My mother, Madame Meng, said with a sneer, What does that mean, guilty? Guilt is the result of human conduct and its application a human prerogative. I tell you now, seducing the Emperor may be easy, but no easier than slicing off your nose, gouging out your eyes, and tossing you into the Cold Palace.

All this I learned much later, thanks to my loyal slave Swallow. During the time that Hui Xian was confined in Beamless Hall in one of the palace wings, we were reduced to exchanging lovesick notes, with Swallow as our messenger.

My endless pining over the girl from Pinzhou created a

desire to write poetry. Throughout that vexing spring I had no interest in governing, content to spend my days in Cultivation Hall, virtually transfixed as I poured my emotions onto paper and designed all sorts of palace stationery. Then, at night, when all was quiet, Swallow delivered them into the hands of Hui Xian in Beamless Hall. This work held me spellbound, though in truth it was really a sad sort of game. My feelings were complex and quite absurd. On quiet spring nights, as tears wetted my cheeks and I recited the lyrics of Li Qingzhao's "Note to Note" to the bright moon and winking stars, I ceased being the illustrious ruler and was transformed into a love-struck, frustrated scholar who pined for the woman of his dreams. This transformation caused me great anxiety and melancholy.

My sentimental musings were eventually collected into a volume entitled *Records of Cultivation Hall*, which was disseminated all over the Xie Empire and to many neighboring countries. Literati and rich men copied palace stationery that Swallow and I had created, including chrysanthemum stationery, red peony stationery, gold sprinkles stationery, and five-color powdered stationery. These valued papers were quite popular as gifts for a while, but that is a story best left for another time.

One drizzly, breezy night Swallow led me quietly through a hidden gate behind a grove of speckled bamboo to the vast Beamless Hall, which was the magnificent legacy of master craftsmen from an earlier age, constructed without roof beams and devoid of windows and doors. Its most imposing feature was a gigantic altar behind several biers that contained the heroic spirits of the founders of the Xie Empire. Why, I wondered, had Madame Huangfu and Madame Meng chosen this remote hall in which to confine Hui Xian? Maybe it was the absence of roof beams, which precluded her from choosing the traditional expression of defiance by women—self-strangulation; or maybe the two women had exiled her to this dark, dank, and remote hall, where they would call upon their feminine patience and, with careful premeditation, wait for her to simply waste away. Then again, maybe it was nothing more than an offhanded means of punishment. I simply couldn't say. These thoughts bore down heavily on my heart, and as my fingers brushed against a mossy wall, a cold, slippery sensation traveled throughout my body, as if I had touched death's gate.

The light of a candle suddenly illuminated the vast interior of the hall, and the girl appeared in the light, all bones, facing a stack of stationery, downcast and sad. I saw eighteen birdcages arrayed neatly alongside her, all empty. Over each of the previous eighteen days I had sent Swallow to Beamless Hall with a different species of bird to keep Hui Xian company throughout her frightful ordeal, never anticipating that all eighteen would be set free. My heart was as empty as the cages. I held my tongue until Hui Xian suddenly realized what was on my mind.

Forgive me, Your Majesty. Your slave released all the birds, but not in defiance of Your Majesty's generosity.

Why then? Did you not say you love birds?

Your slave is guiltless, as are the birds. I simply could not bear the thought of their suffering with me. Wrapping her arms around my legs, Hui Xian fell to her knees and began to sob. In the many days that we had been apart, her voice had changed from that of a young girl, crisp and still immature, to that of a grown woman, husky and recriminating. She said, I beg Your Majesty not to believe that I have rejected your favors. Your slave has lost her looks and her heart has died. She has allowed her pristine body to remain alive only for Your Majesty. I entrusted my true feelings to the freed birds and sent them to Your Majesty. Had I not, I would have died with everlasting regret.

I blame you for nothing. I do not know who to blame. But one of the birds was a domesticated oriole, and since it cannot fly far, it will die before it gets to wherever it is going. You should not have released the oriole.

The oriole died, and since your slave had no place to bury it, I entombed it in my makeup case. Hui Xian reached behind the altar and reverently brought out a sandalwood makeup case. She opened the lid to show me what was inside.

I don't need to look. It's dead, so just throw it away. I shook my head. The smell of rotting flesh from the dead bird was heavy in my nostrils, but Hui Xian continued holding the box as if it were a sacred object. Her imaginative way of entombing the bird filled my head with thoughts, and in the dim light of the candle, I took the girl's hands and looked into her eyes. In the pallor of her face, I saw an inauspicious shadow. It was a single feather from a beautiful dying bird that floated past her lovely face and left its shadow behind. I reached out to caress that delicate, icy face, once, twice, several times, until my hand was wet from her tears.

Hui Xian's tears gushed like a fountain as from memory she recited the poems I had written, interrupted often by sobs. When she finished the last one, "Shorter Magnolia," she swooned in my arms. I held the poor girl tightly, waiting with boundless affection for her to regain consciousness. The sound of a flute floated into Beamless Hall that night, chilling and distant. The smell of rotting wood in the hall mixed with the orchidlike fragrance of the girl, lending the atmosphere a dreamy quality. I knew then that I had truly fallen into the chrysalis of what transpires between a man and a woman.

I am determined to elevate this girl to the status of First Imperial Concubine, no matter what, I said to Swallow.

That decision led to a major palace incident, when I coerced the two women into elevating Hui Xian to the status of First Imperial Concubine. It all came about after Swallow related to me a popular tale. In it, in order to take a prostitute as his wife, Scholar Zhang cut off one of his fingers in front of his parents. I did not know if the unduly clever Swallow was hinting that I should adopt the same strategy, but there was no question that I found the story illuminating.

I still recall that stifling midday in Splendor Hall when I took aim on the middle finger of my left hand with the blade of my sword, turning the two women pale with fright. Their expressions went from alarm to anger, and from there, gradually, to frustration, accompanied by silence. My mother, Madame Meng, rushed up and snatched away my sword, while Madame Huangfu cowered on a pile of sable furs and sighed sorrowfully, over and over. My shocking behavior had the effect of a violent assault on her aging body. Her white old head rocked hilariously from side to side, as ancient tears snaked across the wrinkles of her gaunt face.

By all appearances, I'd miscalculated. Madame Huangfu wiped away the tears and vented her worry and despair on the leopard cat beside her. How could the ruler of an empire turn out like this? she said. It looks as if the Xie Empire and all its territory will crumble and die by Duanbai's hand.

Our eunuch scribe looked to one side and then the other, finally coming to the realization that the elevation of the First Imperial Concubine signified a dramatic and irreversible change. The name of Hui Xian, the girl from Pinzhou who until that moment had been unknown, was entered into the Imperial Genealogy, thus becoming the sole imperial concubine chosen not by others but by me.

Lady Hui had been born on the edge of my imperial sword. The spot at the rear of Beamless Hall, where she had lived for six years, was converted into a small tower and given the name Singing Oriole Pavilion, to memorialize the joys and sorrows of partings and reunions.

T HE TIME HAD COME FOR ME to marry, and even the common citizens of the empire of Xie knew the political advantages to be had by my taking a girl from the empire of Peng as Empress. The gradual decline of Xie and flourishing of Peng had created a political chessboard, and the threat of white pieces being taken by black had already been, or was about to be, realized. In the spring of the fourth year of my reign, unsettling reports of fighting by Xie and Peng armies in the border regions came with increasing frequency. Farmers from those regions were fleeing into the interior and the large cities with their plows, hoes, and other farm implements, bringing with them even more horrific news. The arrogant, tyrannical Emperor Shaomian of Peng stood on the outer wall of the occupied border city of Nizhou and pissed in the direction of the Xie capital, proclaiming loudly that it would take the armies of Peng no more than eight days and nights to capture the Xie Palace.

And so my wedding became an important piece in this dangerous chess game, the last hope of relieving a perilous state of affairs. During those days, I was on pins and needles, no different from any ruler at a dangerous moment in his empire's history, as I sat on the throne in Abundant Hearts Hall and listened to my military and civil ministers and officials engage in battles of words without being able to mediate. I had no illusions that I was anything but a figurehead, and that everything ultimately rested in the hands of Madame Huangfu, Madame Meng, and Prime Minister Feng Ao. So I kept my mouth cautiously shut.

The envoy chosen to travel to the empire of Peng and discuss wedding arrangements was the Imperial Censor, Liu Qian. Censor Liu enjoyed the reputation of a man who had a silver tongue and a knack for diplomacy, both within the walls of the palace and beyond. The ministers and officials differed greatly in their judgment of his task, but my grandmother, Madame Huangfu, placed this last stake on Liu Qian's mission. She loaded his chariot with six chests of gold, silver, and precious gems, including many priceless national treasures. Then, just before he departed, she promised a reward of a thousand hectares of fine land and ten thousand taels of gold if he was successful in his mission.

No one so much as took notice of my passivity or pessimism, and no one realized that the ostensibly illustrious Xie Emperor played only an insignificant role during this crisis at court. Over the days that followed, while all awaited the speedy arrival of news, I tried to imagine the lovely visage and elegant bearing of Princess Wenda of Peng, hoping that she possessed the extraordinary bearing and redolence of Hui Xian and the musical talent of Dainiang, as well as the wisdom of Juekong and the warm generosity of Swallow. But it was not to be, for I received word that Princess Wenda was a young woman of mediocre looks and eccentric behavior, and that she was three years older than I.

Liu Qian returned in three days, bringing with him one of Princess Wenda's embroidered incense pouches. The atmosphere in the Xie Palace was one of unalloyed joy, from top to bottom. As I walked back from Abundant Hearts Hall following the imperial audience, I spotted several eunuchs and palace girls chattering in the corridors, their faces adorned with silly grins. Struck by an inexplicable gorge of anger, I ordered Swallow to drive them all away.

I forbid them to laugh, I said to Swallow. Slap the face of anyone who laughs. No one in the palace is to laugh for three days.

Swallow did as I commanded, reporting back later that altogether more than seventy laughing palace denizens were slapped, so many that his arm was sore.

On the eve of my wedding I had a series of strange dreams. I dreamt that I was hopping around the palace like a little bird, quickly passing through all eighteen gates. I dreamt of a vacant piece of blurry land over which a white light flickered, and around which a sea of dark, shadowy human figures assembled. A tightrope walker's rope stretched tautly above my head, and a voice echoed in the air above the people: Grab hold of the rope, climb up, walk the rope, climb up, walk the rope. I grabbed hold and flew skyward as effortlessly as a little bird, landing perfectly on the taut rope. Then my body, the rope, and I all began to sway; I took three steps forward, then one back, light as a feather and exhilarated, puffs of thin mist rising in my soul as I walked the rope.

I disliked Empress Peng; Empress Peng disliked my First Imperial Concubine, Lady Hui; and Lady Hui disliked my other concubines—Han, Lan, and Yun. I knew that since time immemorial emperors and kings needed to be surrounded by beautiful women, and that open conflict and veiled struggles in imperial harems usually gushed like fountains, with little hope of stopping them. Over the years I tried everything to avoid getting caught up in the squabbles among the Empress and my concubines, but I was not always successful, and there were times when, planned or otherwise, I was dragged into a whirlpool of silly female strife.

In the observant eye of my Chief Eunuch, Swallow, the Empress and my concubines formed alliances almost immediately. Lady Peng and Lady Lan joined forces, and were favored by Madame Huangfu. Lady Han and Lady Yun were cousins, nieces of my mother, Madame Meng, and openly viewed her as their protector, a fact that did not go unnoticed by court denizens.

What about my Lady Hui? I asked Swallow.

Lady Hui is proud and aloof, but is the beneficiary of Your

Majesty's patronage, and that is all she needs, Swallow said with a smile. In my opinion, fortune has smiled upon Lady Hui.

I fear only that she is an ill-fated beauty, and that my patronage may not be powerful enough to ward off attacks from all quarters, open or veiled. Deep in thought, I sighed and reached into my shirt, removing a small embroidered pouch that held cosmetic powders and a lock of Lady Hui's hair. Sometimes when I opened the pouch, an inauspicious illusion appeared before me—the lock of hair would rise up into the air and float aimlessly in the rafters of Cultivation Hall, eventually disappearing in the darkness. I am afraid that she is a bird that has landed on the wrong perch, I said to Swallow, voicing my anxieties, and sooner or later she will be knocked down into the mud.

Neither the Empress nor any of the concubines could tolerate my affection for Lady Hui, and none believed that their beauty was inferior to hers. So they inferred that Lady Hui resorted to black magic in her dealings with the Emperor. I received word that Lady Peng had taken her case to Madame Huangfu, accompanied by Lady Han and Lady Yun, tearfully requesting that Lady Hui's use of black magic be verified. In an expression of generosity, Madame Huangfu gave her permission. I could not keep from laughing, for try as I might, I found it impossible to explain away the women's laughable actions. But when the news reached Lady Hui, she shed tears of anger. As she dried her eyes, she asked me what she should do. Rumors are born and die on their own, I said, and you need not be concerned. Even if you did practice black magic, I would willingly

be the object of your sorcery. Since ancient times, the private
lives of emperors and kings have been sacrosanct, and no one
can keep you and me from sharing a bed. She only half believed
me, but finally I saw a smile break through the tears.

Then one day, the existence of an eavesdropper in Singing
Oriole Pavilion led to one of the most scandalous affairs in the
palace. I do not know how the poor palace girl Gui'er managed
to slip under the imperial bed, and she might well have secreted
herself there for hours. When Lady Hui got out of bed to fetch
hot water, she spotted the hem of Gui'er's skirt poking out from
under the bed. Thinking it was a yellow scarf that had fallen to
the floor, she reached down to pick it up, and dragged out the
girl's foot. I can still hear Lady Hui's piercing squeal, which
brought panicky sentries bursting into Singing Oriole Pavilion.
Gui'er was shaking like a leaf, scared witless and unable to
speak. She pointed to the window, wanting us to know that she
was acting under orders.

Who told you to do this? Holding Gui'er by her coiled knot
of hair, I forced her head back until she was looking up at me.

Empress Peng. The words were barely out of Gui'er's mouth
when she began to wail. Spare me, Your Majesty, she sputtered
amid tears. Your slave saw nothing, I honestly saw nothing.

What did Empress Peng want you to see? I knew without
asking, but wanted to make her disclose everything.

To see how Lady Hui bewitched Your Majesty with her
black magic. But your slave saw nothing. Your slave girl's only
sin has been her greed for nice things, and that is why I did what
I did. I beg Your Majesty to spare me.

What did Empress Peng use to buy you off? Lady Hui asked.

A pair of silver bracelets, a phoenix filigree, and a pair of jade earrings, that's all.

A truly despicable slave girl, that's what you are! Lady Hui cursed between clenched teeth. Is that little bit all it took to tempt you to do something that could cost you your head? As I see it, that jewelry was Empress Peng's funeral gift to you.

The palace girls dragged Gui'er out of Singing Oriole Pavilion like a lamb being led to the slaughter, leaving in her wake weak protestations of innocence. Lady Hui and I exchanged silent looks as the brass hourglass showed the time to be the end of the third watch. The palace was still, and Lady Hui's face had the pallor of new snow, as tears of humiliation slipped from her dark eyes.

Has Heaven decreed that there is no place for me in the Great Xie Palace? she asked.

I do not know.

Has Heaven decreed that my place is now beside the Emperor? she then asked.

I do not know. I honestly do not know.

The following day, the little palace girl, Gui'er, was tied into a cloth sack and flung into the Imperial Stream. On Lady Hui's instructions, palace menials first placed the bribery items given to the girl by Empress Peng in the sack with her. The official in charge then opened the sluice gate to let the sack and its human cargo float past the palace wall and out into the river that flowed through the capital. This, the most common form of capital punishment by the Xie court, was known as a floating farewell.

That night a troupe of actors entered the palace to perform an opera. As I sat in the first row beneath the stage set up in the eastern garden, there in plain view, sitting beside Madame Huangfu, was the author of this living drama, the Lady Peng. A round, silk fan with a peach wood handle covered half her face. She sat unperturbed, while Lady Han and Lady Yun grieved over the death of Gui'er. When Lady Han asked me why Lady Hui hadn't come out to enjoy the performance, I replied that she was not feeling well, and that she had no desire to watch opera. But I then heard Lady Han whisper to Lady Yun, Nothing has happened to the person who caused all this, over which poor Gui'er lost her life.

Empress Peng's quarters, Misty Sunset Hall, was only a hundred paces from Cultivation Hall, yet it was a distance I seldom traveled. The occasional night spent in Misty Sunset Hall was but to satisfy a requirement for palace etiquette. I could not abide the barbarous speech that came from Lady Peng's mouth, and found her unpredictable temper unbearable. There were occasions when I saw the shadowy outlines of wild Peng Empire beasts crouching in her hair ornaments or woven into her temple hair, which gave rise to shameful, disgraceful feelings in me. I once admitted to Swallow, For a powerful monarch to prostitute himself this way is both unspeakably absurd and deeply pitiful. As time passed, Swallow and I referred to Misty Sunset Hall as the Peng Empire. Each time I set out for Misty Sunset, I said to Swallow, Let the imperial procession set out for the Peng Empire to pay tribute.

The loathsome woman of Peng did not appreciate my make-believe merrymaking. A palace servant I had secretly placed in Misty Sunset Hall to be my eyes and ears reported that the Empress often made disparaging remarks about the administration of the Xie Empire in front of palace retainers, ridiculed me as incompetent, and cursed Lady Hui of Singing Oriole Pavilion. None of that surprised me. What I had not anticipated was news that the Lady Peng had secretly written to Emperor Shaomian of Peng. The messenger, who was stopped on the public road beyond the palace, handed over the urgent missive, into which three wild goose feathers had been tucked.

In the letter, which was filled with grumblings and spiteful remarks, Lady Peng complained that she lived a pitiful existence of constant abuse, ending her litany, incredibly, by begging her father to send a squad of crack soldiers to ensure her status in the Xie Palace.

I was livid. After secretly ordering the execution of the messenger, I summoned her to Cultivation Hall, where I had a palace eunuch read the letter aloud, so, amid my disgust, I could observe her reaction. At first panic showed on her face, but that gave way to a smug, insulting smile. She held a bright red cherry between her lips the whole time.

Exactly what is it you want? I asked, keeping my anger in check as best I could.

Nothing, actually. I knew that you would seize my messenger. I wanted to remind the Emperor that while Wenda may be only a woman, she is not someone who will tolerate being ill-treated.

That is a wild accusation. You are the Empress. I have treated you with utmost respect. Who, I ask, has ill-treated you?

I may be the Empress, but one who has been mistreated by a lowly concubine. The Lady Peng spat out the cherry pit, then covered her face with her hands and wept bitterly, stomping her feet and protesting, Back home in Peng, my father and mother treated me like a precious pearl. Never once, even as a child, was I bullied by anyone. I was totally unprepared for what awaited me in this miserable empire of yours when I was sent over in marriage, only to be mortified by a lowly woman. Who does Lady Hui think she is? She's a fox fairy, an evil demon, and the Xie Empire can accommodate only one of us: if not me, then her, and if not her, then me. I ask the Emperor to choose.

Is it Lady Hui's death you seek?

Either hers or mine, the decision is the Emperor's.

What if I choose to have you both die?

The Lady Peng stopped crying and looked at me with surprise in her eyes. But once again the derisive smile I hated so much appeared on her tear-streaked face.

I see the Emperor likes his little jokes. But I am sure that the Emperor will not jeopardize the future of the empire by a simple joke, she said as she glanced to her left and then to her right.

If not for the future of the empire, I would hand you a piece of white silk and order you to hang yourself.

Deeply angered, I turned and left Cultivation Hall, leaving Lady Peng sitting all alone. I stood for a long while out in the garden, the array of spring blooms bereft of their fresh beauty in my eyes. Even the chirps of purple swallows that skimmed the ground in front of a nearby wall sounded dry and dissonant in my ears. I crushed a cluster of plantains with my feet, then another, as I felt heat build up around my eyes. I reached up to touch them; my hand came back cold.

The campaign against Lady Hui by the Empress and my concubines grew increasingly vicious; aided by the support of Madame Huangfu and Madame Meng, the campaign, in word and deed, had gone about as far as it could go. But nothing shocked me so much as what happened one day in the peony garden, when Lady Hui was humiliated and set upon in ways I could never have imagined. Viewing the peonies was a major event in palace life, a once yearly procession out to the garden by all the palace ladies, led by Madame Huangfu. I recall that when the invitation arrived at Singing Oriole Pavilion, Lady Hui had a foreboding that something terrible would happen. Seized with fear, she asked if it would be all right for her to send her regrets, pleading illness. I am terrified whenever they are around. I could not agree to her request. They would not make things difficult for you on such an occasion, I said, and I think you had best go. You don't want to further incur the wrath of Madame Huangfu. A look of anguish appeared on Lady Hui's face, though all she said was, Since Your Majesty wishes me to go, I shall, assuming they will spare me their anger.

A vast gathering of women, dressed and made up as if vying to see who was the loveliest, formed in the peony garden and quickly fell in behind Madame Huangfu's gilded carriage. None of the women had flower watching in mind, as they whispered

in groups of two and three, spreading all sorts of gossip. Lady
Hui drifted intentionally to the rear of the procession, falling
under the spell of the radiant peony blooms in spite of herself.
Drinking in the beauty of the lovely flowers, she paid little heed
to where her lotuslike bound feet were taking her, until, quite by
accident, she stepped on the dress hem of Lady Lan, who was
walking just ahead of her. The disaster she had feared was not
long in coming.

You blind bitch, Lady Lan cursed as she turned and glared at
Lady Hui, then spat in her face. As if on cue, all the other palace
ladies stopped in their tracks and turned to look.

Fox spirit, said Lady Han.

Demon, said Lady Yun.

Shameless little trollop, said Empress Peng.

Absentmindedly, Lady Hui wiped the spittle from her face
with her mandarin duck lovers' sash, then stuck the end of the
sash into her mouth as she fearfully surveyed the faces of the
four imperial ladies who were united against her. She could
hardly believe what she had heard. But when she looked down at
her foot, she was forced to believe that it had been the cause of
the venomous verbal abuses.

Are you cursing me? Lady Hui asked with earnest anxiety as
she grabbed Lady Lan's hand. I stepped on your hem, but it was
only an accident.

An accident you say? You were trying to make me look bad.
With a sneer, Lady Lan flung Lady Hui's hand away, adding a
final barbed comment: And what good will it do you to take my
hand? If it's a hand you want, go take the Emperor's.

She has grown used to holding someone's hand. Not having a hand to hold makes her uncomfortable. All the sluts from Pinzhou are like that. Empress Peng glared at Lady Hui, hoping to provoke her.

Like an autumn weed blown over by a gust of wind, Lady Hui settled slowly to the ground, and as she did she saw that all the palace ladies in the peony garden had stopped and turned their gazes on her. She wanted to fight back, but her counterattack sounded weak and vague, like talking in her sleep. The clusters of peonies suddenly emitted a powerful red light that enveloped the swooning Lady Hui. It was not till later that someone reported that Lady Hui had shouted Save me, Your Majesty, over and over that day. But at the time I had secretly left the palace with Swallow to watch the performances of a circus troupe in the city square. There were no daring tightrope walkers that day, and I returned listlessly to the palace at dusk, when I learned of Lady Hui's humiliation.

That spring, in the third month, Lady Hui took to a sickbed in Singing Oriole Pavilion. The wrinkled brow that told of her suffering only made me love her more, and I summoned the Imperial Physician to come care for her. What he told me after the examination came as a wonderful surprise. Congratulations, Your Majesty, he said, the First Imperial Concubine is more than three months pregnant.

The joy of impending fatherhood washed over me for the first time in my life, dispelling all the gloom that had held me in its grip. I rewarded the Imperial Physician handsomely and asked when the little prince was due. He counted on his fingers.

The child will be born soon after the beginning of autumn. Can you tell if it is a boy or a girl? I asked. The graying old physician stroked his beard and thought deeply for a long moment before saying, In all probability it will be a prince. But the First Imperial Concubine is weak and frail, and there is always the risk of a miscarriage. Only through proper nutrition and care can that possibility be avoided.

I went up to Lady Hui's bed, took her dainty hands in mine, and placed them against my chest, my most common expression of affection toward women. I saw that even though she was bedridden, Lady Hui had tucked a red flower behind her ear, and that she had spread a layer of rouge over her cheeks to cover up the pallor caused by her weakened condition. The melancholy that lay behind her smile was obvious, even to me, and the sense I had of her that moment was of a lovely paper figurine, partly pressed up against my chest and partly floating in the air before me.

You are already three months pregnant. Why did you not tell me?

Your lowly servant was afraid.

Afraid of what? Do you not realize that this is the most wonderful news for the Xie court?

Your lowly servant was afraid that if word got out too early, it might invite disaster.

Are you afraid that Empress Peng and the concubines will be jealous? Afraid they will harm you?

Yes. Your lowly servant is deeply afraid. They have never approved of me, so how could they let me be the first to carry a dragon child? They would be bereft of glory. I know there is nothing they will not do.

Don't be afraid. After you give birth to the heir to the throne, I will find a way to dispose of that venomous Peng woman and will make you Empress. That is precisely what my ancestors did.

But your lowly servant is afraid nonetheless. Lady Hui covered her face with her hands and began to sob. She fell into me like a willow bent by the wind. What your lowly servant fears most of all, she said, is that the pregnancy will end badly, and that it will all be nothing but a dream. I will have failed to live up to Your Majesty's high expectations. Your Majesty is unaware that there have always been schemes to end pregnancies or exchange newborn infants in the palace, and your lowly servant is afraid that she will be the victim of one.

Where did you hear such wild talk?

I heard some and guessed the rest. Nothing in the world is as mean as a woman's heart. And only a woman can see the dreaded viper that lives in another woman's heart. I am deeply afraid, and only Your Majesty can do what has to be done.

What would that be? Tell me what you would have me do, and I shall do it.

If Your Majesty were to move to Singing Oriole Pavilion or move me into Cultivation Hall, where I could remain under your protection day and night, there might be a chance that I could avoid misfortune. Lady Hui looked at me with hope in her tear-filled eyes, then, without warning, banged her head against the edge of the bed in a supplicating kowtow. I beg Your Majesty to keep mother and child safe.

Dumbstruck by her plea, I turned my head to avoid her gaze. As ruler of the Xie Empire, I knew for certain that this was wishful thinking on her part. It violated court etiquette and went far beyond the bounds of propriety for any ruler. Had I agreed to turn this fantasy into reality, I would have met fierce opposition in the palace, from top to bottom. And even if I had granted Lady Hui's request, there were no guarantees I could have carried it out. And so, as gently as possible, I denied her request.

Lady Hui's sobs turned to heartrending wails, and nothing, it seemed, could stop them. I could not say or do anything to lessen her sadness. I dried her tears with the back of my hand, but that did not stem the flow. Finding her interminable wailing irritating, I shoved that sorrowful body away and walked over to stand on the other side of the painted screen.

Moving into Singing Oriole Pavilion is out of the question, and moving you into Cultivation Hall would bring utter disgrace to the Xie court. I can, however, honor any other request.

Lady Hui's sobs shuddered to a stop and were replaced by the sounds of anger born of desperation. Your slave asks that Your Majesty settle accounts by punishing Ladies Lan, Han, and Yun. If Your Majesty truly loves me, he will also reprimand Empress Peng. Only when they are given a hundred lashes, two hundred lashes, as many lashes as it takes to kill them, will I be happy.

I was aghast, incapable of believing that such loathing had fallen from the lips of Lady Hui. I returned to her bedside, where I saw her face, made ugly by grief, and her eyes, which burned bright. What I could not believe was how simply I had, until that moment, judged women. I found it impossible to believe that this woman was the artless and gentle Lady Hui, and wondered if the year she had spent in the rear quarters had changed her or if I had spoiled her by favoring her so single-mindedly. I remained standing silently for a long while before walking out of Singing Oriole Pavilion without a word to its occupant.

An empire is treacherous, as is a palace; but neither is as treacherous as a woman's heart. As I walked down the jade steps, sadness welled up inside me. If Lady Hui remains as she is now, I said to the eunuch behind me, truly calamity will soon befall the Xie Empire.

Without thinking, I had repeated the late attendant Sun Xin's prophecy. The significance was lost on the eunuch, but the unintentionally uttered comment frightened me.

I did not settle accounts for Lady Hui by subjecting the palace ladies to a whipping. Yet the suspicions engendered in her by the pregnancy left me with some doubts. In private, the court historian divulged to my horror that there were ample cases of induced abortions and exchanged infants in the courts of all nations. The only precaution I could take was to conceal Lady Hui's pregnancy from others, and to admonish the Imperial Physician and the eunuchs and the palace girls in Singing Oriole Pavilion to guard our secret zealously.

Events would prove the futility of my scheme. A few days later, I went to dally briefly in Lady Han's Fragrant Joy Tower.

After Lady Han's tender ministrations, she put her mouth up to my ear and whispered, I hear that Lady Hui is pregnant. Is that true?

Startled, I asked, Where did you hear that?

Madame Meng told Lady Yun and me, she revealed proudly.

From whom did Madame Meng hear it? I insisted.

Madame Meng is Your Majesty's mother. Does she have to hear such news from anyone? When we were on our outing in the peony garden the other day, one look told her that Lady Hui was pregnant. Lady Han sneaked a look at me to see how I took the news. With a forced little laugh, she said, Why does Your Majesty look so troubled? Like your slave, Lady Hui is but a concubine, yet this is glorious news for the court.

Shrugging Lady Han's arm off my shoulder, I grasped the railing and looked off into the distance, where Singing Oriole Pavilion was partially hidden by green willows. Was the woman who lived there still crying into her pillow? Spring sunbeams lit up the red roof tiles of Singing Oriole Pavilion, but the woman inside slept in unremitting darkness. I struck the railing with my hand and sighed, sensing that a foreboding red aura was rising in the air from Singing Oriole Pavilion.

Why are you all intent on harming Lady Hui?

How could Your Majesty believe your slave capable of anything like that? Lady Hui and I are as close as well water and river water. Why would I wish to harm her? With characteristic glibness, Lady Han deflected my probing question. Flicking the wide sleeve of her red silk gown in the direction of Misty Sunset

Hall, she said, This is not a matter for someone as lowly as I. Your Majesty should take it up with the Empress.

I assumed that since even Ladies Han and Yun had learned of the news out of Singing Oriole Pavilion, Lady Peng was sure to know it as well. Not surprisingly, the next day, Lady Peng came to Cultivation Hall to offer her congratulations on Lady Hui's pregnancy. I found her forced smile and resentful tone of voice intensely upsetting. Not at all inclined to explain the situation, I responded with a curt, Since something seems to be clawing at your heart, why don't you go back to Misty Sunset Hall and cry your eyes out? Momentarily staggered by my comment, Lady Peng quickly pulled herself together, produced a meaningful smile, and said, Your Majesty underestimates me. How could I, the Empress, lower myself to vie with a concubine? Throughout the three palaces and six courtyards, only the Lady Hui carries a dragon child, and she appears to enjoy considerable good fortune. I shall have to look after her like an elder sister.

Lady Hui was on tenterhooks during her pregnancy, like a bird that hears the twang of a bow. She treated every morsel of food brought to her with suspicion, fearful that the palace ladies had conspired with the Imperial Chef to secrete poison in her meals. Only after one of her serving girls had tasted the food would she eat any of it. The pregnancy sapped her beauty, as her complexion turned increasingly sallow, layer by layer. Faint lines of sadness formed in the space between her once lustrous eyes and mothlike brows; it was a face turned bleak. Whenever I went to see Lady Hui, I was confronted by someone as fragile as a sheet of paper swept up in a breeze. Strangely, the image of the poor soul being swept up in a breeze did not instill in me the power to ward off the winds about to bear down on Singing Oriole Pavilion.

Lady Hui told me she fed all the food Lady Peng sent over to a leopard cat. Lady Peng was well aware of that, yet continued to send over all sorts of edibles every day, rain or shine.

I do not know what sort of game she is playing, Lady Hui said, her eyes turning red again. Why does she keep sending it if she knows I won't eat it? One bowl after another, plate after plate. Does she really expect to win me over that way, to soften my long-hardened heart?

I looked down at the leopard cat as it slept atop one of the carved railings, showing no trace of having been poisoned. Women's minds are a bewildering mystery. Nothing I said or did could dispel the unyielding paranoia of Lady Hui, nor was there any way I could fathom what game Lady Peng was playing.

I was an Emperor who had been sucked into the maelstrom of feminine life. As I rushed among the three palaces and six courtyards, my crown and slippers were spattered with spots of rouge and sprays of perfume, that and fouled water from mud-slinging. It was all quite natural.

SEVEN

IN THE SPRING OF THAT YEAR a plague of locusts descended upon the fields and villages in the southern reaches of the Xie Empire. It was like a black wind sweeping across the southern half of the empire, and in a matter of days the insects had denuded the fields of all their seedlings. Grief-stricken farmers howled before the devastation that was once their fields and cursed the heavens for sending down this calamity at the beginning of the planting season. Picking dead insects up off the ground, they protested the unfairness of vermin dying from overeating while they were on the verge of starvation. With anger leavened by feelings of hopelessness, they stacked the locust corpses into piles and set torches to them. There were reports that the locust fires burned for two days and nights, and that the stench carried all the way to the cities of neighboring empires over a hundred li distant.

Ministers blanched as talk of the locusts rose in the palace, for they feared that the effects of the lost harvest in the south would cause a nationwide famine after the advent of fall, stirring up food riots among the citizenry. During the morning audiences all I heard was Locusts, Locusts, Locusts, until I began to itch all over, as if a cloud of the pests had invaded Abundant Hearts Hall. I fidgeted on the Dragon Throne and cut short the interminable memorial by Prime Minister Feng Ao. No more talk of locusts, I demanded. Can't you ministers and senior officials discuss other affairs of state? Talk about anything you like, except locusts. Feng Ao, struck mute by my command, stepped back silently, his place taken by Yan Ziqing, head of the Ceremonial Rites Board, who handed up a written memorial. The magistrate of Pei County, Zhang Kai, died in the service of his people during the locust plague. I ask that Your Majesty commend Magistrate Zhang and reward his family to extol the virtues of a caring local official. How did Magistrate Zhang die in the service of his people? I asked. Was he bitten to death? Yan Ziqing reported ebulliently, Magistrate Zhang was not bitten to death. He died after ingesting a mound of locusts. He had led a procession of prefecture officials to local fields to save the crops by ridding them of insects, and when he realized that he was powerless to bring relief to the farmers, he took leave of his senses. Every locust he caught he chewed up and swallowed, so moving the commoners who witnessed the event that they wept bitter tears. I could hardly keep from laughing when Yan Ziqing finished his report. I mumbled an assent. The locusts ate the vegetation, and the County Magistrate ate the locusts. Nothing is too bizarre for this vast world, but this is bewildering.

I was truly bewildered. I did not know if it was appropriate to commemorate the magistrate of Pei County as a man of high moral principle and selfless virtue for the bizarre yet heroic act of eating a bunch of locusts. I often found myself in similarly awkward situations during morning audiences, and could only respond by giving irrelevant answers.

Has either of you ever seen a tightrope walker at one of the circuses? I blurted out to Ministers Feng and Yan.

That caught them by surprise, as anyone could see. While they stood there, puzzled by my question, mouths agape and tongue-tied, a commotion arose outside Abundant Hearts Hall. Palace guards rushed outside to see what it was. It turned out that an unauthorized individual had managed to enter the imperial grounds, and had been apprehended by sentries. I heard his husky shouts:

Get out of my way, he protested in a southern accent. I want to see the Xie Emperor.

I was just curious enough that day to order the guards to bring the man into the hall, which they did. Middle-aged and shabbily dressed, he was obviously a peasant, his skin darkened by the sun. Fatigue was written on his face, but he had the keen, intimidating eyes of a predator. I noticed that his clothes were in tatters, thanks to the whips and clubs that had been used on him, and that there were bruises on his toes from being dragged by guards.

Who are you? How dare you attempt to enter an imperial hall?

I am a peasant, named Li Yizhi, and I have braved death to plead on behalf of your subjects. We beg Your Majesty to forgive this year's seedling tax, head tax, and irrigation tax in districts affected by the locust plague.

It is right and proper for those who till the fields to pay taxes. Why should I violate this principle for you?

Your Majesty is astute and discerning. In the wake of the locust plague down south, all the rice seedlings have been devoured. The fields are barren, so how can we pay a seedling tax? The same logic holds true for the irrigation tax. And there could be nothing more unreasonable or cruel than a head tax, for the people down south now survive by eating weeds and the leaves of trees. Death by starvation and exposure to the elements is a daily occurrence. Abject misery is the lot of these people, but rather than come to their aid and relieve them of their suffering, the Crown imposes a heavy head tax. Tax collectors are relentless in demanding payment, and the people have nowhere to turn. If Your Majesty does not issue an immediate edict to exempt the people from paying taxes, popular feeling in the south will surely turn ugly.

The situation in the Xie Empire is ugly enough already, I interrupted Li Yizhi's reproach. How much uglier can it get? Just how ugly do you think popular feeling will get? I asked.

Brave and righteous warriors will head a popular revolt against a corrupt government, and as the empire sinks into turmoil, avaricious and unscrupulous officials will line their own pockets as they bully the weak and deceive the powerful. Even worse, the chaos will provide invading armies and domestic bandits with an opportunity to fish in troubled waters, to satisfy their greedy appetites by usurping power and overthrowing the throne.

How dare you, a piddling peasant, utter such alarmist sentiments in my presence. I laughed and ordered Li Yizhi out of the hall. The penalty for unauthorized entrance into an imperial hall is immediate execution, I said. But I shall reward your courage in risking death to make your case by sparing your life. Go back home and till your fields.

Li Yizhi backed out of the hall, tears of gratitude filling his eyes. But at the last moment, he took a tiny cloth bundle out from under his garment, unfolded it, and laid it on the floor. What the peasant left was the dry, dark carcass of a dead locust. He offered no explanation as he walked out of Abundant Hearts Hall under the stares of the assembled officials, who began whispering among themselves. Once again all I could hear was Locust, Locust, Locust.

I assumed that Li Yizhi would take advantage of my generosity to return to his home. How could I have known that sending him off like that would create an internal danger, and that the result would be a mockery of enormous proportions?

During the fourth lunar month, thousands of peasants and craftsmen from four counties—Pei, Ta, Yu, and Jian—raised the flag of rebellion on the banks of the Red Silt River. Calling themselves soldiers of the Heavenly Sacrifice Society, they headed west from the Red Silt River, and as they passed through three prefectures and eight counties they recruited volunteers and bought warhorses, quickly growing into a great army of more than ten thousand.

Reports reaching the court sent shock waves through the palace. Never in the two-hundred-year history of the Xie Empire had the peasants been anything but docile and law-abiding. This sudden eruption by the Heavenly Sacrifice Society threw the court into chaos. A tense, unsettled atmosphere prevailed.

Prime Minister Feng Ao told me that the Heavenly Sacrifice leader was the peasant who had disrupted the audience that day, Li Yizhi. I recalled the intimidating look in the swarthy man's eyes and was reminded of his bold remonstrance and daring actions. How I regretted my ill-advised act of releasing a tiger back into the mountains.

Has this rebellion arisen from the plague of locusts? I asked Feng Ao.

It has arisen from the taxation that followed the plague. Most of the rebels are residents of the locust-ravaged south who have always been opposed to oppressive taxation. Li Yizhi has stirred up popular sentiment with his call to gain relief by refusing to pay taxes.

That should be easy. Since the people down south are unwilling to pay taxes, I can issue an edict to exempt them. What else, other than opposing taxes, concerns them? Do they plan to attack the Xie Palace?

Opposing taxes and gaining relief are mere pretenses by the

Heavenly Sacrifice Society. Li Yizhi, who enjoys a reputation as a brave warrior in villages down south, is an ambitious man. He has contacted kindred souls of many sects and schools among brigands in the south, and I fear that he desires to overthrow the throne and establish a new dynasty. Internal rebellions are always more dangerous than outside aggression, so Your Majesty must not take this lightly.

There is but one way to deal with these rebels and brigands, I said. Kill!

Spitting out that familiar word made me strangely dizzy, much like reliving the bout of fever I had suffered years before. But the most inconceivable occurrence was how Abundant Hearts Hall itself seemed to quake, accompanied by a rustling sound. Then there appeared a hazy red light, in which I saw the bloody, headless corpses of the Yang brothers, alternating between lying still on the ground and swaying upright. Kill. I repeated the word, trancelike, and watched as a gust of wind billowed the pearl and jade beaded curtains and caused Yang Dong's pale yellow hide to float up into the air, circle the Golden Dragon Throne, then slowly fly back and forth in front of my face, finally forcing me to jump up out of the throne and wrap my arms around Prime Minister Feng Ao.

Kill. Kill. Kill. I reached out with both hands, but grabbed only thin air. Kill him, I screamed at Feng Ao. Kill them.

Be patient, Your Majesty, Prime Minister Feng Ao said calmly. Let me talk things over with the two venerable ladies. His eyes followed the movement of my hands as I groped the air around me, but he could not see the frightful pale yellow human hide, saw nothing, in fact. Only I could see the ghosts and demons in the Xie Palace, things hidden from view of others.

Just before Guo Xiang, head of the Military Board, set out with an army on his southern expedition, he submitted a military pledge to the court: Nothing short of total victory in this southern expedition will suffice, he said. Anything less and I will slit my own throat with a Dragon sword given by the Emperor. Guo Xiang enjoyed the reputation of a valiant general and military genius, and all the officials at court, civil and military, viewed the southern expedition with great optimism. Imagine our surprise when, barely half a month later, disheartening news arrived from the south. Guo Xiang's troops had been routed at the Red Silt River, his officers and men suffering grievous casualties. The bodies of the dead were then stacked up on the banks of the river by the Heavenly Sacrifice soldiers, where they formed a pair of flesh-and-bone dikes.

Apparently, Heavenly Sacrifice soldiers lured the enemy deep into their territory south of the Red Silt River. Guo Xiang, obsessed with thoughts of victory, ordered boatmen on the northern bank to build bamboo rafts overnight. At dawn, his troops boarded the rafts and began to cross the river. But halfway to the other bank, the rafts began coming apart, and the northern soldiers, strangers to water, fell into the river, where they fought over the floating bamboo. Guo Xiang's troops were in total disarray when, on the opposite bank, Li Yizhi and a hundred of his archers launched a barrage of arrows, accompanied by wild laughter. Shrieks of agony rose from the Red Silt River, and bloody corpses began floating downriver, carrying the Black Panther banner of the Xie Empire with them.

In the confusion Guo Xiang swam back to the northern bank, mounted a horse, and rode to a fishing village on the river, where he killed several of the men who had made the rafts. Having never tasted defeat before, Guo Xiang took leave of his senses. Holding three of the boatmen's severed heads, he rode back to the capital as fast as his horse could take him, weeping pitifully the whole way. Three days later, Guo Xiang, hair matted, face grimy, blood-spattered, appeared at the city gate. He flung the three heads into a trench, climbed down off his horse, and walked up to one of the sentries.

Do you know who I am? Guo Xiang asked.

You are General Guo, head of the Military Board. You led a southern expedition to punish the Heavenly Sacrifice Society, the guard replied.

That's right. And now it is time for me to slit my own throat. Guo Xiang drew the Dragon sword, smiled, and said, I am telling you and you are to tell the Emperor that Guo Xiang has been defeated and the future of the Xie Empire is in peril.

Guo Xiang's last words spread through the nation like wildfire and enraged many officials, civil and military, at court. In the days immediately following the Guo Xiang debacle at the Red Silt River, people came to Abundant Hearts Hall every day requesting a military assignment. All of them, major and minor officials, expressed unbridled contempt for Li Yizhi and his

Heavenly Sacrifice Society. They believed that our defeat was a direct result of Guo Xiang's reckless attempt to cross the river, and that if a crack underwater force were formed, the Heavenly Sacrifice scourge could be eradicated within a month.

As I saw it, all those requests for battle assignments were fabrications that masked a host of personal desires—either promotions in rank or overnight fame. My suspicion that the requests for battle assignments were vainglorious fictions caused me to vacillate when it came time to seek out commanders for a southern expedition. From her sickbed, my aging grandmother, Madame Huangfu, made known her deep dissatisfaction, for she was fearful that one day Li Yizhi and his Heavenly Sacrifice soldiers would storm Splendor Hall and take her life. Ultimately, she personally selected a candidate to lead the expedition, the great warrior general Duanwen, summoning him back from his garrison command in the northwest.

I was powerless to countermand Madame Huangfu's order, and besides, I could think of no one more qualified for the task. I wondered what would be on the mind of my half brother, the bitter enemy with whom I shared a bloodline but nothing else, when he returned to the Xie Palace after so many years of banishment.

As the date of Duanwen's return neared, I was in emotional turmoil, and each time the image of his dark, clouded, ruthless face surfaced, my heart filled with a strange heaviness. During that period, I bestowed my favors on the glib and keenly perceptive Lady Han. It took little effort for her to gauge my mood as we lay together on a splendid bed, and she tried to get me to tell her why I felt as I did. Since I did not want to reveal much to her, I put her off with a terse witticism:

A wolf will soon return to sink his fangs into someone, I said.

Is the great Xie Emperor afraid of a wolf? Lady Han asked, hiding a smile with her hand. She glanced at me out of the corner of her eye, the look coquettish yet clearly intended to probe my feelings. I heard Madame Meng say that Your Majesty's elder brother is on his way back to the palace. If Duanwen is the wolf of which you speak, by sending him into battle with rebellious subjects and bandits, he is certain to die or suffer grievous wounds. Then Your Majesty will win on both counts, won't he?

Rubbish. I am sick to death of women who think they are so clever, I cut her off unhappily. Heaven alone knows how things will turn out, I said. Man can only wait and see. Duanwen is no common, mediocre man, and he has at least an eight out of ten chance of subduing the Heavenly Sacrifice armies on this southern expedition. I do not wish for him to die, but if he is to die, that must not happen until after he has returned victorious to the palace.

Actually, I had already revealed my intentions to Lady Han, and I was straining to devise a plan to attack the wolf. As an Emperor who had ascended to the throne as a child, I was ill informed on a great many national affairs and had a poor understanding of palace ins and outs. The one thing I did possess was sensitivity and concern in identifying ambition and schemes, an indispensable trait in the life of an emperor. I was convinced that Duanwen was a wolf, and I knew that a wounded predator was the most dangerous of all.

So what should have been an enjoyable night in the lovely confines of Fragrant Joy Tower turned to silence with dripping water measuring time, and everything as unreal as if cut out of paper. I heard the wind blow, I heard the grass at the base of the palace walls rustle in the wind, and I was reminded of something the monk Juekong had once said years before: You must not assume that the Xie Palace will stand strong and sturdy for all time. Winds from all directions can, in an instant, turn it into flying rubble. If you ascend to the throne one day, he went on, and enjoy the company of beautiful women and untold wealth, one day, inevitably, you will experience a sense of emptiness and will feel like a leaf floating in the wind.

The great Guangyu general, Duanwen, reached the city gate, where he was greeted by an explosion of firecrackers on the city wall and a musical welcome by court musicians—hail to the conquering hero. Doubtless, this had all been arranged by his brother, Prince Duanwu, who leaped to the ground from his carriage, wearing a silk shoe on one foot and nothing on the other. He ran toward his brother, shouting the whole way. The sight of Duanwen and his brother embracing amid loud wails at the city gate had people sighing tearfully for a very long time. In me it created a profound sense of loss.

Duanwen was not my brother. I had ministers and I had subjects, but no brothers.

I did not follow Madame Huangfu's instructions to present Duanwen with a military seal. Instead, thanks to the strategy of my Chief Eunuch, Swallow, I welcomed him home with an altogether different ceremony. It was, quite simply, a duel, winner to receive the seal. The dueling swordsmen were to be Duanwen and Zhang Zhi, a staff officer who, on several occasions, had volunteered to lead the southern expedition. Swallow's stratagem perfectly conformed to my mood, which was too complex even for words. It was both a warning and a deterrent to Duanwen, as well as a reasonable assault on him. As for me, regardless of who won and who lost, a good fight would provide me with considerable amusement.

I saw Duanwen at the prescribed place in the rear garden in the morning. Swirling sand in the winds sweeping in from the northern outposts darkened his normally pale cheeks and, at the same time, seemed to add heft and brawn to his thin, frail body. He had obeyed the imperial decree to come with his sword, and was accompanied by his rather simpleminded and consistently lecherous brother, Prince Duanwu. A unit of armed guards stood beside their mounts in front of a line of trees. I discovered in the bearing and demeanor of Duanwen, whom I had not seen in a long time, a mysterious, distant air, and saw that his gestures and manner of walking looked more than ever like the late Imperial Father.

I have returned and have obeyed all Your Majesty's commands. Duanwen walked up, head held high, and stopped three feet from me to kneel in the grass. I noticed a stiffness in his knee as he went down.

Do you know why I have summoned you back to the palace? I asked.

I do. Duanwen looked straight into my face. What I do not

know, he said, is why Your Majesty has changed his mind about placing the weighty responsibility of a southern expedition on my shoulders, and why I am to duel General Zhang to see who gets the military commander's seal.

The reason is simplicity itself. You are a mortal man who must successfully navigate critical junctures if you are to make great contributions and accomplish tasks worthy of ascending the imperial throne, I replied after a long sigh. A duel with General Zhang is the first of those junctures. I then summoned the master swordsman, General Zhang Zhi, from where he stood behind me. The lives of two men rest on the outcome of this duel. The victor will command a southern expedition, the vanquished will become a specter that roams the cemetery. If either of you wishes not to accept the challenge, that man has leave to withdraw now.

I will not withdraw, General Zhang said. I agree to a fight to the death.

I most certainly will not withdraw. A familiar cold glare emanated from Duanwen's long, narrow eyes. As he took a quick look around the garden, a contemptuous sneer settled on his face. I was summoned to the palace from far away for the sole purpose of determining whether I am to live or to die. Duanwen and Duanwu exchanged smiles. If I should perish by General Zhang's sword, he said, Duanwu will claim my body, per my instructions.

Prince Duanwu was seated on a stone bench, dressed, as always, in the strange and seductive attire of an opera performer: a phoenix robe in the bright red worn by the top candidate at the annual examination, a fur cap in the shape of a boat, and a gold-inlaid sash; on his feet he wore a pair of black, thick-soled boots. He invariably reminded me of those unspeakable palace intimacies that I found so disgusting. Duanwu was muttering something to himself. I assumed he was cursing me under his breath, but I was not about to engage in a verbal contest with that wastrel.

I was then treated to a palace battle so glorious it defies description. It was deathly quiet in the garden that day, except for the labored breathing of the combatants and the clang of steel on steel. Light glinting off of the two men's blades turned the crisp, clean garden air dense and crackling dry. Many of the onlookers' faces took on a bewildering red glow. Duanwen and Zhang Zhi circled a large cypress tree, exchanging sword thrusts. I could see that Duanwen had inherited the White Gibbon swordsmanship of a court warrior. His footwork was nimble and unhurried, his sword thrusts powerful and accurate; General Zhang Zhi, on the other hand, employed the Plum Blossom style that was popular among itinerant swordsmen, characterized by speedy, ferocious thrusts. His Plum Blossom rapid attacks, like falling petals, sent resounding shudders off of Duanwen's shield. I saw Duanwen driven back, fending off one attack after another. He jumped up onto the waiting coffin, which was covered by a straw mat; Zhang Zhi followed, and at that moment, I sensed that the duel had entered the endgame stage, that one of the combatants already had one foot in the grave.

Spotting a momentary opening as Zhang Zhi jumped up

onto the coffin, Duanwen thrust the tip of his sword into Zhang's throat. Duanwen's triumphant shout drowned out the dull slurp of his sword as it buried itself in the exposed flesh. Zhang Zhi slumped onto the coffin, his defeated head lolling to one side, eyes staring into the sky above the garden, frozen in stunned blindness. Blood spurted from the wound in his neck, falling onto the straw mat and from there dripping to the ground. Shouts of joy erupted from Duanwu and the northern soldiers lined up in front of the trees. The game was over. Duanwen had won.

The sight of all that dark blood puddling on the grass made me light-headed. I turned to look at Swallow, the Chief Eunuch of the Imperial Household, who raised the bronze canister in his hands and walked up to Duanwen, to whom he handed the Black Panther military commander seal. At that moment, I could no longer doubt that Duanwen was the only one qualified to lead a southern expedition against the Heavenly Sacrifice armies. It was the will of Heaven. I had the power of life and death over my ministers and subjects, but not the power to defy the will of Heaven.

Now that the life-and-death battle in the garden had ended, the early morning mist dissipated in the faint spring sunlight that fell on the flowers and the grass, as well as on the coffin resting on the ground. Palace servants pulled back the straw mat and carefully laid General Zhang Zhi's corpse into the coffin. I saw Duanwen, his face spattered with blood, walk over, reach out, and lay his hand on Zhang Zhi's open eyes. Close your eyes, he said, the sound of weariness and sorrow in his voice.

Since time immemorial, he went on, heroes have always wound up as wronged underworld spirits. So many people have been sacrificed to conspiracies and to politics. There is nothing unusual about this sort of death.

A sentry picked a handkerchief from the ground and offered it to me, informing me that it had fallen from General Zhang's sash during the fight. The handkerchief was embroidered with a black hawk and Zhang Zhi's name. The sentry asked if it should be given to Zhang Zhi's family as a memento. No need for that, I said. Throw it away. The sentry's hand froze in midair and his fingers twitched. Then I watched as Zhang Zhi's handkerchief fluttered to the ground like a dead bird.

On the ninth day of the fourth lunar month Duanwen set out at the head of a vast and mighty army. The aged and sickly Madame Huangfu personally saw him off at the city gate, something that was talked about throughout the Xie Empire. The commoners then witnessed Duanwen cut his own left wrist and spatter his blood on the Black Panther banner of the Xie Empire. There was talk that tears streaked the face of my grandmother, Madame Huangfu, while the people ringing the scene at a distance sighed with emotion. One even shouted, Long live General Duanwen.

I was high up on a battlement that day looking down on the scene, silent the whole time. I felt as if I could foresee that Duanwen's blood would be richer than ever, that he would grow even more frenzied and more ambitious than before. That made me more uncomfortable than I could say. I suffered from a splitting headache and a cold sweat that soaked my underwear. I could not stop fidgeting beneath the yellow canopy propped up by a curved pole, and when the bugles sounded for the army to set out, I jumped into my Imperial Chariot. Take me back to the palace. My voice sounded mournful, even to me. I actually felt that I was about to cry.

EIGHT

⚮

SPRING DAYS IN THE PALACE GREW increasingly spare. The first cicadas of the year began their songs in the junipers and cypresses outside Cultivation Hall. On the battlefield down south, there was a stalemate between the two forces—ours and the enemy's—as casualties mounted on both sides; but there was no stopping. Singing and dancing in the Xie Palace masked the reality that spring was on its way out. As before, another sort of gunpowder hung in the air amid the redolence of face powder, rouge, fallen petals, and new lotuses: It was the smell of interminable battles in the women's quarters at the rear of the palace.

A shocking piece of news emerged from Singing Oriole Pavilion: Lady Hui, pregnant for all those months, had miscarried in the night, and the dead fetus was a snowy white fox. The little eunuch who brought me the news stammered for the longest time before I understood what he was trying to say. I vented my anger with a resounding slap across his face. Who told you to come to me with such nonsense? She was doing fine, how could she miscarry? And how could a human give birth to a fox? The little eunuch dared not debate the issue, and could only point frantically in the direction of Singing Oriole Pavilion. Your slave knows only what he was told. The Empress and the Empress Dowager have asked Your Majesty to come see for himself.

I rushed over to Singing Oriole Pavilion, where Madame Meng and all the imperial concubines were sitting in the anteroom whispering back and forth. The expressions on their faces varied, but they turned as one to look at me. I went straight to the stairway without a word to any of them. Madame Meng called out my name from behind. Don't go up there. You must avoid inauspicious airs. She then told one of the serving girls to go fetch the dead fox. The pain in her voice betrayed a sense of panic. See for yourself, Your Majesty. One look and you will know what sort of demon you have in Lady Hui.

The serving girl trembled as she opened the cloth bundle, and what popped into view was indeed a tiny, bloody white fox. A repellent odor emanated from the dead animal's body. I took a step backward and broke out in a cold sweat, while the concubines in the anteroom shrieked and covered their noses with their sleeves.

Can you prove that the fox came from Lady Hui's body? I asked Madame Meng after regaining my composure.

Three palace girls who kept watch through the night and the

Imperial Physician, Sun Tingmei, witnessed the event, she said. If Your Majesty does not believe me, she continued, we can summon Physician Sun and the three palace girls to testify to what they saw.

There was something fishy about all this, I sensed, but did not know what to do about it. I could see the disgusting Empress Peng out of the corner of my eye. Dressed in festive attire, she was sitting with the concubines and reaching out with a toothpick to spear a cherry on a plate in front of her. With calm grace, she placed it in her mouth, and I saw a suspicious shadow cross her face.

Poor Lady Hui, I sighed as I headed up the stairs, ignoring Madame Meng's attempts to stop me. At the top of the stairs, I discovered that a yellow brocaded curtain had been strung between the corridor posts, the commonly employed palace method of placing a site off-limits. I tore it down and flung it to the feet of the concubines. As I was doing that, it occurred to me that I had been neglecting Lady Hui for quite some time. I rushed into the room, where I smelled the familiar subtle aroma of orchids and saw her eyes, filled with such worry and sadness they seemed about to fly out of Singing Oriole Pavilion like shooting stars. Lady Hui's dreaded premonition had come true.

Lady Hui was breathing feebly as she lay in bed, seemingly in a stupor. But as I drew near, I watched one of her hands rise slowly and grope in the air until it took hold of my sash. I bent down and was chagrined to see how a once lovely and voluptuous Pinzhou maiden had been reduced to a withered branch on a dying tree. In the afternoon sun, her face emitted a frigid glare. I reached out to touch her dark eyebrows, the only things that seemed not to have changed, and this gesture instilled in her a mystical power, for I saw her eyes open slowly beneath my hand. Several tears slipped between my fingers, like pearls.

I'm dying. They attacked me all at once. They said I'd given birth to a white fox. Her hand tightened around my sash, and I wondered where she found the strength. Her vacant eyes looked up at me, pleading. Your Majesty, for the sake of the feelings you once had for me, help me now. I knew they would chase me down relentlessly, but I never dreamed they would stoop to such malicious, degrading means to achieve their purpose. They actually said I gave birth to a fox, a white fox.

That is what they say, but I don't believe them. I am going to question Imperial Physician Sun and the three serving girls, and I shall get to the bottom of this.

You needn't waste your time, Your Majesty. Imperial Physician Sun and the serving girls have been bought off by Empress Peng. They are a shameless lot who want only to curry favor with those in power. Without warning, Lady Hui burst into tears. They have been planning this for a long time, she sobbed, and I am no match for them. All the precautions in the world are of no use. Ultimately, they have me cornered.

Did you actually see the dead fetus?

No. The serving girls said they could find neither candles nor a lantern, so it was pitch-black at the time. When I felt the puddle of blood on the bed, I passed out, and by the time I revived, candles had been lit and Imperial Physician Sun was at my bedside. He said I'd miscarried and that the fetus was a fox.

I knew he was lying, I knew that Empress Peng and the others had cast their net. By this time, Lady Hui was bathed in tears. She struggled to climb out of bed, kneel on the ground, and wrap her arms around my legs. Your slave cannot escape her tragic fate and will never be able to wash away the wrongful accusation. All I ask is that Your Majesty examine the details carefully and tell me what I must do to survive. She gazed up at me. Her lips looked like a dead fish as they nibbled their way up my coiling dragon robe, producing a cheerless soughing sound. She stopped crying, as the light of martyrdom emerged from her eyes. Your Majesty, she said finally, supreme ruler of the Xie Empire, please tell me, am I to live or am I to die? Is it best for me to die? If so, I beg Your Majesty to bestow upon me the gift of a white silk hanging sash.

I wrapped my arms around Lady Hui's cold figure, feeling as desolate as a pool of water. Since the beginning of spring, each day had seen this angelic maiden of Pinzhou drift farther and farther from me, and I envisioned a pair of shapeless hands mercilessly pushing her toward her grave. Why was I powerless to pull poor Lady Hui back? She begged for my help, but my hands seemed tied. With tears in my eyes, I tried to comfort her, but even then I withheld an Emperor's promise to help.

Secretly, I summoned my Chief Eunuch, Swallow, to Cultivation Hall to ask what I should do about Lady Hui. Apparently, he had already worked out a scheme. But first he asked me to tell him honestly if I still loved her. I said I did. Then he asked if I wanted her to live or to die. I said of course I wanted her to

live. All right, then, he nodded and said with a smile. I can get
Lady Hui out of the palace and send her someplace where no
one will ever find her, a place where she can live out her years in
safety. We can tell the venerable old lady and the other palace
women that Your Majesty ordered her to take her own life and
that her corpse was floated out of the palace.

Where do you plan to have her hide? I asked Swallow.

A Buddhist convent just outside of Lianzhou. My aunt is the
abbess there. The convent is on a high mountain surrounded by
dense woods. Outsiders are seldom seen there, and no one will
ever know what really became of her.

Ask Lady Hui to shave her head and become a nun? I nearly
shouted in alarm. You are asking the noble First Imperial Concubine of the Xie Empire to join a convent? Is that the best you
can come up with?

The only way for Lady Hui to live, however humbly, is to
leave the palace. And once she leaves, she can never return nor
can she remarry, which leaves shaving her head and becoming a
nun her only alternative. I ask Your Majesty to consider this
plan carefully.

As I listened to cicadas in the junipers and cypresses in front
of the hall sing a few notes, the fragile, paper-thin image of a
beautiful girl floated in front of my eyes. It was my poor Lady
Hui, whose heart rose as high as the heavens, but whose life was
thinner than paper. She would, it seemed, live out her days by a
solitary window under the weak light of a Buddhist convent
lantern.

We will do as you suggested, I said at last to Swallow.

Heaven has decreed it. Perhaps Lady Hui should never have come into the palace, and perhaps she was fated to be a nun all along. My hands are tied. I may be the supreme ruler, Emperor of Xie, but what can I do?

A serving girl called Pearl, who bore a resemblance to Lady Hui, was selected to take her place. Swallow's plan was to drug Pearl and stuff her into a yellow cloth sack; we heard light snoring from inside as the serving girl—whom everyone else thought to be Lady Hui, the First Imperial Concubine—was given the floating farewell from the palace. The Imperial Executioner's resonant shouts hovered above the Imperial Stream, alongside which the people lining the bank and the floating yellow sack were that early morning's most arresting sight.

And it was early that same morning that the real Lady Hui, in the disguise of a palace eunuch, slipped out of Bright Xie Gate in the bed of a horse cart ostensibly on its way to market, returning to the outside world. Swallow, who accompanied her out of the palace, described the trip by saying she never uttered a word, even though he tried to get her to talk. She kept her eyes fixed on the shifting scene in the sky above the whole time.

Swallow returned to the palace with all the gold, silver, and jewelry I'd given Lady Hui. He said she could not accept my gifts. I am going to a Buddhist convent, she said to Swallow, so what good will these things do me? None whatsoever.

She was right, of course. She had no need for any of those things. I thought for a moment, then asked him, Did she really take nothing with her?

Only a gilded makeup box that held a sheaf of poems, nothing else. I assumed they were the poems Your Majesty wrote to her. She had kept them all.

Poems? I was reminded of the days when she was confined in Beamless Hall, and we could only exchange love poems. Moved by the recollection, I heaved a sigh. The emotional, ill-fated girl deserved better than she got.

Feeling particularly downhearted the day Lady Hui was spirited out of the palace, I could only walk aimlessly and alone among the flowers. They seemed to sense how I felt, for a warm, perfumed wind on the path carried with it deeply sad emotions. As I walked, I composed a poem I called "Charms of a Slave Girl" to commemorate the passionate love and devotion Lady Hui and I had shared for a brief moment in time. My stroll took me to the bank of the Imperial Stream, where I leaned against the railing and looked off to the west. The palace grounds were in the shade of leafy green trees. Peach and plum blossoms had only recently fallen from the limbs, while the many varieties of peonies by the pond were still decked out in gorgeous purples and reds. Old haunts, old relationships, a girl who had run like a bird beside the Imperial Stream had left me and gone so far away. I found it odd that yesterday's affairs had already begun turning to mist and leaving behind only fragments of dirgelike verses.

In the distance I noticed two figures on the swing set. It was Empress Peng and Lady Lan, accompanied by palace girls who stood beneath willow trees, hands at their sides. As I walked up, Empress Peng swung back and forth a couple of times before jumping off and shooing away the serving girls. Go back inside, she said. Lady Lan and I will entertain His Majesty a while.

I do not need to be entertained, I said indifferently. Keep at what you're doing. I would like to watch you on the swings, see how high you can go.

His Majesty seems distressed. He must be sad over Lady Hui. Is it possible that His Majesty does not know that she did not die, that it was a serving girl named Pearl who was given the floating farewell? Empress Peng stood beside the swing set and lightly tapped the metal frame with her gold bracelet. I detected a crafty smile at the corners of her mouth.

You know everything. Too bad what you appear to know is preposterous and idiotic.

If you must know, having her die was not what we desired, for since she was born a fox, she belongs back in the wild. We were content all along to drive her out of the palace so she could take her evil airs with her. Empress Peng turned and gave Lady Lan a knowing look. Do you have any thoughts on the matter, dear Lady Lan?

What Empress Peng said is true in every respect, Lady Lan said.

Why must you always parrot what others say? I rebuffed Lady Lan angrily. You may have a pretty exterior, but your belly is filled with straw. You are incapable of differentiating between true and false, black and white.

Having spoken my piece, I flicked my sleeve and walked off, leaving the two women to stand woodenly beside the swing sets. After taking only a few steps, I parted some willow branches to take a look behind me. They were speaking softly to each other, occasionally holding their hands over their mouths and giggling. Then each of them sat down on one of the swings, and began swinging, going as high as they could, skirts billowing in the wind, jewelry clanging musically. They looked perfectly carefree and happy. Higher and higher they went, their bodies seeming to grow thinner and more fragile, until I felt that they too were little more than paper figures, and that one day a strong wind would sweep them up and carry them off to some distant, unfamiliar spot.

News from the southern front caused joy one moment and anxiety the next. Duanwen's troops had driven Li Yizhi's Heavenly Sacrifice forces into a valley some eighteen li east of the Red Silt River. Nearly out of arrows and desperately short of provisions, one group of Li Yizhi's soldiers stayed behind to defend the mountain pass while the remaining men and horses crossed Pen Holder Mountain and dispersed into the woods of Yu and Ta Counties.

Duanwen captured Li Yizhi's wife, whose name was Cai, and two of his children. After placing them in the center of a ring of fire as bait, he beat a signal log to entice Li Yizhi to come down the mountain to rescue them. But the bait produced results no one had anticipated. A torrent of arrows suddenly rained down on the mother and her children, who perished inside the ring of fire. Everyone who witnessed the event blanched in terror and looked off in the direction from where the arrows had come. What they saw was a man on a white horse dressed in funeral hemp, a bow in one hand, his face cov-ered by the other, emerging from the dense foliage and gallop-ing off.

They said it was the leader of the Heavenly Sacrifice Society, Li Yizhi himself.

I could no longer recall what Li Yizhi, who had forced his way into the audience hall that day, looked or sounded like. Some afternoons, while I napped in Cultivation Hall, I would see him, a sorrowful, angry figure in muddy straw sandals stomping heavily on the imperial bed, a specter as amorphous as a water stain. It was Li Yizhi, but it was also Commander Yang Song and his brother, and it was unquestionably my half brother, Duanwen. A water stain that filled every corner of Cul-tivation Hall and startled me out of my nap.

My early afternoons in the palace were long and lonely, so sometimes I wandered over to the dusty storeroom where the cricket jars I'd played with as a child were stacked neatly beneath the window, and felt with deep emotion how happy the days of childish innocence had been.

The attempted assassination by an actor occurred in front of a crowd of people. An opera troupe that had achieved some fame in the capital came to the palace that day. Several of the young actors who played female roles captured the hearts of palace women. I recall that I was seated in a gazebo with Madame Meng, Ladies Yun and Han to my left and Empress Peng and Lady Lan on my right. The looks of besotted infatua-tion and nonsensical comments as they watched the play struck me as comical. In the middle of a heart-wrenching aria, I saw an actor called Little Phoenix Pearl reach into his sleeve and pull out a short sword. He sang and he danced around the stage. The officials and their families burst into an uproar, struck by the thought that this was a strange play indeed. Just as I realized that I was about to be the target of an assassination attempt, Little Phoenix Pearl jumped down off the stage and ran toward me, sword raised.

Amid the terrified shrieks of the imperial women, members of the Imperial Guard rushed up and seized Little Phoenix Pearl. The young actor's face was hidden behind a layer of powder and rouge and above a pair of seductively painted lips, red as maple leaves. The eyes alone were those of a man, and they emanated rays of madness. I knew without being told that only assassins and one's enemies had eyes like that.

Death to you, a muddle-headed, debauched, pleasure-seeking emperor. Give way to a bright new world, with an empire that is strong and where the people are at peace. That is what Little Phoenix Pearl sang in an impromptu aria as he was dragged out of the garden, his voice loud and resonant in its sorrow.

I received such a fright that I lay ill for days. I had no strength and no appetite. The Imperial Physician came to tend to me, but was stopped outside Cultivation Hall. Since it was only a fright, I had no need for his potions, which seldom did any good anyway. But I wanted to know why a frail little actor would want to kill me.

Three days later, Little Phoenix Pearl was taken to the execution ground outside the city and beheaded in front of a huge crowd. People could see traces of powder and rouge on his face, and noted that he was still wearing his stage clothes. Those who were familiar with the Pear Garden—the world of theater— found it impossible to link Little Phoenix Pearl with the condemned man tied to the rack, and everyone presumed that a sinister plot lay hidden behind the incident.

I too ran through all the possibilities of why he had wanted to assassinate me. I suspected that Duanwen and Duanwu were behind it all; or that Fengqin Prince Duanxuan and Shouqin Prince Duanming were responsible; or that Little Phoenix Pearl was a member of the Heavenly Sacrifice Society; or even that the neighboring Peng or Meng Empires had arranged it. But the interrogation of Little Phoenix Pearl by the Punishments Board failed to produce an answer, for he sat through it, hot tears streaming down his cheeks, and filled the room with a guttural sound that resembled singing but was not, and that sounded like speech but made no sense; it was not, however, as loud and sonorous as before. That is when they discovered that his tongue had been cut out; whether by accident or by design was impossible to determine. After three frustrating days, they publicly executed Little Phoenix Pearl to bring the affair to a close.

Historians exaggerated the significance of the assassination attempt, which grew into one of the great mysteries of the Xie court. Strangely, the reports all included memorials and eulogies to the renowned actor, Little Phoenix Pearl, while I, the target of the attempted assassination and the sixth Emperor of the Xie Empire, somehow escaped the historians' attention.

. . .

When pomegranate flowers began blooming in the fifth lunar month, my grandmother, Madame Huangfu, fell ill and was quickly on the decline, like a lantern about to run out of oil, flickering weakly in Splendor Hall. Not even heavy doses of perfume could mask the smell of death rising from her body. Privately, the Imperial Physician told me that the venerable lady would not likely hold out until the arrival of summer.

Madame Huangfu summoned me several times to her deathbed, where she reminisced about her life in the palace. Her recollections were tedious and freighted with trivial details, her voice weak, her speech slurred. But her face glowed pink as she excitedly relived the past. I entered the palace at the age of fifteen, and in all the decades since have gone out through Bright Xie Gate only twice, both times as part of a funeral cortege for a deceased Emperor, Madame Huangfu said. I know that the third time I leave the palace it will once again be to travel to the Imperial Tombs at Brass Rule Mountain, but this time for me. Are you aware that in my youth I was not a natural beauty, but that I washed my private parts every day with a mixture of crushed chrysanthemum petals and antler fuzz, a secret concoction with which I captured the Emperor's heart? There were times, she said, when I wanted to change the dynastic name to Huangfu, and times when I contemplated delivering all you princes into the Imperial Tombs. But I was always too kindhearted, too loving, and could never bring myself to carry out such cruelties. As she spoke, her body stirred beneath the foxskin covering her, and I heard her pass gas. Then, with a wave of her hand, she said harshly, Get out of here. I know that you and the rest of them cannot wait for me to die.

I had just about run out of patience with this old woman and her death struggles. Whenever she started talking, her voice weak but her tone cruel as always, I counted silently—one, two, three, all the way to fifty-seven—hoping that when I reached the number of years she had lived, I would see those ancient, purple lips come together one last time. But no, they kept flapping, and her muttered reminiscences went on and on and on. I had to believe that this laughable, muddled state of affairs would not end until she was laid out in her coffin.

The fifth month was coming to a close, and the old lady's life neared extinction. Palace eunuchs and serving girls in Splendor Hall heard her call out Duanwen's name in her sleep. I guessed that she wanted to hold on until the southern expedition army returned in triumph before giving up the ghost.

News that Duanwen had captured Li Yizhi reached the palace early one morning. The messenger rode up carrying Li Yizhi's red helmet tassel and a hank of his hair. The happy news appeared to arrive just in time, for it sparked one last return to consciousness by Madame Huangfu. The day had finally come that the enormous phoenix coffin was carried up to the door of Splendor Hall, while inside the hall people stood solemnly and caged birds stopped singing; danger lurked beneath the surface of the holiday-like airs.

At first, Madame Meng, Empress Peng, Duanxuan, Duanming, and Duanwu kept a vigil by Madame Huangfu's bedside, but she sent them all away, leaving me alone with her. She was sinking fast. She gazed up at me for the longest time, a strangely sorrowful look in her eyes. At the time, I recall, my hands and feet turned cold, as though I knew what was about to happen. Are you the true Xie Emperor? Madame Huangfu raised her hand slowly to caress my forehead and my cheeks. Her touch felt like the sands of winter passing through my veins. Then she pulled back her hand and began tugging at the sachet at her waist. I have worn this sachet these past eight years, she said with a smile. The time has come to give it to you. Cut it open and see what it holds.

When I cut open the mysterious sachet, I discovered it held nothing fragrant, in fact held only a sheet of tightly folded paper. I unfolded it to reveal a second edict from the late Emperor, announcing the Imperial succession. The edict, in the late Emperor's own hand, read: My eldest son Duanwen is to succeed me as ruler of the Xie Empire.

You were not to be the Xie Emperor, the old woman said. It is I who put you on the throne.

I stood there clutching the Imperial edict, wide-eyed and slack-jawed, suddenly feeling like a stone that had been flung down a deep well.

I never liked Duanwen. I never liked you either. This has all been a joke that I played on you, the men. I created a false Xie Emperor, one that I could control. A beaming smile spread across the old lady's withered face. I ruled the Xie Empire for eight years, she said at last, and have lived to the age of fifty-seven, not bad for one life.

But why, why did you decide not to take proof of this plot,

this crime, to your grave? Why reveal it to me now? All of a sudden, my chest filled with anger and a sense of misery. I reached down and shook the old lady's body. But she was beyond caring about my disobedient act. I heard a death rattle settle in her lungs. I felt like laughing, but what erupted from me instead was an uncontrollable series of wails.

The old lady was dead, and once the eunuch passed the word out beyond the pearl curtain, waves of confused sounds spread through Splendor Hall and the grounds outside. I placed a night-luminescent pearl in the old lady's mouth, which protruded and was sunken around the edges of her dead face, forming what looked like a sarcastic sneer. Before people swarmed up to the deathbed, I spat into that dead face, but immediately sensed that this was an inappropriate way for an Emperor to behave. Nonetheless, that is what I did, the sort of thing women often did.

I was back at the Imperial Tombs again, after eight years. Green pines and emerald aspens at the southern foot of Brass Rule Mountain gave a sense of the passage of an entire life. During the imposing funeral rites for Madame Huangfu, I spotted some rare gray sparrows perched calmly on nearby tombstones and grave mounds, obviously not frightened by the people or the sounds of the funeral dirges. I wondered if they were possessed of Madame Huangfu's wandering spirit.

The funeral cortege formed a sea of mourning white that obscured the blanket of green on the ground. Nine smaller red coffins awaited burial with the elder Empress Dowager, a number that exceeded that of the late Emperor's funeral eight years earlier. It was the old lady's final display of power and grandeur for those left behind. I knew that the nine serving girls lying in those red coffins had died willingly. Having served Madame Huangfu in life, they preferred to accompany her in death, so on the night of the day she died, they swallowed gold nuggets before hurrying to climb into the nine waiting red coffins. They would continue to serve their mistress on the road to the Yellow Springs.

The bronze drums were struck ninety-nine times, accompanied by the wails of the imperial family and court dignitaries. The jumble of wails reverberating across the heavens made me laugh, since the sound came from an array of people for whom any sinister design was possible. I could tell which of the wails were shouts of joy, which of the sorrowful howls were cries of resentment, and which of the sobs were in reality laments and jealousy. I simply lacked the desire to expose their hypocrisy, the sort that had been around since antiquity.

Hazy scenes like those of eight years earlier appeared before me: I saw Madame Yang's ghostly image above a grave mound on the left side of the Imperial Tombs. A look of eternal bitterness on her face, she was waving an Imperial edict in the direction of the gathering, and I once again heard the spectral sound: You are not the Xie Emperor. Eldest Prince Duanwen is the true Emperor. I then saw the gray sparrows rise suddenly into the sky above the grave mound, where they assembled into a strange rectangular form before flying off.

The sparrows had been frightened off by another group of

mourners. These uniformed men, helmets still resting on their heads, had hurriedly draped white mourning silks over their horses' backs; carrying with them the stink of blood and sweat, they drew exclamations of incredulity from those who had arrived before them.

No one dreamed that Duanwen would ride day and night to get there in time for Madame Huangfu's funeral. I looked up at him astride his red-maned warhorse. The last rays of sunrise fell on his face, on which was written the pallor of exhaustion, and above which fluttered the Black Panther flag and a funeral banner. Duanwen, eldest Prince Duanwen, great General Duanwen, Commander of the Three Armies of the Southern Expedition Duanwen, my half brother and my lifelong foe, was once again there before me. I still recall the first strange thought that crossed my mind at the time. Why did it have to be the clip-clop of Duanwen's horse that frightened off those fearless, spectral sparrows? This was also the only question I put to the conquering hero who had suddenly returned to our midst. I pointed up to the western sky and demanded of him, Who are you, to have frightened off that flock of gray sparrows?

NINE

THE FINAL DESPERATE BATTLE at the foot of Pen Holder
Mountain ended in a complete rout of the Heavenly Sacrifice army. Stepping on the bodies strewn over the battlefield, the
victorious soldiers planted the Black Panther flag on the mountain. They then launched a pincer movement on remnants of the
Heavenly Sacrifice army on the hidden ancient plank road built
along cliffs on the other side of the mountain, where they captured the Heavenly Sacrifice leader, Li Yizhi, who had thrown
down his bow and tried to flee.

Under a cloak of secrecy, Li was spirited into the capital,
where he was thrown into a water dungeon at the Punishments
Board. During three futile interrogations, he steadfastly denied
that the Heavenly Sacrifice Society was a gathering of outlaws,
and insisted that it existed solely to bring relief to the common

people. When Li's interrogators discussed his fate, they agreed that the traditional state punishments were too good for him, and devised a series of extreme and unprecedented punishments to get him to confess to his crimes. My Chief Eunuch, Swallow, as an invited palace observer of this brutal interrogation, later described for me each of the unique tortures imposed upon the prisoner.

The first one was called Backward Disrobing Primate. Swallow told me they made a barrel out of a sheet of metal, with sharp needles lining the inside. The barrel was wrapped around Li Yizhi. Then, as one of the executioners held the sheet metal around the prisoner, a second one grabbed Li by the hair and pulled him through it. Swallow said he heard Li cry out in agony as the needles shredded his skin and released rivulets of blood. A third executioner, standing by with a bowl of brine, asked if he was ready to confess. Li Yizhi stubbornly shook his head, so the executioner slowly poured the salty liquid over his torn and bloody body. Swallow said the pain had to be excruciating, like piercing the heart and boring into bone, because he heard a second painful cry from Li Yizhi before he passed out.

The second punishment was called Immortal Rides the Mist, a seamless complement to the first torture, which was used to quickly bring Li back to consciousness, so he could suffer a new and different form of agony. The executioners hung him upside down over a vat of boiling liquid. What do you think was in the vat, Your Majesty? Swallow giggled. It was filled with vinegar, a brilliant idea. As soon as the lid was removed, sour, acrid steam curled up into Li Yizhi's face and jerked him awake. That had to have been a hundred times more agonizing than what made him pass out.

Next came Hollow Out the Eggplant, Swallow said. It was the simplest, most clear-cut of all. They cut Li Yizhi down, then two executioners spread his legs, while a third drove an incredibly sharp dagger up his rear portal. Swallow paused and then, in an ambiguous tone of voice, said, What a pity that a manly, valiant fellow like that had to share the bitter experience of a powdered catamite.

When his narrative reached this point, Swallow stopped abruptly. I could see he was feeling awkward, and suspected that the description had brought back unpleasant memories, as he relived his own painful past. Don't stop now, I urged. It's just starting to get interesting.

Does Your Majesty really want to hear the rest? Swallow asked, back to normal. He looked at me, trying to gauge my reaction. Doesn't Your Majesty feel that this is all too cruel and heartless?

What do you mean, cruel and heartless? I snapped at Swallow. Am I supposed to concern myself with propriety and morality when dealing with brigands and highwaymen? Keep talking, what other ingenious tortures did they come up with?

There was one called Wearing a Palm Cape. For this they melted some lead and poured it along with boiling oil over his back and shoulders, Swallow said. I watched as Li Yizhi's skin slowly cracked and split, mixing blood and oil that sprayed everywhere. Li Yizhi's body really looked like it was wearing a big, red palm cape, I mean it really did.

The fifth torture was the true eye-opener. It had a wonderful name: Hanging Embroidered Balls. First they had a blacksmith make a special dagger, with four or five little barbs hanging from the blade. It went in without any trouble, but Li Yizhi's flesh got hooked on the barbs and went flying when the executioner jerked it out, like bright red meatballs.

I left after the fifth torture, Swallow said, but I hear they put Li Yizhi through eleven kinds altogether, ones with names like Shouldering a Gourd, Soaring Dragonfly, and Scraping a Boot. But since I didn't see them with my own eyes, I cannot describe them to Your Majesty.

Why did you leave before it was over? Why not stay and watch all eleven tortures?

Because one of those meatballs from Hanging Embroidered Balls landed on my face and scared me so much I couldn't bear to watch any more. I know that was wrong, and the next time they torture someone, I will stay to watch to the end and then report back to Your Majesty.

If I'd known it was going to be that interesting, I'd have gone to see for myself, I said half in jest. Surprised by my unexpected fascination with the torture of Li Yizhi, I was reminded of the similarly sinful punishment I'd meted out to banished concubines in the Cold Palace in my youth. I'd had a fear of blood and killing for many years, and this instinctive return to that earlier time must have emanated from my mood and my trying circumstances. So I closed my eyes to conjure up images of the remaining six types of torture, until I could almost smell Li Yizhi's blood spreading through Cultivation Hall, and I grew somewhat light-headed, the sort of impotent, feminine light-headedness I hated so much.

Did Li Yizhi really go to his death without confessing? After eleven kinds of torture, did he really not say anything? I asked Swallow.

He uttered a single sentence. Swallow hesitated before continuing softly. He said, When torture becomes this cruel, humans are worse than wild beasts, and the Xie Empire is in its final days.

What a coincidence, that Li Yizhi's curse so closely resembled that of Sun Xin, who had been dead all those years. That was perplexing and terrifying.

Duanwen spent his first half month in the capital in the palace of his brother Duanwu, the Pingqin Prince. Someone I'd sent to spy on them reported, A blue lantern signifying no visitors is hung over the gate to the imperial quarters, but there is a steady stream of royalty and court officials entering to offer their congratulations. The record of visitors my secret scout handed me listed all the important individuals, dozens of people: that included my brothers, Fengqin Prince Duanxuan and Shouqin Prince Duanming; Northwestern Duke Dayu; Head of the Ceremonial Rites Board Yan Ziqing; Head of the Civil Service Board Huangfu Bin; Vice Head of the Military Board Li Yu; Imperial Censor Liu Qian; Wen Qi; Zhang Hong; and others. It also included six academicians in the Hanlin Academy, all of whose ranks I'd bestowed upon them the year I ascended to the throne.

What are they up to? I asked Swallow, pointing to the name list.

Your Majesty needn't concern himself. Bearing congratulations is just their way of socializing.

Wolf cubs have savage hearts, that's clear, I said with a sneer as I drew circles around the names and put a line through them. What does this look like to you? I asked Swallow.

It looks like a string of locusts, Swallow said after a moment's thought.

No, not a string of locusts. It's a pair of iron shackles. These people are secretly plotting the overthrow of the dynasty, I said. That is both loathsome and infuriating. And when you pull it all together like this, it's a pair of shackles they are planning to fasten around my wrists.

Then you should fasten shackles around their wrists first, Your Majesty, Swallow blurted out.

Easier said than done. I paused, heaved a sigh, and continued, What kind of dog-shit Xie Emperor am I? The weakest, least competent, most pitiful Emperor under the sun. In my childhood I was manipulated by nannies, eunuchs, and serving girls; after I began to study and learn things, I was manipulated by the monk Juekong; then since I became Emperor, I've been manipulated day in and day out by Madame Huangfu and Madame Meng. Now the empire has undergone great changes, chaos reigns among the populace, and it's too late to do anything about it. I don't have to be told that a sword aimed at my neck is inching closer and all I can do is sit around and sigh. Tell me, Swallow, just what kind of dog-shit Xie Emperor am I?

The moment my emotional outburst ended, I began to wail. This had hit me without warning, but the tearful release had been building up inside for a long time. Swallow stood there wide-eyed and slack-jawed. His first thought was to quickly close my bedroom door, knowing it was a bad omen for an Emperor to cry in the palace.

But the serving girls and eunuchs outside my door heard me cry, and one of them ran off to Hidden Pearl Hall to report this extraordinary event to Madame Meng, who rushed over, followed by that gaggle of sneaky, nosy palace women. I noticed that on this particular day, they were all made up identically: their faces had a crystalline tinge of purple, their lips were painted crimson, either dark or light, and to me they looked like those chicken-blood stones you find in the water.

What have you all come here for? I asked, feigning nonchalance.

What was Your Majesty doing just now? Madame Meng asked in return, looking angry.

Nothing. What makeup style is that? I turned and asked Lady Yun, who was closest to me. Plum blossom? Black moth? To me you look like chicken-blood stones, so from now on, let's call it chicken-blood style, how's that?

Chicken-blood style? That's an intriguing name, Lady Yun clapped her hands and said with a giggle, which she swallowed the instant she saw that Madame Meng was glaring at her.

Madame Meng told one of the serving girls to fetch a bronze mirror. Hold it up to His Majesty, she said, so he can gaze upon his Imperial countenance. The serving girl held the mirror up to me. Madame Meng heaved a sigh; her eyes reddened for some strange reason. When the late Emperor was alive, she said, I never once saw a look of great joy or great sorrow on his face, and certainly never saw tears.

Are you saying I am not fit to be the ruler of an empire? I flared up. With a single kick, I sent the mirror flying. You don't want me to cry? I said. Then I ought to be able to laugh. If I cannot cry, fine. I shall fill the palace with laughter, and there is nothing for any of you to worry about.

You may not laugh either. The twenty-one-day anniversary of Madame Huangfu's passing has not yet arrived. How can Your Majesty think of violating your filial responsibility by unrestrained laughter?

I cannot cry, and I cannot laugh, so what can I do? Kill someone? You don't seem to care how many people I kill, but you won't let me cry and you won't let me laugh. What kind of dog-shit Xie Emperor am I? With that I threw my head back and laughed loudly. Then I removed the Black Panther Imperial Crown and tossed it to Madame Meng. I am not going to be a dog-shit Xie Emperor anymore. You do it. Anybody who wants to can do it.

This dramatic change caught Madame Meng completely by surprise and quickly had her in tears. I watched her tremble as she hugged the crown to her bosom, tears coursing through her makeup, which became a mottled mixture of red and white. On a signal from Swallow, the Empress and concubines backed out of my bedroom, and I heard Empress Peng say to Lady Lan, her voice dripping with sarcasm, His Majesty has suffered a bit of madness recently.

After so many years, an assembly of little white demons crept back into my dreams. They came in through the southern window on the wind, dragging a blurry, mysterious light behind them. They hid on both sides of my quilt and under my night-clothes, where some stayed still and others danced and jumped around. When they wept they sounded like those resentful women at the rear of the palace, and when they were angry, they sounded like battlefield warriors. I nearly suffocated from the forced intimacy.

There was no one to come drive those little white demons away. The monk Juekong was far off in Bitter Bamboo Monastery enjoying his dreamless sleep, and when I managed to fight my way out of my nightmare, I was face-to-face with the panic-stricken Lady Yun. Covering herself down below with a piece of silk, she was standing barefoot at the far end of my bed, a puz-zled, terrified look in her eyes. I knew I had frightened her by shouting out in my dream.

Something is wrong with Your Majesty's imperial body. I have already summoned the Imperial Physician, she said tremulously.

I don't want the Imperial Physician. Get me someone who can catch demons. I was awake, but I could still see the little white demons, except that in the candlelight they were a little smaller, and less well defined. They were now standing on large-waisted vases, on flower stands, and on windowsills, their shouts as shrill as ever. Can you see them? I asked Lady Yun, pointing to the white figures on one of the flower stands. Those little white demons are what I'm talking about. They've come back, and calamity will soon befall the Xie Empire.

Your Majesty is seeing things. Those are potted all-season crab apples.

Take a closer look. The little white demons are hiding under the crab-apple leaves. See that one turn its face toward you? It's mocking all you foolish, know-nothing women.

Your Majesty, there is nothing there, I promise you. Your Majesty is seeing moonbeams.

Lady Yun was so frightened she began to cry, and in between sobs she shouted out the name of the eunuch standing guard on the other side of the door. Imperial Guardsmen burst into the room. I heard a series of loud crashes in the air of Refinement Hall, and saw the little white demons disappear one by one under the guards' swords, like bubbles bursting.

No one believed that I had seen demons while I was wide-awake. They would rather believe in far-fetched ghost stories than accept my meticulously detailed descriptions. I could see that in the sleepy looks on their faces. To my surprise, they now looked at me with wariness. A supreme ruler, an Emperor whose every utterance is worth more than gold and jade, was it possible they knew that I was not the legitimate heir to the Xie throne?

My nights and my days were troubling. The curse uttered by the madman Sun Xin rang in my ears. You will see ninety-nine spirits, and calamity will soon befall the Xie Empire.

The plan to assassinate Duanwen began to ferment one night after much drinking. The conspirators at the liquor-enhanced feast included Qiu Wen, head of the Military Board; Liang Wenmo, vice head of the Ceremonial Rites Board; Ji Zhang, the Palace Inspectorate-General; and my Chief Eunuch, Swallow. I was a bit drunk when I blurted out what was bothering me. Perplexing looks appeared on the faces of my loyal followers. They exchanged glances. Then, cautiously, they mentioned Duanwen's name and brought up a range of rumors they had heard about him. At that moment, I recall, I flung a white jade cup at the feet of Qiu Wen. Kill him, I thundered tersely, immoderately, so shocking Qiu Wen that he jumped to his feet. Kill him, he echoed my command. The conversation then took on a head of steam and a secret plan began to take shape. The conspirators agreed that it would not be difficult to carry out, and that the only real concern was that it might infuriate members of the late Emperor's family, all those feudal lords spread throughout the empire. Their conflicts with the Xie court had magnified since the passing of Madame Huangfu, especially Western Duke Zhaoyang, whose close relationship with Duanwen was cause for concern.

Kill him. I terminated the discussion among my overly cautious conspirators, as a rush of excitement swept over me. I want you people to kill him. I banged my fist on the table and then reached out and pulled the ears of all four men, one after the other, leaning over and shouting, Did you hear me? I am the Emperor, and I want you to kill him.

Yes, Your Majesty. If you want him killed, he is as good as dead. Ji Zhang fell to his knees and wept. Your Majesty, he said, summon Duanwen to the palace tomorrow, and I will fulfill this wish for you.

The next day, Swallow carried a summons over to the Pingqin Prince's palace. With his white horse tied to a tethering stone, peddlers and ordinary citizens out on the street quickly gathered round until the area was so densely packed that even water couldn't pass through. They wanted to see what the reigning castrato looked like, and were even more eager to lay eyes on the elegant bearing of Duanwen. They said that when Duanwen got down on one knee to receive the summons, he acted strangely, slapping the floor with the palm of his hand three times, the dull rumbling sound surprising Swallow, who had no way of guessing what Duanwen was up to. Meanwhile, Duanwen's brother, Duanwu, stood in front of a screen wall facing the gate and cursed the onlookers in particularly coarse language.

Duanwen led his horse across the red threshold of the Pingqin Prince's gate. Except for his long, narrow, cold eyes, his face was covered by a piece of black cloth. He mounted his horse and made his way through the crowd, a masked man looking straight ahead, unmoved by the shouted encouragement and scattered comments from the people around him. People wondered why an illustrious hero, author of celebrated exploits, would ride through town with his face covered.

Swallow later described an unanticipated incident that occurred near the marketplace. An old beggar known for roaming the city streets in tatters materialized in front of Duanwen's horse, reached out with a cane he used to ward off dogs, and flicked the black cloth off of Duanwen's face. It happened so fast it caught everyone by surprise. Duanwen screamed and tried to snatch the piece of cloth out of the air. But it was too late. People closest to him discovered that two words the size of tadpoles had been tattooed on his pale forehead, which was suddenly exposed in the sunlight: Xie Emperor.

Indescribable chaos erupted in the street. Duanwen reared back his horse and turned to leave, holding one hand over his forehead and, with a sword in the other, driving the crowd back. A look of agony mixed with ferocity showed on his face; a roar of anger pounded into the people's heads like a blunt instrument. Duanwen galloped off on his jade hare horse, but his way was blocked by Swallow and a squad of uniformed Imperial Guards. Yet even that did not stop him. A shamefaced Swallow reported that Duanwen had kicked him off of his horse, and all he'd caught was a single hair from the jade hare horse's tail. So, amid the chaos, Duanwen had gotten away.

Archers that Ji Zhang had deployed in the watchtower waited all afternoon, but all they saw was Swallow and his entourage returning in defeat, and they were ordered to put away their bows. At the time, I had a premonition that my plan had been foiled by some mysterious force, and when Swallow's imperial tablet fell weakly to the floor as he faced me, the tension that had gripped my heart actually fell away.

The gods have spared his life, it is Heaven's will, I said to Ji Zhang. If I want him to die, and Heaven wants him to live, then he will be spared.

Should I send troops to seal off the city gates, Your Majesty? I suspect that Duanwen is still in the city, and since we have already beaten the grass to startle the snake, we might as well simply arrest Duanwen as a traitor, Ji Zhang suggested.

But the tales of Duanwen's heroism had already spread to every corner of the Xie Empire. The people were beginning to entertain doubts about their Emperor and had learned to distinguish the true from the false, the good from the bad. As for me, I had never pretended that black was white or that a deer was a horse, yet my susceptible nature said to me, You must kill the heroic figure who commands the wind and the clouds. That's all there was to it, but I had no interest in explaining myself to Ji Zhang.

The heavens have decided for us, I said to the conspirators as they gathered round. Maybe Duanwen is the true Xie Emperor, for it seems that some powerful force is aiding him. If he is to die, let him die. If not, let him live. Let us simply treat this all as one of my drunken quips.

The four conspirators stood in the watchtower, hands at their sides, and exchanged glances. I saw both doubt and shame on their faces. Obviously, they were disappointed by my indecisiveness and wished I hadn't abandoned the chase halfway. The watchtower bell rope swayed in an afternoon breeze, causing the clapper to brush against the inner surface and create a hum that swirled in the air. Everyone in the watchtower cocked their ears to listen to this strange sound, and none dared break the uncomfortable silence, though in the mind of everyone present, myself included, great changes seemed inevitable in the future of the Xie Empire. In the blazing sunlight of that summer afternoon I saw the white beams of calamity spreading across the red glazed roof tiles and green tree canopies arrayed below the watchtower.

Members of the Imperial Guard searched the city for two days and two nights, without finding a trace of Duanwen. On the third day, they returned to the Pingqin Prince's palace, where they discovered the mouth of a tunnel in an abandoned well at the rear. Two of the guards entered the tunnel with torches and groped along until they emerged in the midst of an old haystack and discovered that they were standing in a wooded area beyond the city's northern gate. The torn edge of a sleeve hung from the branch of a tree, and when they examined it, they saw two lines of writing in blood: The day Duanwen returns to the capital/Will mark the extinction of Duanbai.

They brought the torn white sleeve back to Cultivation Hall and handed it to me as the sole evidence of his crimes. A pain struck deep in my heart as I stared at the two bold lines of blood script. A diabolically cruel means of revenge formed in my head as I destroyed the sleeve with a pair of scissors. Summon

Duanwu to the palace, I shouted to the palace eunuchs. I shall make him eat this funeral banner.

Duanwu was as arrogant as ever when he was brought to Cultivation Hall. He stood on the jade steps and glared at me defiantly, refusing to kneel. So guardsmen rushed up to force him to his knees, but he called upon his martial training to send three of them sprawling.

Kill me if you must, he shouted, but I will never kneel.

How can I get him to kneel? I asked Swallow.

Smashing his kneecaps with a hammer is the only way, Swallow answered softly.

Then have them fetch a hammer. I insist that he be punished for Duanwen's crimes.

An agonizing shriek tore from Duanwu's mouth when his kneecaps were shattered, and I watched as he crumpled onto the jade steps. A pair of guardsmen rushed over to catch him under the arms and prop him up, while a third wrapped his arms around his waist and forcibly bent him over. An odd way to get him to kneel before me, perhaps, but it worked.

Now I want him to swallow the torn sleeve, a tasty morsel left for him by Duanwen. I had a big laugh over that. I walked down the steps and patted Duanwu on the shoulder. You are going to find that delicious, don't you think?

With considerable difficulty, Duanwu raised his head and looked up at me, the arrogance in his eyes replaced by bracing despair, as if drops of blood were about to ooze from the sockets. You are not the Xie Emperor, he said in what sounded like a dreamy voice. Duanwen is the true Emperor. The day Duanwen returns to the capital/Will mark the extinction of Duanbai.

Yes, that was one thing we all believed absolutely. My smile disappeared. I reached down, picked up the piece of cloth and, grabbing his chin with one hand, stuffed it into his mouth with the other. But I am the Emperor at this moment, I said, and I can do whatever I please. If I do not want to listen to you, then you may not speak.

I avenged myself on Duanwu for two hours, until I grew tired. By the time the guards let go of his arms, he had already lost the capacity to stand, and he crawled around the floor for a while, dragging his legs behind him, like logs. He suffered the dry heaves as he crawled up and grabbed the hem of my python robe. At that moment I noticed an innocent, unaffected smile on his face.

Did you see the words tattooed on Duanwen's forehead? Duanwu asked.

No, but people on the street did. Everyone knows of Duanwen's desire to usurp the throne.

Do you know who tattooed the words Xie Emperor on his forehead?

I was just about to ask you. Was it you? Or did he do it himself?

Neither. It was the spirit of the late Emperor. One night, the late Emperor's hand came to Duanwen in a dream, and in it he saw a glistening needle. When he awoke the next morning, the two words were there on his forehead.

That's rubbish. Duanwen was outrageously arrogant to

think he could come to the palace in such a provocative manner. If I had actually seen that accursed forehead, do you know what I would have done? I would have carved those words out little by little, until he woke from that dream of his.

No, they are a reappearance of the late Emperor's sacred spirit, and no one, not you and not Duanwen, can obscure those words, no one can erase them from Duanwen's forehead.

Duanwu released a bold and impassioned laugh, then let go of my python robe and rolled down the jade steps. Guards came up and dragged him out of Cultivation Hall, leaving a wavy trail of blood from his shattered knees that, from a distance, looked like a snake. Even after he was out of sight, I could still hear his wild laughter, and the sound made my hair stand on end.

The late, glorious Emperor, my father, after years of dwelling in the land of immortals, had now returned to cast his heavy shadow over me. Many versions of how he died had surfaced over the years: Some said he had died from ingesting an ersatz longevity pill; others said he had died in the bed of the bewitching concubine Dainiang; and there were even those who secretly advanced the theory that Madame Huangfu had murdered her own son by poisoning his wine. I, on the other hand, had confidence only in my own judgment, which was that anxiety, fear, and carnal desires formed a life-threatening rope that, at any time and at any place, was capable of carrying a person down into the underworld. I believed that the Imperial Father had died by his own hand, that he had grabbed that rope and held on tightly.

From that summer on, the Imperial Father's enormous,

hairy hand appeared to me many times during my morning audiences in Abundant Hearts Hall, floating amid the high-topped hats and broad waistbands of the assembled officials like a cloud. It cast a moldy, dark, larvae-covered rope, whistling in the air as it came at me. The hand appeared even more fre-quently in my dreams. I dreamed that it gently stroked the fore-head of one of his sons. It was his eldest son, Duanwen, and I saw that it held a needle, with which it tattooed the words Xie Emperor on Duanwen's forehead.

You are a pretender, my father, the late Emperor, said.

The true Emperor is Duanwen, my father, the late Emperor, said.

They told me that Duanwen had fled to Pinzhou by hiding in a coffin to elude capture by military patrols. It was the coffin of Governor Li An of Qing Prefecture, who had died unexpect-edly. The pallbearers had carried the coffin to Li An's hometown of Pinzhou for burial, and people said that Duanwen had lain under the body all the way to Pinzhou.

Pinzhou, of course, was Western Duke Zhaoyang's baili-wick. Zhaoyang had always been especially fond of Duanwen, and was one of the four feudal lords who had argued forcefully for his ascension to the throne. So it was a certainty that Duan-wen was now licking his wounds in the residence of the Western Duke, having found safe haven at last.

My mother, Madame Meng, and I were both very much on edge; she knew, with absolute clarity, that Duanwen's departure could only bring calamity to the palace, and after voicing her complaints and unhappiness, she sent an urgent summons for Prime Minister Feng Ao to engage in secret discussions. Either the fish dies, she said, or the net breaks. Under no circumstances can we allow Zhaoyang and Duanwen to wear the same pair of pants. Duanwen must die, of that there can be no doubt, even if the Western Duke himself perishes in the process.

Prime Minister Feng Ao rushed over to Hidden Pearl Hall. His views were poles apart from Madame Meng's, but strangely, as he and Madame Meng probed more and more deeply into the situation, somehow I became an observer only. I was reminded of the time years earlier, when Swallow and I had traveled around Pinzhou incognito, and how we had found ourselves in the midst of a boisterous crowd of people during the Twelve-Eight celebrations. I could picture the circus troupe, which had come up from the south, the exhausted but happy performers and their various equipment—clappers, teapots, pitch pots, plates, balancing logs, and puppets—surrounded by crowds. It was all so beautiful and richly fanciful. Then a tightrope took shape before my eyes: It looked like a rainbow that stretched from Hidden Pearl Hall all the way to Pinzhou. I saw a tightrope walker, all in white, arms sticking out straight and smiling as he took three steps forward, then one step backward. With consummate skill, he gracefully courted danger. He turned his head to acknowledge the cheers from below, and I saw that it was my parallel body and parallel soul.

Western Duke Zhaoyang had an army of twenty thousand

troops under the command of courageous generals, and any attack on Pinzhou by imperial forces might well be beaten back. The Western Duke is the most powerful of all the eight feudal lords, Prime Minister Feng Ao said. A single cold day cannot produce three feet of ice. When the late Emperor was alive, he saw Zhaoyang as a potential danger, but had no way of blunting the man's spear. These days, both the court and the commonality are under siege from within and from without, and no sooner was the Heavenly Sacrifice Society uprising quelled than a rebellion broke out in Tang Prefecture and the city of Fengzhou. Dealing with Pinzhou is something that can only be done on paper, I'm afraid. Feng Ao finished his comments with an ambiguous smile, and his crafty gaze swept past Madame Meng's face to land on the carved latticework of a window in Hidden Pearl Hall, where a buzzing fly was flitting around. Your Majesty and Your Ladyship both dislike flies, I assume, he said by way of analogy. Well, the best way to deal with a fly is not to hit it with a flyswatter, but to open the window and let it fly away.

And what if it doesn't want to fly away? Madame Meng said. What if it decides to fly right into your face?

Then you need the finest flyswatter there is, Feng Ao replied with a sigh. Unfortunately, I have never seen the finest flyswatter, so perhaps it is best to close one eye and let it fly around.

Our wise and resourceful Prime Minister Feng. Madame Meng was visibly upset, and the usual sad, melancholy look on her face was abruptly replaced by a menacing sneer. I saw her grab a glazed green teapot from a peach wood table by its handle and fling it at Feng Ao. Do you expect us to sit tight in the palace and wait to die? she demanded as she jumped up from her chair and pointed a finger at Feng Ao. I don't trust any shitty thing you cowardly little imps say. I'll show you what this old lady can do.

Humiliated, Feng Ao covered his scarlet face with his sleeve and did not say another word. I was shocked by Madame Meng's gutter language. It was the first time in years she had revealed her common origins in front of senior court officials, and I suspect that it was a sense of unavoidable dependency that had caused her to explode in nearly crazed anger, the way I often did.

I let Madame Meng's street talk and indecorous behavior pass, but Prime Minister Feng Ao, a man of enormous self-respect, apparently could not endure suffering humiliation at the hands of a woman who had come out of a harem at the rear of the palace. A few days after this incident, news that Feng Ao, prime minister to two imperial reigns, had resigned from office and returned to his hometown, spread throughout the capital.

The eighth lunar month. Imperial envoys who had called on the eight feudal lords returned in failure. They brought with them memorials to the throne that were virtually identical in content: Eastern Duke Dajun and Southwestern Duke Daqing pleaded illness as a reason for not journeying to the capital; Southern Duke Zhaoyou could not break free from a welter of administrative duties; while Northeastern Duke Dacheng was leading a military expedition out in the hinterlands, or so it was said, to collect long overdue taxes in several prefectures. I could tell that the similarity in the memorials from the feudal lords was not coincidental, and that this was a sign of extreme danger. It appeared that my desire to turn the might of the other feudal lords against Zhaoyang was naïve wishful thinking.

The only one to heed my summons to return to the palace was Northwestern Duke Dayu, who had no real power and ruled in name only. He had, by then, spent many years in idle residence in the capital, so besotted and lascivious that he was incapable of straightening himself out. Seeing him weave drunkenly into Abundant Hearts Hall, a telltale bit of redness on one cheek, I guessed that he had come straight from one of the singsong palaces.

Only one person had shown up, that one a drunken womanizer, so perhaps he was the one with whom I was fated to discuss affairs of state. Suppressing a wry smile, I ordered the servants to hand Dayu a sobering-up tablet, which he promptly crushed between his fingers and let fall to the floor, insisting that he was not drunk. He said he had never been more sober, and I watched as, with faltering steps, he sidled over to a chair and sat down, releasing an impertinent belch as he did so.

You may leave after you have rested there a while. The others did not come, and will not come. I stared at his disgustingly blotchy face, and knew there was no point in attempting to discuss anything with him. Belch a few more times and then you may leave.

Has Your Majesty heard of a girl they call Azure Bondmaid

at Oriole Pavilion? She is Persian, and beautiful beyond description. She makes music, she dances, and she has an astonishing capacity for alcohol. If Your Majesty is interested, I can escort her into the palace. Not to disappoint, Dayu belched twice. He then came up close to me, where I could smell the liquor on his breath and the feminine fragrances clinging to him. In a tone of voice that passed for sincere, he said, Even though every concubine in Your Majesty's harem is a bewitching beauty, none can hold a candle to Azure Bondmaid. Is it even remotely possible that Your Majesty has no desire to experience the Persian girl's amorous qualities?

I am willing to see for myself. Bring her to the palace tonight.

Dayu responded with a joyful laugh. I knew that he enjoyed arranging amorous liaisons within the palace confines, for that was yet another of his hobbies. The strange part was my attitude, for at a time when deteriorating circumstances had turned my mood ugly, I let myself get caught in Dayu's illicit sex trap.

And so, for the moment at least, Duanwen and Zhaoyang were forgotten. Since earliest times, countless monarchs have consoled themselves by holding beautiful women in their arms as they sat atop a rumbling volcano. So, I thought, I won't be the first to make that particular mistake. That night, Dayu quietly escorted Azure Bondmaid into a side room of Cultivation Hall. On her voluptuous body, silky smooth like white jade and nearly as translucent as fine crystal, she carried the smell of impending death. She wore golden bracelets and silver anklets that made beautiful music when she danced. The bold and sensually beautiful Persian woman performed the famed belly dance of her homeland. She leaped to the floor from a low table, danced from there up next to Northwestern Duke Dayu, and from there into my arms. She flirted openly with her blue-black eyes, while her passionate hands created heart-thumping movements. I watched wide-eyed and slack-jawed, sensing that the beautiful goddess of death was stroking me gently, starting at my head and my heart and working her way down slowly, like icy flowing water, and I heard a muted sorrowful sound emanate from somewhere deep in the canopy of heaven: The Xie Emperor is mired in debauchery and calamity will soon befall the Xie Empire.

I had received no news of Lady Hui after she'd left the palace, and every once in a while, when crossing the stone bridge over the Imperial Stream, I caught myself looking down. Everything was where it should be, except for the person: no girl in white running next to the water like a bird about to take wing in the midst of all that lush undergrowth beneath willow trees. I thought about the girl from Pinzhou and how she had by now entered the Buddhist realm, and as my thoughts turned to the deep affection, the abiding love, that she and I had shared, I felt utterly dejected.

Meanwhile, bickering and infighting among the concubines continued unabated. Those ignorant, shallow women never quite understood the dire predicament facing the Xie Empire; they were too caught up in issues of beauty, clothing, gossip about who might be pregnant, and, in the process, behaved in

an absurd, comical manner. Once I saw Lady Lan rub rice vinegar all over her face and then sit upright in the sun in front of
Orchid Splendor Hall. Her eyes watered nonstop from the vinegar, which turned them red, puffy, and infected, a sorry state of
affairs that lasted for several days. I later heard from a serving
girl that she'd tried this beauty secret, which was popular
among the masses, only to suffer unspeakably. The serving girl
who applied the vinegar to her face was rewarded by Lady Lan
with three angry slaps across the face.

Even more laughable was the secret potion that found its
way into the women's quarters. The potion, it was said, was a
magical elixir guaranteed to induce conception, and when I was
in Abundant Hearts Hall suffering through the impassioned
complaints of my ministers, my concubines were cooking up a
batch of the potion around a little clay stove. During that
period, no matter which of my women I visited, my nostrils
were assailed by a strange, rank odor. Finally, one night, I
learned from Lady Han that the potion had been passed around
from her hand. She was, I saw, enmeshed in a farce of her own
creation. In a mischievous, self-congratulatory voice, she said,
They are jealous of me, wouldn't you say? They have nearly
gone mad wanting to bear Your Majesty's heir, wouldn't you
say? Well, I dreamed up this potion. It cannot kill them, and I
have given them hope. And I don't have to watch them staring at
my body day in and day out, drooling with envy.

I took a look at the scribbled prescription, which listed ten
or more herbal ingredients, including goldthread rhizomes,
aniseed, divaricatum, fritillary, angelica, sinensis, frankincense,

forsythia, knotweed, honeysuckle, and cistanche. But the final ingredient was evidence of Lady Han's canny manipulation and vengeance against her fellow concubines: that ingredient was, simply, swine piss. Probably, it occurred to me, the source of the rank odor emerging from the medicinal pot.

Poor wretches. I felt like laughing, but couldn't, as I ripped the prescription to shreds and conjured up an image of them holding their noses while they swallowed the potion. I looked down at proud Lady Han's protruding belly, reached out and rubbed my hand over it, then said, You must be quite happy now.

Of course I am, Your Majesty. How could I not be? In two months you will have your prince and heir. Happiness showed on her face, which glowed pink. Proudly, she turned my question back on me. Is it possible that Your Majesty is not happy?

Only the heavens knew whether I was happy or not. I turned to avoid Lady Han's mawkishly passionate gaze and lowered my head to fiddle with the jade *ruyi*, the symbol of my power. Are you afraid? I asked her. Afraid of an unanticipated calamity? Afraid you will one day wind up like Lady Hui?

No. With the protection of Your Majesty and Madame Meng, they would not be so reckless as to attempt to harm me. If an unanticipated calamity were to occur, Your Majesty and Madame Meng would support me, wouldn't you? Lady Han walked up to sit on my lap, but her bloated body made her coquettishness appear clumsy and insipid, and at that moment I sensed the complex and fearful nature of the pressures bearing down on me. They were like boulders swept down in a mountain torrent to crash, one after the other, into my imperial crown.

The calamity will come from beyond the palace walls, and if even the Xie Palace is brought down by outside forces, everyone is in peril. No one will be able to come to anyone else's aid. That day is nearly upon us. I stood up and pushed Lady Han away, then rushed out of her quarters as if fleeing from danger. On my way out I was overcome by rage, and took my anger out on the beaded curtain of Moon-Watching Tower by kicking it wildly. Tell those slutty women, I shouted at Lady Han, who stood there terrified, to loosen their underwear and wait by the palace gate, for Duanwen is on his way. Duanwen will be here soon to impregnate you all.

More and more I avoided the beds of my harem of women, spending the nights alone in Cultivation Hall. Impotence had unexpectedly come upon me, a turn of events that was likely linked to my mood of dejection and despair. I had no desire to seek pharmaceutical help from the Imperial Physician, no matter how efficacious. I pretended to be unaware of anything the women did to find out what was wrong and rebuffed all their advances. I became a sort of martyr as I awaited the inevitable end of the empire.

During those, my final days as Emperor, my heart was like dead cinders. My loyal slave Swallow never left my side, standing in for all those beautiful women. I recall one stormy night when he and I were talking by candlelight, and we reminisced about the days in the palace when I was a naïve youngster. Naturally, most of the talk centered on that time in Pinzhou when we had ventured out to see the sights, and we realized how deeply the Twelve-Eight celebration had affected us both. As thunder rumbled through the night, Cultivation Hall shuddered under an assault by torrential rains; my bedside candles flickered and went out. I jumped down off the imperial bed as lightning shattered the darkness, intending to go close the window. But Swallow took my hand and held me back. Don't be afraid, Your Majesty, he said, it's only lightning, and lightning has never entered an emperor's quarters.

No, this lightning is aimed at me. Fearfully, I stared out at the trees swaying in the wind just beyond the window. I believe in nothing any longer, I said to Swallow, except that calamity is drawing ever nearer to the Xie court and that the final days of the Xie Empire will soon be upon us.

Swallow stood in the darkness, his body slightly bent, as always. I couldn't see his face, but I could hear his sobs, like those of a weeping woman, and I knew that he understood my fears and my sadness.

If I could somehow survive the calamity about to engulf me, if I could somehow leave the Xie Palace alive, Swallow, guess what I'd do out there.

You would go looking for the Pinzhou circus and become a tightrope walker.

Right, I would find that Pinzhou circus and become a tightrope walker.

If Your Majesty became a tightrope walker, your slave would become a log balancer.

I threw my arms around Swallow's shoulders and held him tight. On that inauspiciously stormy night, a eunuch of low birth and I held each other in our arms and cried in sorrowful anticipation of the end of eight years as Emperor even before it occurred.

TEN

ON THE TWENTY-SIXTH DAY of the seventh lunar month, the illustrious general Duanwen and Northwestern Duke Zhaoyang passed through the Pinzhou city gate at the head of a spirited army that stretched for several li, banners and flags so numerous they all but blotted out the sun, the sound of bugles blanketing the northwestern plain. This vast, indomitable army marched toward the Xie capital, reaching the city of Chizhou, some sixty li distant, on the third day.

The Battle of Chizhou, one of the most renowned military engagements in the annals of the Xie Empire, occurred on the morning of the third day. Ten thousand imperial troops deployed to defend the city engaged in hand-to-hand fighting with the rebel troops, scattering human flesh and blood among the fields outside the city and into the river. The battle raged for a day and a night, with heavy casualties on both sides. The next day, soldiers who had made it through the night threw the bodies of their dead comrades into the river so as to clear the battlefield for one final deadly clash. There were so many corpses they stopped up the river and formed a series of shifting, floating bridges, over which deserters made their escape before the final battle, carrying the stink of blood and gore on their bodies as they fled to their homes, abandoning their weapons by the roadside, swords and spears that were scavenged by local peasants and converted into farm tools and axles for their carts, in the process creating a diffuse and eternal memorial to this battle.

My favorite general, Ji Zhang, was knocked from his horse by Duanwen's Thunder Lance, signaling the beginning of the defeat of loyalist troops in the Battle of Chizhou. Duanwen lashed Ji Zhang's corpse under his horse and galloped with it up and down the riverbank, the mystical words tattooed on his forehead shining brightly under the noonday sun. Wherever his white horse passed, surviving loyalist soldiers looked up and saw those words—Xie Emperor—and were cowed into submission: Xie Emperor, Xie Emperor. They were like blades of grass bending down in the wake of Duanwen's whirlwind passage on his white steed as they knelt in abject surrender.

The territory more than sixty li from the Xie Palace was permeated with the aura of death, and from where I stood on one of the watchtowers, I looked off into the distance and could see a large covered wagon standing in front of Empress Peng's Misty Sunset Hall, and several black-clad Peng warriors busying themselves around the wagon. They had come on orders from

Shaomian, Emperor of Peng, to fetch the princess and take her home, safe from the upheavals of war. Dimly I heard the raspy sound of Lady Peng's crying. I didn't know who she was crying for, and maybe she simply realized that she would never be coming back, but for the very first time, I felt a bit of pity for this shrewish, arrogant, willful woman; for she was no different from any of my women in the palace, who had been unceremoniously awakened from their powder and rouge dreams into the reality that they were fated to accompany a feckless Emperor into a dark abyss from which there would be no return.

At midday I stood on the watchtower and leaned against a railing as I gazed off to the west, where, under a royal blue sky and above a panorama of gray urban rooftops, all I could see were a few isolated clouds of dust from roads where merchants were spurring their horses on; residents of the city, knowing that the cataclysm of war was bearing down on them, barricaded themselves behind the doors of their houses. There was nothing to see. I could not witness the final battle some fifty li in the distance and saw none of the cotton-clad residents of my city, who would normally be swarming over the streets and marketplaces like ants; my heart was empty. After a while, I heard the watchtower bell ring out, and I knew it was a death knell; but I was alone on the watchtower, and there was no wind. Who, then, had rung the bell? My attention was caught by the woven hemp rope attached to the clapper. It was swaying magically in the dead air. Then I spotted eight little white demons clinging to the rope. Inconceivably, they had come out in broad daylight, attaching themselves to the rope to sound a chilling death knell.

. . .

Somewhere, I forget where, I picked up the dusty copy of *The Analects*. It had been years since the monk Juekong had left, insisting on his way out of the palace that I finish reading the renowned, sagely text; but the thought hadn't crossed my mind since. I placed the heavy tome on my knees, yet saw nothing, and I knew there was no time left for me to finish reading *The Analects*.

Weeping and wailing was the dominant sound emerging from the women's quarters, as ashen-faced palace eunuchs and serving girls flitted in and out of the maze of buildings like headless houseflies. My mother, Madame Meng, appeared in the boudoirs of the palace ladies, followed by eunuchs carrying strips of white silk. There was no need to explain the ritual of presenting hanging silks to women by the Emperor, and a teary-eyed Madame Meng personally watched as Ladies Lan and Yun hanged themselves from the rafters. She then carried the last remaining silk over to Moon-Watching Terrace.

Lady Han, who was pregnant, rabidly resisted Madame Meng's gesture, refusing to die. People said she cut up the white silk with a pair of scissors. I cannot die before the prince is born, she pleaded, wrapping her arms around Madame Meng. Do not make me do it. If I must die, present me with another piece of white silk after the prince is born.

How can you be so foolish? Madame Meng said, choking on her tears. You are so very foolish. Do you honestly think that day will come? Even if I were to spare you, Duanwen would surely not, and he and his army will soon enter the city.

Do not make me do it, I am bearing the prince, I cannot die. By then Lady Han's voice had grown shrill as she ran barefoot out of Moon-Watching Terrace. Madame Meng watched as she fled toward the Cold Palace, hair flying in all directions, and guessed that she hoped to hide among the castoff concubines who lived there. Madame Meng stopped the eunuchs from going after her. Foolish child, she said with a sad smile, she will die a far more horrible death this way, for the women who live in the Cold Palace will tear her limb from limb.

The place where Lady Han chose to hide in her confusion did indeed become her final resting place. I learned later that when she burst into Dainiang's cell, she asked Dainiang to cover her with straw, which Dainiang did. Long shorn of her tongue, Dainiang was unable to speak, and since all ten of her fingers had been lopped off, covering Lady Han with straw was a slow, laborious process. Once that was done, Dainiang used her feet, about the only parts of her body that were still intact, to stomp madly on the straw-covered figure of Lady Han. Slowly but surely, Lady Han's cries for help died out, and the straw blanket that covered her turned red with sticky blood.

I did not go to the Cold Palace to see Lady Han's body, which was laid out on top of the straw, and so I never saw how my own flesh and blood had been stomped out of its womb by a crazed castoff concubine. I passed my last day in the Xie Palace in frozen silence. My copy of The Analects in hand, I waited for the calamity to fall, my heart as placid as a pool of water. From the direction of Bright Xie Gate came the thuds of a battering ram against the barricaded wooden gate. I looked up. Swallow was standing at the door, hands by his sides. In a voice devoid of passion, he reported, The Empress Dowager is dead, Lady Han is dead, Ladies Yun and Lan are dead.

What about me? Am I still alive?

Your Majesty will live on forever, Swallow said.

But it feels like I am dying, bit by bit, drop by drop, and it looks as if I will not have the time to finish *The Analects*.

Finally, the sound of hoofbeats spilled into the palace grounds through the shattered Bright Xie Gate like a flood tide. Pointing to my ear with the tip of a finger, I said, Hear that? It is the sound of the calamity that is about to befall the Xie Empire.

I met my half brother Duanwen once more under the palace walls after the passage of eight years. The look of loathing and the gloomy countenance were, by then, gone. Having emerged victorious in the protracted battle of Imperials, he now wore a tired yet meaningful smile. The moment we laid eyes on one another, wordlessly, all that had happened in the palace during those years flashed before my eyes, and there was no doubt that the indomitable, heroic figure who rode a white steed was the embodiment of the late Emperor.

You are the Xie Emperor, I said.

Duanwen laughed loudly and knowingly, and I recall that it was the only way I'd ever seen him laugh. Then he scrutinized me silently, a strange look of pity and affection in his eyes.

Nothing but rubbish, a walking corpse. Unfortunately for you, back then they forced the Black Panther Imperial Crown onto your head, which was then unfortunate for all citizens of Xie. Duanwen dismounted from his white steed and walked toward me. His black cape flapped behind him like wings and sent a sour smell into the air. The two dark characters tattooed on his forehead emitted a veiny light that nearly blinded me. Can you see what is written on my forehead? It is a sacred edict placed there by the spirit of the late Emperor. I had hoped you would be the first to see it before going quietly to your death. I never imagined that a beggar's cane for warding off dogs would change the nature of events. So now you are the last to see it. Who is the true Xie Emperor?

You are the Xie Emperor, I said.

I am the Xie Emperor, it is my true identity, as the entire world has informed you. Duanwen placed one hand on my shoulder and, with the other, made an astonishing gesture. He stroked my cheek, like an ordinary older brother, and, in a calm voice that indicated he had considered his words carefully, said, Climb over the palace wall and go make your way through the world as a commoner. That is the ideal punishment for a false Emperor. Go on, climb the wall, and take your loyal slave Swallow with you, Duanwen said, so you can begin your life as a commoner.

As I stood on Swallow's soft shoulders, I rose up like a torn and tattered flag and slowly began distancing myself from the place where I'd lived for twenty years. Grass growing wild atop the palace wall covered my hands, its sharp edges cutting into the skin. I looked out at the city beyond the palace wall, a seething sun suspended in the sky above the streets, the houses, the dense forest; it was a scorching, unfamiliar world. I saw a gray bird fly by overhead, its strange cry slicing through the sky.

Wang—Wang—Wang.*

*Literally "Die," but a homonym for "Ruler."

THREE

ELEVEN

I N THAT HOT, MUGGY SUMMER I began life as a commoner. The air hung heavily in the capital. People out on the street stank of sweat as they baked under the blazing sun, while dogs belonging to officials slept peacefully beneath the eaves of great houses, occasionally lifting their heads and showing their bright red tongues to passersby. Shops and public houses were all but deserted. Rebel soldiers in black and bearing the designation West passed in groups. I spotted Western Duke Zhaoyang on his date-red horse with its black mane and tail riding at the head of his fearsome army, led by five tiger generals under the protection of the Black Double-Ring banner. The eyes of the white-haired Western Duke flashed as he rode through the city with confidence and ease, the picture of a man who has achieved all that he desired. These people, as I knew, were Duanwen's allies in overthrowing the Xie throne. What I did not know was how they planned to carve up the imperial crown or how they planned to carve up my rich territory and enormous wealth.

By then, Swallow and I were dressed no differently than the common people around us. Perched on the back of a mule, I gazed up into the sun-bleached sky, then looked around at the devastation caused by war. Swallow, a money bag over his shoulder, walked ahead, leading the mule, so that I was following a heaven-sent slave of undying loyalty who was taking me to his home in Caishi County, for that was the only choice left for me.

We left the city through the northern gate, which, like all the city gates, was heavily guarded by Western soldiers who subjected everyone entering or leaving the city to a rigorous search and interrogation. I watched as Swallow wrapped two silver ingots in a piece of silk and slipped it under a sergeant's uniform. We passed through the gate without incident. No one recognized me, for who could have imagined that a young merchant wearing a conical bamboo hat to ward off the blistering sun's rays and riding a mule was in fact the deposed Xie Emperor? When we reached a hill five li north of the capital, I turned to look back at the Xie Palace. The majestic, imposing home of emperors was nothing but an empty yellow shell, blurry as a mirage, calling forth illusory memories.

The road to Caishi County would take us to the southeastern corner of the Xie Empire, the opposite direction to the one I had taken years earlier on my western expedition. The vast plains and dense population of the southeast were unfamiliar, alien even, to me. Everywhere I looked, the land was rich and fertile, and everywhere we stopped, we were surrounded by thatched huts lived in by men who farmed and women who weaved. Villages that spoked out in all directions were like a vast tapestry in yellows and greens that spread out ahead on my road to safety. A river, or a muddy road, or a few odd trees separated me from the lives of the common people, yet they were never far away. Farmers out threshing grain gazed indifferently and bleary-eyed at the travelers on the public road as they beat the ripe grain against rocks; peasant women in black cotton blouses squatted alongside riverbanks washing clothes, their hair casually tied with red ribbons. In groups of three or four, they crowded onto large boulders and, in a rapid-fire local dialect, tried to guess who we were and where we were headed. Every now and then, water from their wooden mallets would splash on my face while they were beating clothes.

He's a salt merchant, a woman said.

Nonsense, a salt merchant would be followed by a horse caravan carrying salt. I think he's a young scholar who has failed the civil service examination, a second woman said.

Who cares who he is, a third woman said. You wash your clothes and let him travel his road. Besides, you're all talking nonsense, she added. I think he's a sixth-rank official who's lost his job at court.

I was the recipient of more judgments than I could count as I traveled to safety, and after a while they no longer left a prickly feeling on my back. Sometimes I responded to their uncalled-for comments from across the river. I am your ruler, I would reply loudly. That always drew a hearty laugh from the peasant women out washing clothes, and maybe a shrill warning: Careful, or the government will separate you from that dog head of yours. I'd look at Swallow, and we'd both laugh as I slapped the mule on its flank to get it moving again. Only the heavens knew if the jocularity that passed between me and the peasant women was a sign of happiness or of sorrow.

Throughout the long journey, I constantly brushed up against the realities of a commoner's life: I was disgusted by the dirty, dusty road leading to Caishi County; disgusted by the fly-specked, maggot-ridden manure vats by the roadside; and particularly disgusted by the squalid, tumbledown inns where we were forced to spend our nights and endure the constant buzzing of mosquitoes and unpalatable food. On the bamboo mat at one roadside outpost, with my own eyes I saw three fleas pop out of the cracks and a big, fat, squeaking rat emerge from a hole in the wall. Fearlessly, they all leaped onto my body and stayed there, despite my frantic screams and flailing arms.

Nameless lumps that appeared on my arms and legs itched horribly. Every day Swallow applied a liquefied solution of plantain seeds to the affected areas. All part of Heaven's plan. Even the fleas are joining forces to humiliate me, I mocked myself, but not without a trace of bitterness. Swallow said nothing in reply as he carefully applied the balm to my skin with a piece of cloth, gently, skillfully. You know, you could humiliate me if you wanted to, I said as I grabbed his hand and fixed him with a hard stare. So why don't you? Still he said nothing. His eyes flashed momentarily, and then turned moist. I heard him heave a sigh. Things will be fine once we reach home. Once we reach home, Your Majesty will never again be humiliated by those filthy creatures.

Those nights spent in roadside inns have left indelible memories. A weary traveler snores sprawled atop a bamboo mat; outside the window moonlight bathes the open fields; summer insects chirp in the grass; frogs croak incessantly in the ditches and paddies. The eastern regions of the Xie Empire are unendurably hot. Even at midnight, rural inns made of mud and straw are like steamers inside, and as Swallow and I slept in the one bed, I heard him talking in his sleep, his words crisp and choppy: Go home, go home, buy land, build a house. There could be no doubt that returning to his ancestral home in Caishi County had long been Swallow's cherished hope, and that I was little more than a package he was taking home with him. All part of Heaven's diabolical plan. I began to feel that every person in that rural inn was luckier and happier than I. That, even though I had once been the supreme ruler of all the land.

We were waylaid thirty li east of Caishi County. As dusk was falling, Swallow led the mule up to a ditch to drink, while I rested on a roadside boulder. A deep, dark oak forest began on the far side of the ditch, and I was startled by a flock of crows that burst forth from amid the trees, followed by the sound of hoofbeats racing in my direction. Leaves parted to reveal five speedy horses and their masked riders. Like streaked lightning they bore down on Swallow and the gray mule, which was carrying saddlebags with our baggage.

Run, Your Majesty, they're highwaymen, Swallow cried out in alarm. He tugged on the mule's reins to get it over to the public road, but it was too late, the five highwaymen had him surrounded. The robbery took hardly any time at all. I watched as one of the highwaymen cut the saddlebags from the mule's back and flung them to one of his mounted comrades. Since their prey was a pair of travelers incapable of resisting, the process was the epitome of simplicity and ease from start to finish. One of the highwaymen walked up to Swallow and, following a curt interrogation, ripped open his shirt. I heard Swallow plead desperately with the man in a shrill voice, but without acknowledging his protests, the man cut the money bag from the sash around his waist. My mind was a blank as I remained frozen on the boulder, aware only that they had stolen everything I owned, stranding us penniless.

The five highwaymen whipped their horses and galloped into the forest, quickly vanishing in the evening mist. Swallow lay sprawled alongside the ditch without stirring for a long while until he was overcome by spasms. He was crying. The frightened mule had run off to deposit a puddle of soupy excrement. The animal sounded as if it were moaning. I went over and picked Swallow up off the ground; tears had turned the dirt on his face to mud. I could see that he was utterly forlorn.

How can I go home without any money? Without warning, he began slapping himself, over and over. Damn, I've ruined everything. I thought Your Majesty was still Your Majesty and I was still the Chief Eunuch. How could I have kept all the money on me?

What else could you have done with it? We have only one mule, we had only one set of saddlebags, and we have only the clothes on our backs. I turned and let my gaze sweep past the open plain around us. Prior to this, I had known only that there were bandits in the mountains and pirates on the open sea. I had never heard of murderous gangs of highwaymen who preyed on travelers on public roads that passed through open plains.

I knew that the Xie citizens were poor and often hungry, and that poverty can turn people into crazed murderers and bandits. So why hadn't I taken precautions against them? How could I have allowed everything I'd saved up my whole life to pass into the hands of bandits with my eyes wide open? Swallow buried his face in his hands and wept. He staggered over to where the mule was standing and stroked its now exposed back with both hands. There's nothing left, he said. What am I supposed to give my parents as a sign of filial respect? What am I supposed to use to buy a house and purchase land? How am I going to take care of Your Majesty?

To me, the trauma of the robbery was like adding frost to snow, no more than that. But to Swallow, it was an attack of mortal dimensions. Perplexed over how to console him, I spotted what I thought were the loose pages of a book under the mule's hooves, much of what remained soiled by the animal's excrement. It was the copy of *The Analects* I had hastily stuffed into the saddlebags just before leaving the Xie Palace. Apparently, the bandits had fished it out from among the treasures in the saddlebags and discarded it. It was now my sole surviving possession. Slowly I retrieved the pages of *The Analects*, knowing that it could serve no practical purpose in my life as a commoner, but that Heaven had made it known to me that I must carry it with me wherever my exile took me.

As dusk fell, the sky turned murky and dark clouds hung low over the squat, densely packed residences of Caishi County, promising a downpour any minute. A scant few peddlers were running up and down the streets with their baskets of fruits and vegetables swinging from carrying poles. Swallow had returned to his ancestral home, me with him, grimy from the journey and empty-handed. As we neared White Iron Market, some people recognized Swallow. A woman sitting in her doorway eating dinner stared at the mule's back and pointed her chopsticks at him. She muttered something I couldn't make out. What are they saying? I asked Swallow, who was spurring the mule on. Obviously embarrassed, he said, They want to know why the mule isn't carrying anything and why I'm bringing a pasty-faced dandy home with me. I don't think they've heard what happened in the capital.

Swallow's home was in fact a chaotic, cramped blacksmith shop. Several blacksmiths, stripped to the waist, were hard at work around a furnace, sweating furiously. The blast of hot air spewing from the shop made me recoil. Swallow went up to an older, hunchbacked blacksmith who was just then quenching a piece of hot metal and fell to his knees. The old blacksmith didn't know what to make of that. Obviously, he didn't recognize the son who had been away from home so long. What can I do for you, honored patron? He put down his tongs and tried to help Swallow to his feet. Are you in the market for a dagger or maybe a sword?

Father, it's me, Swallow. Your Swallow has come home. I could see he was on the verge of tears. All the blacksmiths stopped what they were doing and rushed up to him. Just then the curtain leading to the living quarters was flung back, and a woman whose blouse was partially unbuttoned for the sake of a nursing infant in her arms came charging out. Has Swallow come home? she asked joyously. Has my Swallow really come home?

You're not Swallow. My son is serving the Emperor in the Xie Palace. By now he's risen like a meteor, is feasting on delicacies, and dresses in silks and satins. The blacksmith sized up Swallow, who was still at his feet, and smiled contemptuously. Don't play tricks on me, honored patron, he said. How could someone in rags and covered with dirt be my son Swallow?

Father, I am Swallow, I truly am. If you don't believe me, look at the birthmark on my belly. Swallow lifted up his shirt, turned to his mother, and kowtowed. Mother, he said, you of all people should recognize this birthmark. I really am your son, Swallow.

No, lots of people have birthmarks on their bellies, the old blacksmith insisted stubbornly, shaking his head. I don't believe you're Swallow. If you were in the market for a weapon, I could help you. But I'll not let you pretend you're my son, so you'd better get out of here—now. The old blacksmith picked up a broadaxe, kicked Swallow, and roared, Get out of here and don't make me end that dog life of yours with this axe.

I was standing in a shop doorway watching this unexpected

drama unfold in the blacksmith shop across the way. Swallow, who was still on his knees, seemed to be choking on tears when he abruptly stood up, dropped his pants, and cried out hysterically, Then look at this, Father. You castrated me with a white-hot knife. You ought to recognize me now.

What followed was a tearful reunion, as the blacksmith and his wife embraced their son. All sounds of metalworking ceased in White Iron Market blacksmith shops, as men, some stripped to the waist, others wearing work aprons, quickly filled the doorway of Swallow's house to watch excitedly as father and son were reunited. With tears flowing freely, the blacksmith father looked up into the sky and sighed. Everyone said you would return home in fancy clothes, buy some land and build a house, repair the family grave sites and erect a temple. That you would come home empty-handed was the furthest thing from our mind. The old blacksmith dried his clouded eyes, red from weeping, and walked back over to his anvil, where he picked up the piece of steel he had been working on and said, Now what? A man in name only, unfit to work in the fields or in the shop, you'll be my burden from now on.

My presence went completely unnoticed. While I was standing outside the shop waiting for Swallow to summon me, the skies opened up and released a downpour, quickly turning the White Iron Market dirt road into a stinking, muddy mess. The rain bounced noisily off of newly tempered farm tools stacked out in the open; it also fell on my face and my shirt, sending me from one overhanging eave to the next. Bring an umbrella, I shouted to no one in particular out of habit. Hurry, bring an umbrella. They turned and stared at me with a mixture of curiosity and bafflement, probably thinking I was a madman. In the end, as always, it was Swallow who helped me cross the rain-drenched road. There were no umbrellas in his house, so he ran over with a large, black pot lid, which served as a hat as I entered the blacksmith shop.

The blacksmiths all called me Master Liu. Everyone in White Iron Market, including Swallow's mother and father, arrived at a variety of conjectures and theories regarding my background, but they followed Swallow's lead in calling me Master Liu. I doubt that any of them placed any credence in his story that I was hiding to get out of a marriage contract, but my true identity fell well beyond the bounds of these common citizens' capacity to speculate upon.

I awoke each morning to the clang of metal, not knowing for a brief moment where I was. Some of the time I dimly thought I saw the jade burners and latticework windows of Cultivation Hall, while at other times I had the feeling that I was rocking back and forth on the mule's back. Not until my eyes were wide open and I saw the farm tools, old and new, beside the straw mat did I realize that the rope of fate had led me to the humble abode of commoners. When I looked out the window, I could see Swallow on his haunches alongside the well washing clothes, my dirty, sweaty clothes in the wooden tub beside him. During our first few days at the blacksmith shop, his mother had washed my clothes, but then one day she flung them out of the tub with a curse. I, of course, was the real target, and her shrill voice made me feel like a man sitting on a bed of needles.

What am I doing here? I asked Swallow with a mixture of anger and dejection. Did you drag me all this way to your home just so a sharp-tongued old woman could hurl insults at me?

It's my fault for handing our money over to the bandits. If we hadn't lost all our valuables, my mother wouldn't be so rude to Your Majesty. At the mere mention of the robbery, Swallow hung his head and stomped his foot. He knew that was what had placed us in such awkward circumstances. His once fair, plump face had turned gaunt and yellow, thanks to all the tribulations on the road, and the vacant look of isolation in his eyes reminded me of the twelve-year-old castrato during his first days in the palace. Swallow tried to smooth things over. Your Majesty, he said, for my sake try to avoid arguing with my mother. She's busy cooking from morning to night while taking care of my brothers and sisters, and she was hoping that I would return from the palace dressed in finery. She never dreamed that I'd come home penniless and bring along an extra mouth to feed. She's resentful, and she has a right to be. He was holding a bowl of millet gruel; agonizing feelings were causing his face to twitch. All of a sudden I saw his hand shake and his body begin to rock back and forth. The bowl fell from his hand, spilling the gruel all over the floor. What in Heaven's name am I going to do? he exclaimed as he buried his face in his hands and wept. Doesn't anyone care that I am only a eunuch, an inept, utterly dependent castrato, neither male nor female? When Your Majesty sat on the throne, I served you loyally with all my heart, and after Your Majesty fell from grace, I stayed by your side. What in Heaven's name am I supposed to do now?

Swallow's words and actions caught me unprepared. There was no denying that I had always considered him to be a tool at my disposal. I'd nearly forgotten that his loyalty had become a habit, second nature, had nearly forgotten that he was just the sensitive son of a commoner. I scrutinized him with mixed sympathies and thought of the depth of my feelings for him, which had developed over the years and went beyond words. It was like a multicolored silk cord painted with the hues of mutual trust, mutual exploitation, mutual bonding, possibly even mutual adoration. It was a cord that had once bound an emperor and a eunuch together, and I realized at that moment that it was on the verge of snapping in two, which struck me like a knife to the heart.

This has been hard on you, Swallow. Like you, I am now a commoner with a bleak future. There's no need for you to stay by my side and look after me anymore. I guess it's time for me to begin living the life of a commoner, time to get back on the road.

On the road to where, Your Majesty?

To find the traveling circus and learn how to be a tightrope walker. Have you forgotten?

No, that was only a joke. How could a majestic Son of Heaven mix with a crowd of circus performers? If Your Majesty insists on leaving, then go to Tianzhou and throw in your lot with the Southern Duke, either that or travel to the Meng Palace and live under the protection of your mother's brother.

I have no desire to return to a cloistered existence among royals. It is Heaven's will that I shed my imperial gown and become a tightrope walker. That was determined the moment I left the palace walls behind me. I plan to live out my days with the traveling circus.

But we didn't see any traveling circuses on our way here. Those people never stay long in one place. How will you find them, Your Majesty?

I can head south, or maybe southwest. I shall go where fortune takes me, and sooner or later I will find them.

Since there appears to be no way I can convince Your Majesty to stay, I will go with you. Swallow sighed and walked inside to gather his belongings. We must pack for the trip and arrange for travel expenses. I think the best place to borrow money is the Meng Palace. Your uncle is the richest person in Caishi County.

I don't need it. I don't want to borrow anything at the Meng Palace, and I don't want you to go with me. Let me head out alone, let me live the life of a commoner. I'll survive.

Your Majesty, do you want me to remain here at home? Swallow looked at me with panic in his eyes. Are you saying that I failed in my service to you? Once again, he began to sob; he slumped to the ground and slapped a piece of sheet metal with both hands. How am I supposed to spend my life here? If I were a complete man who could marry and have children and earn my own livelihood, or if I had lots of money to buy land, build a house, and hire servants, I could stay here. But I have nothing. He crawled up to me on his knees and wrapped his arms around my legs. Raising his tear-streaked face, he said, Your Majesty, I don't want to hang around here and live off of my mother and father, and while I don't look forward to the trials of travel a second time, I would prefer to spend my life at Your Majesty's side, serving you and waiting for the day when Your Majesty rises to power again. But if that wish can never be fulfilled, Swallow can do nothing but die.

I saw him stumble out of the bedroom, cut through the busy, steamy blacksmith shop, and run out onto the street. Where are you going? his father shouted at his back. Straight to Hell? Without slowing down, Swallow replied, Wherever my feet take me.

I joined the workers in hot pursuit of Swallow, all the way to the river, where he dove into the water over the heads of some washerwomen, sending a geyser of water into the air and drawing excited shouts from the crowd on the riverbank. I watched him struggle and scream in the water and saw several of the blacksmiths jump in after him. They grabbed him like taking a fish and laid him out in one of the wooden washtubs, which they floated over to the bank.

Swallow's blacksmith father picked his nearly drowned son up and held him. Sorrow was written all over his aged, swarthy face. My poor child, did I do this to you? the old blacksmith murmured as he laid his son over his shoulder and pushed his way through the crowd of onlookers. What are you looking at? he demanded. Eager to have a look at his crotch? Then tear open his pants and have a look, there's nothing to see. The old blacksmith thumped Swallow on the back as he walked, until a stream of water spewed from his mouth, marking their wet passage. Well, the little eunuch has come back to life, one of the onlookers said. But that did not stop the old blacksmith from walking and thumping his son on the back. He stopped when he reached where I was standing and aimed a hostile glare at me. Who are you anyway? the old blacksmith said. My son isn't your woman, is he? The way you two are together disgusts me.

I didn't know what to think about Swallow's womanish suicide attempt. There were times when even I felt a measure of disgust over our relationship. It seemed perfectly reasonable in the context of the palace, but somehow out of place, contemptible even, in Caishi County's White Iron Market. I didn't know how to begin explaining matters to the old blacksmith, and all I could do was hope that Swallow didn't die. He lay on a rush mat, where his mother covered his privates with an infant's red stomacher. Once he'd emptied his lungs of the water he'd taken in, he regained consciousness, and the first thing he said was, I'm so wretched, so despicable. Just what am I anyway?

I took advantage of the confusion in the blacksmith shop to climb unnoticed out the rear window. I found myself in one of White Iron Market's dead-end lanes, which was cluttered with castoff firewood and rusty farm implements, amid which I spotted a sharp knife, either hidden there by someone or else a shop reject. I picked it up and stuck in into my belt before returning to the street out front, the sound of Swallow's groans as he cursed fate ringing in my ears. Just what am I anyway? Swallow was born to be pitied and despised, but compared to him, what was I? Maybe only the wise academicians at the Hanlin Academy could find adequate words to describe me.

I walked up and down the streets of Caishi County looking for a pawnshop, but a local fortune-teller informed me that the county didn't have one. He then asked me what valuable item I was seeking to pawn, and when I showed him the panther-shaped jade pendant I wore around my neck, his one good eye flashed. He grabbed my hand. Where did you come across such a rare and precious jade ornament, sir?

A family heirloom. My grandfather handed it down to my father, who bequeathed it to me. With extraordinary calmness, I asked him, Are you interested in buying it?

In most cases, exceptional panther-shaped jade comes from the Imperial court in the capital, which must mean that you stole this from the palace, am I right? Still holding my hand, he gauged my reaction with his one good eye.

Stole? I smiled, in spite of myself. I guess so. And since it's stolen, I can sell it cheaply. Are you interested?

How much do you want for it, sir?

Not much, enough to cover my traveling expenses.

Where are you going?

I don't know. I'll make that decision as I go. I'm looking for a traveling circus from down south. Have you seen anyone like that pass through here?

A traveling circus? Are you a circus performer? Letting go of my hand, the fortune-teller made a turn around me and said, You're no circus performer. How is it that from what I see I detect the air of an emperor?

In a previous life, perhaps. Can't you see how eager I am to sell this jade ornament for traveling expenses? I looked down at the fortune-teller's money box; there wasn't much in it, but I figured it would be enough for several days on the road. So I removed the Imperial Xie pendant I'd worn since childhood and placed it atop a pile of divination tallies. It can be yours, I said to the fortune-teller, for what you have in that box.

The man helped me dump the silver coins from his money box into my empty money bag, which I then draped over my shoulder. But as I was leaving the fortune-teller's stand, I was shaken by what I heard from behind. I know who you are, he said. You are the deposed Xie Emperor.

That stopped me. The fortune-teller's almost mystical powers of observation gave me a terrible fright. A popular local saying went, Since ancient times, Caishi has been the home of mystics. I was now a believer. The place was unique. Not only had the once powerful Empress Dowager, Madame Meng, come from its citizenry, not only was it the birthplace of favored officials and beautiful concubines, but it was also the home of this fortune-teller, who saw things with remarkable clarity. Glad tidings did not await me in this place, and I knew I must immediately leave this city where danger lurked.

The people of Caishi County were jittery that day; wagons and horses raced up and down the streets as a phalanx of soldiers in purple uniforms streamed out through the county yamen gate and quick-stepped toward an intersection in the northeast corner of the city. Instinctively, I took cover by the side of the road, fearful that I was the target of the military action, that the fortune-teller had placed me in mortal danger. But after the soldiers passed, I heard jubilant shouts of, To the estate of the Imperial Uncle, everyone. They're going to execute him and his whole family.

Relieved at last, I also felt somewhat ashamed. What, I was thinking, did an Emperor who depended upon the sale of a jade pendant to survive in a foreign land have to fear anyway? I clapped a woven bamboo hat on my head and walked out into the midday sun, when all of a sudden it dawned on me that the Imperial Uncle, a member of the Meng imperial family, who was about to be killed along with his entire family, was a blood relation to me. I knew that the Meng family, thanks to the protection of Madame Meng, had once held sway in Caishi County, and that many treasures from the Xie Palace had found their way into the Meng estate, secretly brought there in three boats by Madame Meng. After arriving in Caishi County, I had been ashamed to call on the Imperial Uncle, and now a strange and very dark stirring compelled me to fall in behind the purple-clad soldiers; I was curious to see what Duanwen and Zhaoyang, the Western Duke, had in store for officials who had served the former ruler.

The Meng estate gate was strongly fortified, and soldiers had set up blockades at both ends of the street. So I was forced to stand at one of the intersections, in front of a teahouse, along with a group of men who were enjoying their afternoon tea as they waited for the spectacle to unfold at the Meng estate, which was far off, but not so far that we couldn't hear the sad, shrill wails of women in the compound behind the high wall. One by one, individuals were led out through the crimson gate and past the green stone lions, cangues around their necks. Some of the teahouse customers crowded up to the door and applauded at each appearance. Now we get our revenge. From now on, Caishi County will know peace. The way that particular teahouse customer rejoiced in the suffering of others shocked me. Why do you hate the Imperial Uncle so? I asked him. He was as shocked by my question as I was by his comment. That's a strange question, sir. The Imperial Uncle is a bully who has consistently oppressed the people. Every winter, he requires some infants' brains to build his vital energy, so how could there be a soul in Caishi County who does not hate him? I was silent for a moment before asking, Will executing the Imperial Uncle and his family bring lasting peace to Caishi County? Who knows? he replied. Get rid of the tiger, and the wolf appears. But the common folk can't worry about everything, that's just how the world is. The rich want the poor to die of poverty, so the poor have no choice but to wish for the violent deaths of the rich.

What could I say to that? Unwilling to let these people sense my predicament, I turned to look at the sorry figures of the Meng family as they were led to the execution ground. This was the second time in my life I'd laid eyes on my uncle, Meng Degui; the first time had been at the grand ceremony when I was wed to the Lady Peng, and we had merely exchanged pleasantries. He had left hardly any impression on me, and I never dreamed that the next time I saw him would be under these circumstances. As sadness welled up inside me, I slipped over to the teahouse window to catch a glimpse of Meng Degui as he passed. The white glare of wrath mixed with despair flashed in his eyes; a pallid gloom suffused his face. But his corpulence reminded people of the infants' brains.

Someone in the crowd spat on Meng Degui, and in no time, spittle covered his face. I saw him struggle vainly to move his head within the confines of the cangue to see who was spitting on him, and I heard him release his final helpless yet violent shout, Don't throw stones on someone who has fallen down a well. I am not going to die. No one who spat will get away. Wait till I return. I'll suck your brains dry.

Slowly the commotion at the intersection died down and the teahouse customers began drifting back to their tables, where waiters filled their teapots with freshly boiled water. I remained standing at the window, pondering the ugly reality that had just come and gone. Such a pity, the vicissitudes of life. Some of that sentiment was directed at the members of the Meng family being herded toward the execution ground, while the remainder unquestionably revealed my own internal turmoil. As the pall of steam in the teahouse merged with the sweaty odors of its customers, a sow with a dead rat in its mouth passed quietly by my feet. A noisy, frenzied, roadside teahouse on a blistering summer afternoon with the stench of blood in the air, and I could not wait to get away from these customers and all their grievances. But suddenly, my legs would not move. I felt as if my body had turned to cotton and was floating amid the foul air of the teahouse; suspecting a malarial relapse, I sat down at the nearest squat table and prayed for the protection of the spirits of my

imperial ancestors, asking that I not fall ill in the midst of my
exile.

A dwarfish waiter carrying an oily teapot rushed up to my
table. I shook my head. Unlike the locals, I couldn't put any of
that oily, rich tea in my stomach on such a hot, steamy day. The
waiter laid his hand on my forehead. You're burning up, sir, he
said. But you're in luck. The hot tea of the Mei Family Teahouse
works wonders with convulsions and fevers. Three pots of Mei
Family Tea, and I guarantee you'll be as good as new. Not wanting to argue with this silver-tongued waiter, I nodded, for all I
really needed was rest. I reached into my money pouch for a
sliver of silver to pay for the tea. I had no experience in dealing
with ordinary people, but I knew that once I got back on the
road, people like this would swarm around me like pesky flies,
and I wondered how I'd be able to make my way through them.
It was going to be a problem, since I'd abandoned my loyal slave
Swallow back at the blacksmith shop.

Halfway between sleep and wakefulness, I rested my head
on the rectangular white wooden table. The men at other tables,
who were drinking tea on that scorching afternoon, disgusted
me. I wished they would stop exchanging obscene stories, stop
guffawing, stop mocking the unfortunate members of the Meng
family, in the most spiteful terms, and stop reeking of sweat and
dirty feet. But no one had to tell me that my days in the Xie
Palace were well behind me, and that I had to learn forbearance.
After a while, I dimly heard some out-of-towners relating the
startling news of an upheaval in the capital. They mentioned
Duanwen and Zhaoyang, and told of factional fighting in the

palace that had broken out in recent days. I was staggered by the news that Zhaoyang, the Western Duke, had been put to death.

The old don't stand a chance against the young, one of the newcomers said. Duanwen beheaded Zhaoyang in front of Abundant Hearts Hall on the very day he ascended the throne.

Duanwen had subjected himself to terrible hardships for many years. All for that Black Panther Imperial Crown. Now he'd burned his bridges behind him, since he could not share that crown with Zhaoyang, as I'd predicted. The way I see it, another customer said, Zhaoyang was a fool. A heroic life squandered in a single day. Even worse, he went to his death on the basis of an unjust accusation. I straightened up to look at the exultant or concerned expressions on the teahouse customers' faces, trying to gauge the accuracy of the news. Then I heard my name mentioned. What happened to the little emperor? the dwarfish waiter asked. What do you expect? the out-of-towner said. His head was separated from his body. Dead, that's what, tossed him into the Imperial Stream. The man stood up and dragged his hand across his neck to signal a decapitation.

Another shock. And in that instant my malarial symptoms vanished. I snatched my bag up off the floor and tore out of the Mei Family Teahouse. Running madly toward the distant gate of the county town, I could feel the blazing sun's rays hit the top of my head and shoot off in all directions. People out on the street scattered like panicky birds. The world no longer belonged to me; all it could give me was an overheated, vast and white path to exile.

. . .

In the seventh month, the five stars passed the meridian, and I was wearing a pair of worn straw sandals as I walked through the Xie hinterland, passing through the three prefectures of Bo, Yun, and Mo, and the four counties of Zhu, Lian, Xiang, and Ou, a wonderfully scenic area crisscrossed by rivers and mountain ranges covered with green trees. I'd chosen that particular path to exile just so I could take in scenery over which writers and poets had long rhapsodized. I spent my nights in roadside inns writing poetry by the light of soybean oil lanterns. The dozen or so sentimental poems were later collected into a booklet called *Night Scribblings of Sad Travels*. The desire to write poetry seemed laughable and unreasonable, even to me, but it helped me get through those nights on the road. Except for my dog-eared copy of *The Analects*, tear-filled poems were all I had.

Beside a clear pond in a Lian County village I looked down at the water and watched my face wrinkle, sway, and change shape. I could hardly believe the sunburned peasant's face and wayfarer's stern expression looking back at me. On the surface, at least, I'd become a commoner. I smiled; the face in the water appeared strange and unpleasant, so I leaned down closer and pulled a long, sad face. The face now looking back at me was unspeakably ugly. Instinctively, I shut my eyes and pulled back from the pond and its revealing mirror.

Everywhere I went, people asked, Where are you headed?

To Pinzhou, I'd say.

To trade in silk there?

No, I'm a trader, I'd say, but a trader in myself.

. . .

As I traveled the road to Pinzhou, from the plains in the east to the hills in the west, I often encountered peasants who had been driven off their farms by floods in the southwest or drought in the mountainous west and were blindly heading south, searching for a new life. Anxiety was written on their faces. Many of them—young and old, men and women—were huddled in small clearings in the woods, others bedded down inside local deity temples in the middle of wastelands. Children frantically grabbed sweet potatoes out of their mothers' hands, skeletal old men lay on the muddy ground, some snoring loudly, while others cursed their relatives. I saw a robust young man drop a bamboo basket to the ground; it was filled with soggy yellow raw cotton, which he spread out on the ground with a stick, probably to dry it in the hot sun.

What good is that going to do you on such a hot day? I asked him as I jumped over the spread-out cotton. The floods in Yu County must be bad.

The water washed everything away. A whole year's hard work, and this basket of cotton is all I have to show for it. He looked at me as he absentmindedly stirred the pile of cotton, then reached down, picked up a handful, and held it up to show me. It's good cotton, as you'll see when it's dry. He tried stuffing it into my hand. Why don't you buy it? he cried out. You can have it all for a single copper. No, all you have to do is give my children something to eat. I beg you, please buy this basket of cotton.

What good will this cotton do me? With a sad smile on my

face, I pushed his hand away. I'm running away too, just like you people.

But he stood there blocking my way. He looked over at some nearby trees, then confronted me with another request, this one utterly shocking: Would you like to buy a child, honored patron? I have five of them, he said, three boys and two girls. For eight coppers you can have your pick. Other people sell their children for nine coppers, but I only want eight.

No, I don't want any children. I'm trying to sell myself to a traveling circus, so how could I buy one of your children?

I clutched my money pouch tightly and took off down the road, not stopping to look back until I'd distanced myself from the man, and even then I could hear him cursing me in a loud, gruff voice. I'd never experienced anything like this before, encountering someone willing to sell one of his own sons or daughters for eight coppers. It seemed to me that the entire Xie Empire had gone mad. The look of deranged despair on the man's gaunt face became an indelible stain on my memory.

The little town of Xiang County had the reputation of being a center of sensual activities. Even during calamitous times, bright red lanterns and cheerful music surrounded the town's brothels and pleasure quarters. As I threaded my way through crowded, narrow cobblestone lanes, my nose was besieged by feminine perfumes carried on the hot air. Powdered and rouged women of ill repute displayed their wares in pleasure quarters lining the lanes, singing popular ditties or giggling, and all of them plying their seductive airs on each man who gawked his way past them. As dusk fell over Xiang County, an air of abandonment filled the lanes and byways; procurers waited at road crossings for rich clients, running back from time to time to shoo away beggars and refugees who were trying to sleep in the brothel doorways. You people always pick the best spots to bed down in for the night. There was a happy, almost whimsical quality to their voices. A man stepped down from a carriage, picked out a red lantern on which a name was written, and carried it inside one of the brothels. A moment later, the cheery voice of a madam drowned out the soft music inside: Precious Flower, you have a guest.

I knew that I ought not to have gone ten li out of my way to spend the night here, that coming to a low-class house of prostitution in Xiang County to recapture the amorous mystique of my life in the palace was both laughable and pitiable, not to mention highly inappropriate. But my feet tramped urgently down the cobblestone lanes as I eagerly sought a comforting bed that would not overly deplete my resources. Had I known ahead of time of the sad encounter that awaited me, I'd never have walked those ten extra li to spend the night in Xiang County. But I did, and as chance would have it, I walked into a place called The Charming Phoenix. This, as it turned out, was the greatest mockery and most severe punishment Heaven could have sent down to me.

I heard a door creak open behind me and saw a lovely, heavily made-up prostitute poke her head out and fix me with unblinking eyes. Do you recognize me, Your Majesty? Come inside and see if you can tell who I am. I remember letting out a shout and wanting to turn and run downstairs. But she had already grabbed my money pouch from me. Don't run away, Your Majesty, I'm not a ghost. Come, she said, let me serve you as I did in the Xie Palace. I don't want your money.

It was Lady Hui. It really was her, the girl whose soul was linked to mine, the one who had filled my dreams.

I noticed someone loitering down there, and I thought it was you, even if I couldn't believe my eyes. I knew that if you came upstairs, it had to be Your Majesty, and if you didn't, it would have just been a passerby who resembled Your Majesty. But you're here, and now I'm sure that the dream I had last night has come true. Your Majesty is right here, at The Charming Phoenix.

This cannot be happening, it must be a dream. I took Lady Hui, now a prostitute, in my arms and sobbed unashamedly. I wanted to speak, but overwhelming grief stuck in my throat, and no words came. Lady Hui dried my tears with a silk handkerchief, over and over. She wasn't crying, and the hint of a smile I saw at the corners of her mouth both puzzled and worried me.

I know why you're crying, Lady Hui said. Back then, Empress Peng drove me out of the Xie Palace, and now Duanwen has done the same to you. When I left the palace, I cried until I had no more tears to shed. Your Majesty now should do nothing to bring me sorrow anew.

I forced myself to stop crying and studied the woman in my arms through the mist of my tears. This magical chance encounter, this earthshaking coincidence still had me thinking that it was all a dream. I pulled back Lady Hui's light green jacket to reveal the little red mole I knew so well. At that moment, it occurred to me that something was amiss. You're supposed to be at the nunnery in Lianzhou living a life of Buddhist meditation. I raised her face with both hands, turned it to the left, and then to the right, and asked in a loud voice, Why are you in this place selling your body?

I slept seven nights at the nunnery, but on the eighth I couldn't sleep, and so I left.

Why did you leave? And why come to a place like this?

To await Your Majesty's favors once more. Without warning, Lady Hui flung my hands away, and a mocking smile appeared on her face. There are rumors that the Xie Emperor fled to the Peng Empire to raise an army and return to the palace. Who would have thought that a deposed Emperor would actually be in the mood to seek pleasure in a whorehouse? Lady Hui walked over to her dressing table, picked up a bronze mirror, and began powdering her face. I am a woman without shame, she said, but after observing people inside and outside the palace, men and women everywhere, I wonder who there is who knows the true meaning of shame?

My hands froze in midair; I felt mortally weakened. Being discredited by Lady Hui left me speechless, and in the midst of an unbearable silence, I heard someone stir outside the door, which opened a crack. A wooden basin of steaming water was slid into the room.

Ninth Sister, it's almost dark, time to choose a lantern. It must have been the madam.

Who was she talking to? I asked Lady Hui.

Me, she said as she stood up lazily and walked to the door. I am Ninth Sister. I watched as she stuck her head and shoulders out the door. Don't worry, she said, you can leave the blue lantern. He is going to stay the night.

When *The Secret History of the Xie Court* was published two years later, my chance encounter with Lady Hui at The Charming Phoenix was described in exaggerated, and largely false, terms. The passionate but star-crossed lovers in the book, the joys and sorrows of two people in love, sprang forth from the fertile imagination of an idle man of letters. The truth is, soon after our reunion, our feelings turned cold and enmity crept in; it was this enmity that would spur me to depart without even saying good-bye, to quietly leave Lady Hui, now a prostitute, and the fouled airs of The Charming Phoenix.

For all three of the nights I spent at The Charming Phoenix, the blue lantern, indicating an overnight guest, hung outside the door. Obviously, the madam was unaware of Lady Hui's background, and had no idea that I was the banished Emperor. She merely accepted the ample payments of gold, which precluded any thoughts that I might not be a wealthy client. I knew that Lady Hui had betrayed a cardinal rule of The Charming Phoenix in order to make it possible for me to shed the dust from my travels in such an expensive place.

I was the cause of the real problem. After making tender love, I thought I sensed traces of other men who had taken their pleasure from this full, fair-skinned body, and this drove me to distraction. Beyond that, Lady Hui made love differently than she had in the palace. I assumed that so many coarse, low-class whoremongers had fundamentally changed this genteel girl from Pinzhou, a once lovely girl who had run beside the Imperial Stream flapping her arms like a bird. Now she truly did seem like a bird, one that had flown off, never to return, leaving behind only a degraded body that was beginning to smell.

On the third night, I recall, when the moon was bright and clear, and the dense web of lanes and byways outside The Charming Phoenix had grown silent, Lady Hui slept peacefully in the fancy bed. I gently pulled a red silk handkerchief from her hand and, by the light of the summer moon over Xiang County, on that very piece of red silk, wrote the last poem I would ever present to my Lady Hui and left it beside her pillow. I cannot calculate how many sensual lines of poetry I have penned in my life, but these must surely have been the most sadly sentimental of all, and may well signal the last time I shall engage in such phrasemongering.

The Secret History of the Xie Court described me as an impotent, dethroned monarch who lived off of the earnings of a concubine-turned-prostitute. The truth of the matter is, I stayed in Xiang County only three days, and the further truth is that I continued on to Pinzhou in search of a traveling circus.

Along the way, a great many birds circled the skies overhead and feasted on rice that was not yet ripe in roadside paddies. One bold bullfinch even perched on my bedroll, on which it leisurely left white droppings. As a child I was particularly fond

of crickets, but in my adolescence and early adulthood, it was
these free-flying creatures that captured my fancy. I knew the
names of at least two dozen birds and could imitate their calls.
In my solitary travels I encountered many students and merchants traveling alone, like me, yet spoke to none of them.
When I felt especially lonely, I struck up a conversation with the
birds.

Wang—Wang. I shouted to birds flying overhead.

Wang—Wang—Wang. Their echoing response quickly covered mine.

My observations of the birds only reinforced my desire to
find the traveling circus. There was in me a sense of veneration
for birds and contempt for creatures that walked the earth. As I
saw it, there was no lifestyle closer to that of birds than the magical, consummate skill of tightrope walking: a rope stretches
taut high above the ground, a man rises in the air like a cloud
and, like a cloud, glides across the rope. To my way of thinking,
a tightrope walker was a bird of true freedom.

I detected a strange air settling over the villages near the city
of Pinzhou; here and there I spotted white funeral streamers,
and distant cacophonous horn toots and drumbeats from a
group of musicians spilled over onto the roadway. The road to
Pinzhou, which, in the past, had been heavily traveled, was now
all but deserted, and that deepened my concern. My first
thought was that war had broken out, perhaps a clash between
the newly crowned Emperor Duanwen and the heirs of
Zhaoyang, the Western Duke. But I could see Pinzhou off in the
distance, and there were no signs of battle; the city wall and

moat seemed tranquil and undisturbed in the dying rays of the sun. The dark blue roofs of houses, the earth-toned temples, and the nine-storied pagoda that rose into the clouds were, as always, mysteriously enshrouded in a steamy mist.

A young man holding a long bamboo pole was walking around several old trees. I saw him take aim on a bird's nest high up in one of the trees and leap like a madman, accompanied by a stream of filthy curses. The twigs and clumps of mud that made up the nest rained down. Then he knocked down another one, after which he picked something up from the ground with the pole, and I watched as shards of birds' eggs flew over onto the road; a bit farther off, a nearly featherless bird with a swollen abdomen lay dead on the road. Intrigued by the young man's strange actions, I hopped across the roadside ditch and approached him. He stopped what he was doing and stared at me, wide-eyed, clearly frightened. He lowered his pole and aimed it at me.

Don't come any closer. Do you have the plague? he demanded.

What do you mean, plague? I stood there dumbfounded and just looked at him. How could I have the plague? I said. I only wanted to ask what's happening around here. Why are you knocking down birds' nests? Don't you consider birds to be nature's most magnificent creatures?

I hate these birds, the young man said as he recommenced stirring up the remains of the nests with his pole, a mess of sun-dried flesh and the blackened intestines that had once belonged to a beast of some sort. They're the ones that brought the plague to Pinzhou, he said as he continued what he was doing. My mother said that the plague, which killed my father and my older brother, came to our village with these birds.

Now I understood: the disaster that had hit Pinzhou was, in fact, the plague. I stood transfixed in front of the young man for a long moment without saying a word, then turned to gaze off at distant Pinzhou, where I thought I saw outlines of countless white streamers. I now sensed that the mysterious enshrouding mist over the city walls and moat was in fact the pall of calamity.

A battle had raged in town for eleven days, between the forces of the new Xie Emperor and those of the sons of Western Duke Zhaoyang, I was told, and when it was over, the bodies of thousands of dead soldiers were simply stacked up in the streets. No one was willing to cart them off to the potter's field, so they quickly decomposed and began to stink in the hot sun. Finally, the young man threw down his pole, apparently no longer feeling he needed to be on guard against me, and, with considerable interest, related to me the history of the plague. The bodies decomposed and began to stink, he said, and the town's flies and rats made playgrounds out of their exposed bellies. These birds began flocking into town too, and once those creatures ate their fill, the plague broke out. You understand? That's how it started. Lots of people have died in Pinzhou, in our village too. My father died the day before yesterday, my brother followed him yesterday. My mother tells me that she and I will be dead within a few days.

Why didn't you leave when you had a chance? Run away from here?

We couldn't. The young man bit his lip as a tear slipped

down his face. My mother wouldn't let me, he said as his head sagged. She said we have to stay here to keep a vigil by the coffins and perform our filial duties, and that if we're all to die, we'll die as a family.

An indescribable shiver ran through my body as I took one last look at the filial young man before hurrying back onto the road. Where are you going, sir? he shouted from behind. I felt like telling him that I'd journeyed an entire summer in a single-minded quest to reach Pinzhou and find the traveling circus. I wanted to tell him everything, but it was such a strange, mysterious story that I didn't know where to begin. He was standing amid new grave mounds and several funeral streamers, watching me leave this area of devastation with envy in his eyes. What could I say to him? In the end, I framed my parting comments in the cries of a bird:

Wang—Wang—Wang.

This time Fate had stopped me from visiting Pinzhou, and now, after traveling all summer, I had nowhere to go. The entire trip had been the height of folly, utterly absurd, and as I stood at the crossroads, looking in all directions, trying to decide which way to let my feet take me now, a horse-drawn cart came madly up the road from Pinzhou. The driver, a young man stripped to the waist, was singing a strange impassioned song: Living is good, dying is fine, burial in the yellow earth is best of all. The cart bore down on me, and I saw a swarm of flies buzzing around the driver's head. Finally, he was close enough that I could see he was driving a cartload of corpses. On top of the pile of young warriors and civilians lay a five- or six-year-old child clutching a brass-handled dagger to its chest.

The driver cracked his whip in my direction and split the air with an indescribably mad laugh. Climb aboard, he said, everybody climb aboard. I'll drive you out to the potter's field. Instinctively, I moved to the side of the road to get out of the death cart's path. The driver, it seemed, was a madman who raised his head and laughed loudly as he sped past the crossroads. A moment later, he turned to look at me. Not ready to die? If not, head south. Head south, don't stick around here.

South. Maybe that was where I ought to be going. By now, my escape plans had fallen through, irretrievably. I stumbled off in the direction of Qingxi County, my mind wiped clean of just about everything, all but the rope beneath the feet of a tightrope walker. It undulated before my eyes, like an ocean wave, like an illusory brocade sash, like the last ocean lighthouse on a dark night.

TWELVE

IN FRONT OF QINGXI COUNTY'S PRECIOUS Light Twin Pagodas, I stumbled upon signs that the traveling circus had been there: a pile of monkey droppings and a ripped and torn red felt shoe commonly worn by acrobats. I asked the monk in charge of the pagoda where the circus had gone from here. His reply was indifferent and off target. They came, he said, then they left. I asked him which road they had taken. The eyes of the pure, he replied, see not where the uncouth go. Ask the people strolling through the marketplace.

So I turned and walked up to a fruit peddler, from whom I purchased some pears. Happily, he was as big a fan of southern circus acts as I was, and took delight in describing the magnificent performance several days earlier. He then pointed south with his steelyard and said, What a shame they only put on one

show here in Qingxi. They said they had to head south. The
man in charge said they were searching for a place to pitch
camp where peace and prosperity reigned. Where would a place
like that be? The fruit peddler sighed. The Feng Empire seems to
be the most peaceful these days, so that's probably where
they're headed. It's where lots of people are fleeing to. As long as
you've got money to bribe the border guards, you can leave this
godforsaken Xie territory.

I cut one of the pears in two with the knife I'd found, put
half in my mouth and threw the other half away. The peddler
stared at me in bewilderment. I suppose he thought this was an
unusual way to eat a pear. Why are you so fascinated by a traveling circus? he asked. The way you ate that pear calls to mind a
member of the royalty in the capital. I had no interest in clarify-
ing anything for the peddler's benefit, since I was just then rumi-
nating over how chasing a dream for so long was taking on the
characteristics of a tragedy. As if in repayment for my arduous
travels, the circus had already crossed into the Feng Empire, farther from me than ever.

I guess I'll go ahead anyway, I murmured.

What did you say, sir? the puzzled peddler asked.

Do you like tightrope walkers? I asked him. Remember this:
One day I will be the most famous tightrope walker in the
world.

I returned to the square in front of the Precious Light
Pagodas and sat on the stone steps until nightfall, after the Bud-
dhist faithful had come, burned their incense and prayed to the
Buddha, and gone home. The monks busied themselves sweep-

ing up the piles of ash on the ground around the incense burners and the remains of candles on offering tables. One of them came up to me. Come back tomorrow, he said. The first worshipper of the day enjoys the greatest blessings. I shook my head. I wanted to tell him that rites of worship had lost all meaning for me, that I was facing a dilemma, and that the incense of devotion could not save me. Only I could bring about my own salvation.

With the onset of night, silence and a pleasant coolness returned to Qingxi County. The air here was much cleaner than that in the Pinzhou area, even had a hint of peppermint and orchid, to which I attributed the fact that a lake and a mountain range north of Qingxi kept the plague spores in Pinzhou from finding their way in. Those days, something as simple as a peaceful, ordinary night did not come easily. I was beginning to feel very sleepy. Vaguely I heard the sound of the temple gate thud shut, followed by the dull rapping of hollow wooden blocks—the wooden fish—by the monks inside, and before long, I fell asleep leaning against the temple's earthen wall. Sometime before dawn I had the wispy feeling that someone had draped a thin shirt over me, but I was so exhausted I didn't even open my eyes.

My loyal slave Swallow appeared before me along with the light of early dawn, and the sight of him sitting in front of me, holding my feet to his chest, not moving, his hair moistened by dew, was like a dream. I couldn't believe that Swallow had caught up with me again and that he had spent the night with me under the stars in Qingxi County.

How did you find me?

By the smell of Your Majesty's body. No matter how far away you may be, I can find you by smell alone. Does Your Majesty find that strange? Does Your Majesty think I am some sort of dog?

How far have you traveled?

Exactly as far as Your Majesty has traveled.

Without another word, I took Swallow in my arms. His clothes were rags, and he was wet from head to toe. I held on to him as I would a lifesaving straw, once lost but now found. The talk that followed this moment of reunion included the tiniest details of the most trivial matters, and in the course of our conversation, I became keenly aware that the master-slave relationship between us had vanished into thin air. Now we were like a pair of brothers in difficult straits, our fates bound up together.

It was in one of Qingxi County's roadside inns, packed to the rafters with refugees heading south, that I made the most important, most glorious decision of my life. I told Swallow that my days of drifting from place to place were over, and that I was going to stay in Qingxi, where I would devote myself to the practice of tightrope walking, and that on the Buddhist holiday of Twelve-Eight, I would give a public performance. I said we could form our own circus troupe, and that one day I was assured of becoming the finest tightrope walker in the world.

How will you practice? After a long, thoughtful pause, Swallow trooped out all the practical considerations. Where will you find a teacher? Where will you get the equipment you need and an open space to practice?

I need none of those. I pushed open the window of the inn room and pointed to the pair of jujube trees in the yard. Do you see those two trees? I asked him. Heaven has bestowed them on me as the very best tightrope anchors. All you need to do is find a length of rope the thickness of my thumb, and tomorrow my practice will begin.

If Your Majesty is to become a tightrope walker, then I shall become a log balancer. Swallow flashed a knowing smile. I can find a log anywhere, he said. So while Your Majesty is walking high up on a tightrope, I'll be down on the ground log balancing.

It all began on a morning in late summer, just before the arrival of autumn. I recall that the sky over Qingxi that day was blue and very high, the sun big and bright red. As the first autumn breezes blew past, guests at the inn were still sound asleep when I climbed the jujube tree to the left and took my first step out onto the swaying rope stretched high up in the air. I promptly thudded to the ground. I climbed the jujube tree to the right, and once again thudded to the ground. As I repeated the process over and over, I could hear shouts deep inside me— fanatic, tragic—and saw Swallow, tears glistening on his gaunt, upturned face as he watched me. A sleepy-eyed little girl, most likely the innkeeper's daughter, stood in the doorway watching my earliest attempts at tightrope walking. At first she clapped her hands and giggled, but without warning, obviously frightened, she began to cry. She turned and ran inside. Daddy, she screamed tearfully, come look at this man. What's he doing out there?

· · ·

The other guests at the inn assumed that I was an idler, someone whose family had fallen into decline, and they viewed my determination to walk a tightrope, day in and day out, as eccentric. They sat by their windows and pointed at Swallow and me, making derisive comments or passing judgment. I was oblivious to all this, for I knew that I was high up on a suspended rope, while they were walking corpses doomed to spend eternity stuck to the mud of the mundane world. I knew that only up there could I confidently scorn all living things below me once again; only then was I the master of my own fate, filled with the knowledge that balancing on the rope allowed me to cling to life's ultimate dream.

I discovered that I was blessed with a remarkable, almost magical, sense of balance, and that I learned quickly without the aid of a teacher. One drizzly morning, I walked effortlessly from one end of the rope to the other, and I felt the world at my feet rise silently to greet me. As a gentle autumn rain wetted my face, sad thoughts opened up in my heart like wilted flowers coming back to life. I stood in the center of the suspended rope with tears coursing down my cheeks, body and soul rising and falling with the changing tension of the rope. How much freedom, how much joy this simple skill had brought me. It was a marvelous talent with which I had been born but had neglected in my passage through life. Finally I could fly like a bird. I stretched out my wings and watched as the rain thudded into them. I was flying, at last.

Watch me, all of you, watch me, I shouted at the people below, wild with joy. Watch me carefully. Who am I? I am not

Master Liu. I am not the Xie Emperor. I am an unrivaled tight-rope walker, I am a tightrope walker.

Emperor of the Tightrope—Emperor of the Tightrope—Emperor of the Tightrope. A wave of laughter swept over the guests at the inn; they thought they were too good to share in my joy and excitement. A shrill, mocking voice said, Don't encourage that oddball. He wants us to think he's crazy or dim-witted. I knew that those vulgar people could never understand or appreciate me, so I shouted out to Swallow, Can you see me, Swallow? Can you see that my dream has come true? Actually, he was standing at the base of one of the jujube trees looking up at me, one arm wrapped around a log, the other holding his balancing board. I can see, Your Majesty, I've been watching you all along. Swallow wore a heart-thumping look of compassion.

The innkeeper's daughter, who was called Jade Locket, had turned eight that year. Her hair was combed into tufts behind her ears, and she was wearing a red cotton blouse. She pranced around like a proud little fox, and when she sat alone in the doorway, she looked like a red lotus flower about to open its petals as it floated on the surface of a pond.

Whenever I began to sway back and forth on my tightrope, I could hear Jade Locket's thin shriek. She loved to sit on the stone steps and watch my every move. She was a bashful girl, and her laughter was reserved; but her shrieks were fearfully loud and shrill. The innkeeper's wife, a bony, hot-tempered woman, was, we were told, Jade Locket's stepmother, and every time one of Jade Locket's shrieks split the air, she would burst out from the kitchen or the outhouse, grab hold of one of Jade

Locket's tufts with one hand and slap her across the mouth with the other. You disgust me, you and your demonic shrieks. She would then drag the girl into the outhouse by her hair. I'm wasting my time trying to raise a lazy girl like you, she would say. You run off as soon as you hear the word work. What are you shouting about? If you're so fond of that low-class entertainment, I might as well sell you to a traveling circus.

From my vantage point high up in the air, I could see down into the yard, where Jade Locket looked like a pitiful little bird caught in a net, and whenever that little tear-streaked face sneaked up over the low outhouse wall, she would stare in obstinate fascination at the two guests as they practiced their acrobatic skills. I cannot say why, but she reminded me of Lady Hui when she first entered the palace, and little by little I grew extremely fond of the pitiful little girl.

Swallow was even fonder of her than I was. I saw tenderness and pain in his eyes when he looked at her. I'm afraid of women, but I like this little girl. Swallow's voice sounded sad, and I could not fathom what was on his mind. His thoughts were on someone other than me, a very childish eight-year-old girl. Nothing like this had ever happened before. I recalled a time in the palace when intimacy with children was in vogue, but that something like that could involve Swallow shocked me beyond description.

Jade Locket seemed drawn to Swallow in return, and began pestering him to teach her log balancing when no one was looking. Any time the innkeeper's wife let down her guard, even a little, Jade Locket clasped Swallow's hand and tried balancing on the log. The girl had a natural talent, was smart as a whip, and light as a feather, and I saw how easily the skill came to her; I also watched as a look of pure joy spread across her rosy cheeks and her mouth opened as if she wanted to shriek, as usual. But she didn't dare make a sound, and I watched as she grabbed the tassel on Swallow's sash and put it in her mouth. The way she moved atop the rolling log was both comical and charming, a scene of joy and pity at the same time.

I cannot recall what caused the incident that night, since all that autumn I went to bed early and got up at the crack of dawn to practice on the tightrope during the daylight hours. I had already blown out the candle and fallen asleep, so I had no way of knowing if Swallow tricked the girl into sharing the bed or if she had come on her own. But at about four in the morning, I was rudely awakened by some low and extremely coarse swearing. Standing at the foot of my bed were the innkeeper and his wife; she was cursing something awful in the Qingxi dialect, he was holding a lantern in his hand and shining it on the corner of our bed. There in the dim light of the lantern, off in the corner, lay little Jade Locket, curled up in the arms of Swallow, whose eyes were partially open, and whose pasty face was twisted into a look of pain and puzzlement. The little girl in his arms slept on.

Who do you think you are? the innkeeper shouted angrily, contemptuously. Guests who want a woman go whoring at local brothels, but you, how dare you take liberties with our Jade Locket? She's my daughter, barely eight years old! Who are you people anyway? Where did you low-class bastards come from?

I didn't touch her, Swallow said as he looked down at the sleeping girl. I am not a low-class bastard. I like her, that's all. She's sleeping peacefully, please don't frighten her with so much noise.

You don't like noise? the innkeeper said with a sneer. That's right, you don't like noise. He brushed aside Swallow's hand, which was reaching out to shield the girl from the lantern light, and glared at him. He then abruptly changed the subject. Tell me how you want to handle this scandalous affair. We can take it to a magistrate or we can settle it privately.

I didn't touch her, I honestly didn't. I just held her while she slept. Swallow was stammering.

Save your damned lies for the magistrate. Do you want me to call the other guests in here to witness your despicable actions? the innkeeper asked as he reached out and pulled the blanket off of the girl's body. She was naked. That startled Jade Locket awake. She rolled off of Swallow's legs onto the bed itself, where she cried out shrilly, I don't want you, I want my Uncle Swallow.

I saw Swallow reach out to her with both hands, but he quickly pulled them back and let them fall helplessly to his side. He turned to me, with a look of sadness and indignation, wanting me to come to his aid. Reluctantly, I believed that maybe he had done something he shouldn't have, for in the past I'd heard fantastic tales of powerful eunuchs who owned harems. Anything was possible.

How much do you want? I asked the crafty-looking innkeeper.

If you went to one of Qingxi's brothels to buy a virgin's first night, it would cost you ten taels of silver. The innkeeper's tone of voice had turned mild but salacious. He whispered something to his wife, who was still cursing, and they eventually settled on the amount. Since you've been guests for so long, he said, we'll settle for nine taels of silver. Buying my daughter's chastity for only nine taels of silver is a bargain.

It was cheap. I looked over at Swallow, who hung his head bashfully. Then a wicked but not cruel thought sprouted in my head. How much would it cost to buy your daughter, I said to the innkeeper, and take her along with us?

I doubt that the honorable patron can afford it, the surprised innkeeper said, quickly regaining his composure. With a feigned smile, he raised five fingers. Fifty taels of silver, he said, not one less. Raising her all these years hasn't been easy, and you're getting off cheap for only fifty taels.

All right, I'll get your fifty taels, I said as I walked over and picked up Jade Locket. I dried her tears and then handed her to Swallow. Hold her, I said to him. She's a member of our circus troupe. As of today, she is your log-balancing apprentice. I will also teach her tightrope walking. This poor child now has a proper future.

To raise the fifty taels, Swallow and I set out that night to travel the two hundred li to the Tianzhou estate of Zhaoyou, the Southern Duke. He was surprised and a bit alarmed by my showing up unannounced like that. He was a lily-livered vassal lord who lived in total seclusion, spending all his time studying a perpetual calendar and a horoscope. Even though our meeting

was secret, he was nonetheless accompanied by a pair of enig-
matic astrologers, and not until he was assured of my intentions
did he say, clearly relieved, So it's all about fifty taels of silver. I
thought you might be subjecting yourself to hardships—sleeping
on brushwood and tasting gall, as they say—to plan a return to
the throne. They tell me that the Dog Star and the White Tiger
Constellation are on a collision course, and that a meteor will
soon land on Tianzhou territory. Take the silver and leave
Tianzhou. They tell me that you are a Xie Emperor who has
sunk to the status of commoner. But the fire in you has not been
extinguished, so you must be that meteor, and that is why I must
ask you to take the silver and leave Tianzhou. Please leave and
take the calamity with you.

On the road from Tianzhou back to Qingxi, we did not
exchange a word. We could not completely discount Zhaoyou's
astrological prediction, but there was one reality about which we
had no doubts. At the Southern Duke's Tianzhou estate, I had
fallen from the status of a once-feared Emperor to that of a fearful star of calamity; I was burning as I tumbled downward, bringing new disasters to a disaster-ridden Xie Empire. I had escaped
the world, but the world could not escape me. If that proves to be
true, I shall sense a bitter regret till the end of my days.

On the road from Tianzhou back to Qingxi, our horse carried the silver. I felt no shame and had stopped sighing over having to beg for what I wanted. Across the length and breadth of
the southern grain fields, farmers had brought in the harvests,
and bleakness reigned as far as the eye could see beneath the
canopy of heaven. I saw countless haystacks, blackened by

heavy rainfalls; I saw several young shepherds driving their water buffaloes up over lonely grave mounds. All of a sudden, I understood that man's passage through this life is an arduous journey, much like one of those young shepherds tending his animals out in a field or amid grave mounds, all in order to find a pastureland hidden from others.

On the road from Tianzhou back to Qingxi, I understood, for the first time in my life, that a man represents a constellation. I did not know if I was ascending or descending, but for the first time ever I felt the fires all around me; they were burning faintly in the space between my thin clothes and the hardships of travel, aflame between my limbs and my tranquil heart.

The purchased girl rode a little gray mule away from the inn. She was wearing new purple clothes and bright red shoes, and was chewing loudly on a rice cake. Jade Locket's face was like a spring peach as she laughed and chattered excitedly along the way. Some people recognized her as the daughter of the family who ran the Mao Family Inn and called out, Where are you going, Jade Locket? She would look up proudly and say, To the capital. I'm going to the capital to be a log balancer.

It was the day before the Twelve-Eight festival. The weather was strangely clear and warm. We struck out ahead of schedule onto the path of circus performances, the three of us—me, Swallow, and the eight-year-old Qingxi girl Jade Locket. We'd settled on the capital as the place to where our wandering would take us, for no other reason than to fulfill a long-cherished wish of the little girl Jade Locket. We three rode on two mules, one big and one small, and carried a rope and two logs as we left Qingxi County and headed for the country's heartland as the beginning of what would later be known far and wide as the Tightrope Emperor Traveling Circus.

THIRTEEN

❧

T HE FIRST PUBLIC PERFORMANCE of the Tightrope
Emperor Traveling Circus took place on a street corner in
Xiang County. It was unexpectedly successful. I recall that while
I was hopping lightly on the rope, monkey fashion, high up in
the air, a mystical red cloud floated past and, it seemed to me,
slowly circled the sky over my head as if to keep watch over a
circus performer who had begun life as Emperor. The crowd
that had gathered on the street below to watch kept shouting its
approval, and some of the more charitable and grateful members
of the audience, moved by the performance, tossed copper coins
into an alms bowl on the ground. Someone standing on a
wooden tower was shouting, Walk! Hop! Turn a somersault!
Turn another one!

On that street of carnal desire, where the stench of money

hung in the air, the division of my life into two parts was completed. The part where I ruled as Emperor had fallen like a leaf at the base of a Xie Palace wall to silently rot away, while the part where I became a master performer was born on a tightrope stretched taut nine feet in the air. What did I hear up there on that rope? I heard the sobs and the pleasures of the north wind, I heard the delirious cheers of my former subjects from the ground below: Emperor of the tightrope, walk! Hop! Turn a somersault! And so I did: I walked, I hopped, I tumbled, and when I planted my feet, the rope did not move an inch. What did I see up there on the rope? I saw my real shadow swell quickly under the setting sun of Xiang County, I saw a beautiful white bird fly up from somewhere deep in my soul and haughtily soar through the vast sky above the heads of the people below.

I was the Emperor of the Tightrope.

I was a bird.

Xiang County was a place of pure pleasure, where worries were unknown. Even though the nation was experiencing a winter of natural disasters and unrelenting war, the citizens of Xiang County continued to seek pleasure in a wanton lifestyle. I saw a drunk fellow run madly after every woman who walked through the brothel district, and I saw several sons of rich men surround a dog, stick a firecracker with a long fuse up its bunghole, so that when it was lit, the dog became a crazed animal, running around and yelping madly, sending people scurrying off in fear. I could not understand how people could treat a harmless dog that way, could not understand where they found the fun in that.

A constant stream of traffic passed in front of The Charming Phoenix. Time and again I looked up at shadowy figures at the lamp-lit windows and could hear strains of music from reed pipes and flutes, intermingled with the delicate voices of women I did not know. I also heard the coarse, ribald laughter of the brothel clients. Lady Hui had left The Charming Phoenix by then. The name Fair Ninth Sister of Pinzhou had been removed from the lanterns in front, its place taken by Maiden Li of Tazhou and Maiden Zhang of Qi County. I was pacing the ground in front of the brothel when a waiter walked out and took down one of the lanterns. He gave me a long look and said, Maiden Li has a guest, but Maiden Zhang is available. Would the gentleman care to go upstairs and meet Maiden Zhang?

I am not a gentleman, I said, I am the Emperor of the Tightrope.

A performer? The waiter studied my attire. With a titter, he said, Nothing wrong with a performer, if he has the money. These days there's nothing more worthwhile than paying for a good time. You never know when you might slip and fall to your death, and you can't have any fun after you're dead.

I am the Emperor of the Tightrope, and I'll never fall to my death. Stopping the waiter from going back inside, I asked if he knew where Lady Hui had gone. I'll pay you to tell me where Ninth Sister has gone, I said.

Ninth Sister has gone to the capital, where she earns more

money than she ever could here. Everyone says she's making a killing with her body. Are you aware that she mastered secret skills known only in the palace in order to serve the Emperor? She had a falling out with the local madam and left, just like that. The waiter came up to whisper something in my ear, as if it had just occurred to him. Who are you, anyway? he asked wide-eyed. You've been hanging around here waiting for Ninth Sister, haven't you?

Not knowing how else to explain myself, I blurted out, I'm her man.

The look on the man's face underwent an immediate change, one of shock and curiosity, and he made a strange hissing sound. The lantern fell from his hand. Mother save me, he shouted. You are the dethroned, Emperor Duanbai! You've come to The Charming Phoenix looking for Fair Ninth Sister, a banished concubine, haven't you? Wildly happy, he grabbed my sleeve and pulled me into the brothel. Come upstairs and have a cup of tea, he said. It won't cost you a thing. Who saw to it that I was the first to spot your Imperial countenance?

My sleeve tore off in his hand. The waiter's discovery threw me into a panic. Having broken free of his violent yet enthusiastic grip, I turned and ran down the street. I could hear the man's shouts from The Charming Phoenix doorway: Come back, Emperor of Xie, I'll find your Ninth Sister for you, and I'll do it for nothing. I waved my arm, the torn sleeve flapping in the air, and returned his shout with one of my own—loud and insistent: No, don't try to find her, let her go. Don't ever try to find her.

That was my deepest wish. My beautiful, unlucky Lady Hui

had already been transformed into a free-flying white bird, and from now on we would soar in the same skies, our meetings limited to brief encounters and a wave of the hand; this would legitimize our worshipping of birds and our dreams of becoming one.

We had reached the same goal by different routes.

Now that the inside story of the Tightrope Emperor Traveling Circus had been revealed by the waiter from The Charming Phoenix, Xiang County was all a-roar. On the following day, our quarters in the Dong Family Ancestral Hall were surrounded by local residents; minor county officials, dressed in their finest, had formed two lines outside the ancestral hall and were waiting quietly for us to walk out. They were joined by the county magistrate, Du Bicheng.

The little girl, Jade Locket, was terrified by the boisterous crowd and cowered inside, refusing to come out. So Swallow had to carry her out in his arms. Still sleepy-eyed that morning, I found myself confronted by a crowd on its knees. Someone shouted Long Life, and I didn't know what to do. Magistrate Du, a man in his sixties, was kneeling at my feet, looking ashamed, curious, and frightened all at the same time. Please forgive this county official for having eyes without seeing. I failed to recognize the Imperial Dragon purple aura. County Magistrate Du banged his head on the flagstone step. I beg the Xie Emperor to honor my humble abode with his presence.

I am not the Xie Emperor. Haven't you heard that I've been degraded to commoner status?

The Xie Emperor may have been degraded in status, but will always be of imperial birth, and it is our great good luck that he has stopped off in our county. The people have lost no time in spreading the news, and crowds are swarming in from all directions. To ensure the Xie Emperor's safety, I beg him to take leave of this ancestral hall and come to our humble abode so as not to be harassed by the crowd.

There's no need for that. I hesitated for a moment before refusing the county magistrate's offer. Now I'm nothing but a tightrope performer, and who would want to harm a tightrope walker? I'm not afraid to be surrounded by a crowd of onlookers. For a performer, the bigger the audience, the better. With so many Xiang County residents to cheer me on, I fully expect to walk the tightrope better than I've ever done before.

The vacant lot was packed for that day's performance by the Tightrope Emperor Traveling Circus, which seemed almost supernaturally inspired. The log-balancing exhibition by Swallow and Jade Locket elicited one chorus of approving shouts after another, and when I performed the crane stance on the tightrope, the roar was like thunder and pounding rain. Shrieks of terror and wild shouts erupted from the crowd below: Xie Emperor, Xie Emperor, Emperor of the Tightrope, Emperor of the Tightrope. I knew that I had gained approval as a tightrope walker. It was magical, it was incredibly moving.

Something else echoed faintly in my ear: It came from the throat of a bullfinch that did not know what it meant to be tired; it flew to me from an eave on the roof of The Charming

Phoenix, and left in its wake a familiar cry that drowned out all human noises:

Wang—Wang—Wang.

Beginning in Xiang County, the reputation of my Tightrope Emperor Traveling Circus grew and grew, until we had become quite fashionable. *The Secret History of the Xie Court*, which was published some time later, recorded scenes of entire towns turning out to observe the consummate skills of the Tightrope Emperor Traveling Circus performers. The author, who wrote under the name of The Laughing Scholar of Dongyang, considered the success of the Tightrope Emperor Traveling Circus unexpected and quite accidental: "During the final years of the Xie, the empire was in decline, the people discontented, all occupations had fallen on hard times, and in the realm of entertainment only the Tightrope Emperor Traveling Circus prospered, not because its members possessed divine skills, but because the Emperor of the Tightrope was a dethroned monarch, drawing large crowds of the curious mainly to lay eyes upon the man, to see for themselves how a once powerful ruler had fallen to the status of circus performer. Who would not wish to witness one of history's truly rare events?"

Maybe, for all I know, *The Secret History of the Xie Court* got it right, but I am convinced that no one knows every detail about the second half of my life, that no one is able to really understand my personal story of that period, not The Laughing Scholar of Dongyang, nor anyone else.

. . .

By the spring of the following year, our troupe had expanded to include eighteen performers with twenty separate skills, an unparalleled development in the history of the Xie Empire. Everywhere we went we left behind a populace caught up in a frenzied joy like that which occurred at the end of a century. Men and women, the old and the young, flocked to our shows, wanting to see with their own eyes my transformation from Emperor to performer. I was fully aware that they shouted and jumped for joy because I introduced a bit of happiness into their lives of quiet desperation, breathed some life into cities and villages that were besieged by natural and man-made disasters and over which threatening dark clouds hung. What I found unbearable was how the people paid homage to their dethroned monarch. When faced with the fervent cheers for their onetime Emperor, I invariably thought back to the hoaxes the Black Panther Imperial Crown had perpetrated on the people, who were blinded by imperial sleights of hand. The onetime wearer of that crown had extricated himself from that ancient trap, but the masses of people who lived outside the palace walls continued to be defrauded by the Black Panther Imperial Crown, perennial victims of a gigantic hoax. I had saved myself, but could never succeed in pointing the way for these simple and dim-witted people.

The end of the road for our itinerant troupe appeared to be drawing near. We would soon reach the capital, which the girl Jade Locket had never stopped thinking about, day or night. Our last stop before entering the capital was at Youzhou, where we performed for three days, almost as if delaying, intentionally or not, the date of our return to the capital. For those three days, Jade Locket was like a top spinning around me without letup. She peppered me with questions about the city and the palace, but I refused to answer. You'll know everything when we get there, was all I said. So she ran to Swallow, and I watched as he silently sat her on his knees, a troubled look in his eyes.

Why are you both so unhappy? Jade Locket asked. Are you afraid to go into the capital?

Yes, Swallow said.

What are you afraid of? That the people won't come out to watch us?

No, we're afraid of the unknown.

With that, Swallow voiced my apprehensions. As the day of our return to the capital drew ever closer, I suffered insomnia in the large Youzhou inn where we were staying. I wondered what it would feel like when the ministers and officials who had served me in the past, as well as members of the imperial family, saw me walk a tightrope. I also wondered if my sworn enemy Duanwen had, by now, forgotten all about me. If I were to choose the grassy area behind the palace to put on a show, would an assassin's arrow streak toward me from some hidden corner in a palace watchtower, thus bringing an end to the bizarre life of one who had turned his back on his origins? I confess that I was petrified of the unknowns awaiting us, but at the same time I knew there was no way the Tightrope Emperor Traveling Circus could avoid ending its run in the capital. It would comprise the ritualistic end to our travels.

On the morning of the fourth day, the Tightrope Emperor Traveling Circus pulled up stakes. Eighteen performers, along with their equipment and props, piled into three horse-drawn wagons and left Youzhou for the trip north. It was a hazy morning; the fields in the Xie heartland were a soft, gentle green and exuded the fresh perfume of newly plowed earth. Farmers hoeing their fields caught a glimpse of this performing troupe that soon thereafter would not be seen again. Where are you headed? they asked. There's fighting up north, where do you plan to go?

To perform in the capital, Jade Locket shouted in response from her wagon.

That spring, the Peng Empire launched large-scale attacks on Xie territory. More than thirty battles erupted on both sides of the border that snaked between the two empires. Performers in the Tightrope Emperor Traveling Circus, who had grown used to frequent fighting, made their way north, occupying their time by talking about a variety of lost acts and skills; sometimes the talk would be considerably bawdier, centering on illicit love affairs, cases of incest, or bedroom activity, often punctuated by the uncomprehending laughter of the eight-year-old Jade Locket. When they were on the road from one venue to the next, the performers were always happy; they seemed totally oblivious to the almost inevitable annihilation of the Xie Empire.

The troupe arrived in the capital on the predawn morning of

the seventh day of the third lunar month. According to *The Secret History of the Xie Court*, it was the very day the vast armies of Peng arrived at the gates of the Xie capital, a coincidence that was, by all appearances, exquisitely scripted by the forces of history.

FOURTEEN

D AWN WAS BREAKING WHEN OUR WAGONS reached the southern gate of the city. A familiar, rancid smell of decay from the moat, whose waters carried rotten food and dead animals, rose to greet us. The drawbridge was lowered, the gate opened, and if we had looked up, we'd have seen that the Black Panther banner of Xie had been torn down from atop the watchtower flagpole, replaced by the blue Double-Eagle flag of the Peng Empire. Several soldiers stood in the gateway without moving, staring straight ahead, not even seeing this early morning troupe of performers. Our driver turned to us and said, They're probably drunk beyond caring. They regularly drink themselves half to death, which saves us from having to pay to enter the city.

After traveling all night on bumpy roads, all eighteen performers were too worn out to even notice the strange scene at the gate. When the wagons pulled up in front of the Southgate Inn, some members of the troupe went up and knocked at the door, which was locked. A quaking voice on the other side of the door said, We're closed, go away. Who ever heard of a guest-house that won't take guests? someone asked. We've been on the road all night, so open up and let us in to get some sleep. The door opened a crack to reveal the puffy, petrified face of the inn-keeper. You couldn't have come at a worse time, he said. Don't you know that the Peng Empire has occupied the city? Didn't you see all the Peng soldiers on the watchtowers?

The members of the troupe in the wagons suddenly came to life and turned to look. As the man had said, the top of the southern wall was black with people. The scene frightened the little girl Jade Locket out of her wits and she let loose one of her shrieks. Swallow quickly clapped his hand over her mouth. Don't scream, he said. Don't make a sound, don't anybody make a sound. Those crazy Peng soldiers kill for the fun of it.

The drawbridge creaked back up over the moat and then the Peng soldiers closed the gate. At that moment I sensed that the gate to this dying city had been opened expressly for me and the Tightrope Emperor Traveling Circus. Was this a sign that my long journey was about to come to an end?

Did you see that? I said to Swallow, who was sitting quietly in one of the wagons. They closed the gate. Do you know why the Peng soldiers let us into the city?

Swallow had his hands over Jade Locket's eyes so she wouldn't see anything that would make her scream. They probably saw that we were a traveling circus and want us to put on a show for them.

No, it is an invitation of death. As I looked up at the blue Double-Eagle flag flapping in the morning breeze above the watchtower, the melancholy face of the mad retainer Sun Xin, who had been dead all those years, flashed before my eyes. Calamity has already befallen the Xie Empire. Ever since I was a child, I said, people have predicted this calamity. I was terrified by the thought. But now that it has actually arrived, my heart is empty. Here, feel my hands, listen to my heartbeat. I'm as calm as still water. I'm just a common citizen, a tightrope walker. I'm not facing the ignominy of a ruler who lost his empire. For me it's now a simple decision of life or death, so I have nothing to fear.

We had entered the wolf's den like ignorant sheep, and there was no way out. Once the city gate was closed, Peng soldiers emerged from hiding places in the wall and houses and from behind trees and began converging on the city streets. I saw a young mounted officer draw his sword as he galloped down the street shouting, The Emperor of Peng has given the order: Kill, kill, kill, kill.

I personally witnessed the bloodbath that followed, as Peng soldiers slaughtered Xie citizens from early morning till that afternoon. Blue-clad Peng soldiers in white helmets rode from one end of the city to the other, their drawn swords turned dark red from the blood of their victims, their helmets spattered with drops of blood and strangely shaped pieces of flesh. The cries and moans of dying people were heard all over town. Survivors of the capital massacre ran in all directions, their clothing askew, hair falling over their eyes, and I saw some young men begin climbing the wall in the midst of the chaos, only to fall victim to crack archers and crash to the ground like rocks in an avalanche, trailing forlorn cries behind them.

Just before a squad of mounted Peng soldiers launched an attack on the Southgate Inn, my mind went blank. Thinking back, now I recall how Swallow pushed me into a haystack. They won't find you in here, he said as he tried to hide the little girl Jade Locket in the haystack with me. But it was too small for two people and started falling apart when she tried to squeeze in beside me. Don't be afraid, Jade Locket, I'll hide you in this big vat. Those were the last words I ever heard from Swallow, who quickly gathered up the hay to cover me and left me in darkness.

In my dark hiding place I faintly heard the clomping of horses' hooves in the inn's courtyard. There was a series of pitiful screams by members of my circus troupe, who had hidden in trees and chicken coops and under the wagons. I heard a thud, followed by loud cracks, as someone smashed the big vat with something heavy. I listened to the death throes of at least fifteen members of my troupe. It was obvious from the sounds they made as they died that this savagery had taken these once happy, innocent itinerant performers by surprise.

I was unable to pick Swallow's death screams out from all the others, so maybe he fell victim to the guesthouse butchery without making a sound. Since the first day he entered the palace as a youngster he had always been timid and shy. When it was all over, I found the smashed vat amid the corpses strewn around the courtyard. Swallow was seated on the base, his head lying on the broken edge. The three wounds in his chest had the startling appearance of red blossoms. I lifted up his head so that even in death he could look up into the sky, now that the savagery had ended. The spring sunlight sliced through the blood-sour pall and was reflected off the still wet tears on his cheeks. As before, there wasn't the hint of a beard on his face, and what remained were the unique features of the fetching young eunuch back in the palace.

The water in the broken vat, which had turned pink from the human blood, came up to Swallow's knees. After dragging him out of the vat, I saw there was another corpse inside, the eight-year-old girl Jade Locket; her purple jacket had been stained red, and she was still hugging her little rolling log. I saw no wounds anywhere on Jade Locket, but there was no life in her body, which had turned cold. I assumed that Swallow had shielded the hapless girl from the swords of the Peng marauders, but had inadvertently crushed her in the process.

After all that time, I had finally lost the loyal slave that Heaven had sent down to me. Swallow died for me, thus realizing the solemn vow he had taken that day in Cultivation Hall. I recall how, when he entered the Xie Palace at the age of twelve, he had said, I will die for you, Your Majesty. Now, years later, he was dead, and he'd taken with him the only gift I'd ever given him, the pure and innocent little Jade Locket, whose freedom I'd purchased for fifty taels of silver. It was, I believed, his last expression of love, yet another Heaven-ordained act.

The killing stopped. The Peng soldiers put away their swords and congregated in the town square to begin drinking. A squad of mounted soldiers in black were rounding up the survivors of the massacre and herding them in the direction of the Xie Palace. I squeezed in among the ranks of survivors and walked with them toward the palace; we were frequently forced to step over corpses lying in our path. Some of the survivors were weeping, others were quietly cursing the Peng Emperor Shaomian. As I walked, I kept looking down at the palms of my hands. They were stamped with patches of dried blood, which I could not remove no matter how hard I tried. I knew it was the blood of strong individuals, not just Swallow and Jade Locket, but the castoff concubine Dainiang, Chief of Staff Yang Song, the Imperial Physician Yang Dong, and all the warriors who had died defending the empire's borders. I knew that the dried blood of these people had formed patterns across my palms. So why had the invitation to death excluded me and me alone? Me, a man whose profound transgressions and unpardonable sins could never be forgiven? A sense of sadness gripped my heart, and I joined the chorus of weeping and moaning commoners who had survived the massacre. My very first tears as a common citizen.

The people being herded along suddenly discovered that the sky ahead had turned red.

The Peng invaders had torched the Xie Palace. By the time

the surviving residents of the capital had been herded up to the Bright Xie Gate, flames from the massive wooden archway were already licking the sky. Peng soldiers lined the people up in formation so they could watch the palace burn. An elderly officer with a strong voice loudly proclaimed victory in the Xie-Peng war: People of Xie, take a good look at this conflagration, watch how your filthy, obscene imperial palace becomes a pile of rubble and see how your pitifully weak little empire has been brought into the supreme fold of the Peng Empire!

Dimly I heard sad, forlorn human sounds from somewhere inside, but the raging flames quickly turned the palace into a sea of fire, and the roar of buildings and imperial halls going up in flames, plus the crashing sounds of collapsing structures, drowned out the cries and pleadings of those inside. The sea of fire engulfed the place where I was born and grew up, the place in which the first half of my life was stored, a place of pleasure and of sin; I covered my nose with my sleeve to keep from breathing the suffocating smoke and reached back for some memories before the place no longer existed. I recalled the splendor of the renowned eight major and sixteen minor halls; I recalled the beautiful women who lived in the six compounds, the main building and the imperial bed; I recalled all the precious objects and exotic flora; I recalled every court intrigue while I was on the throne. But for some reason, my thoughts froze, and the scene before me was the Great Xie Palace going up in flames, fire and more fire. And the sound filling my ears was the plaintive cry of the bullfinch:

Wang—Wang—Wang.

. . .

The sixth Xie Emperor, Duanwen, died in flames that consumed the palace. His corpse, burned beyond recognition, was later found in the ashes of Abundant Hearts Hall. They knew it was him by the Black Panther Imperial Crown, which, because it was made of gold and precious gems, survived the fire; it was fixed tightly on the seared skull.

Sixth Xie Emperor Duanwen had sat on the throne for only seven months, the shortest reign in the history of the line, and the unluckiest. Historians would later analyze the historical phenomena and determine that Duanwen was the Emperor who lost the empire; it was his aloof arrogance, his imperiousness, and his unshakable self-confidence that consigned a beautiful empire to history's graveyard.

I had become an outsider. On countless occasions that spring I dreamed of Duanwen, with whom I shared a father, but not a mother. My lifelong bitter enemy. In my dreams we drank together in even-tempered calmness. Our struggle over the Black Panther Imperial Crown finally ended, we realized that we had both been tricked and made fools of by the forces of history.

The ninth day of the third lunar month, the powerful armies of the Peng Empire swept across Xie territory, which was like a sky with scattered clouds. They easily scooped up seventeen prefectures and eighty counties. The legendary successor of the Peng line, Shaomian, stood atop the ruins of the Xie Palace, faced the tearful hordes of survivors of the defeated Xie Empire and personally raised the blue Double-Eagle flag of the Peng

Empire, then announced solemnly: The corrupt and impotent Xie Empire is no more. From this day forward, all the land has fallen under the sway of the sacred and invincible blue Double-Eagle flag.

According to *The Secret History of the Xie Court*, nearly a hundred members of the imperial family and their offspring were slaughtered in the calamitous third lunar month; the sole survivor was the fifth Xie Emperor, Duanbai, who had fallen to the degraded status of commoner, and who made his living as an itinerant tightrope walker.

In *The Secret History of the Xie Court*, The Laughing Scholar of Dongyang recorded in detail how the residents of the Xie court met their deaths. He wrote:

Emperor Duanwen: Died in the conflagration of the Xie Palace.

Pingqin Prince Duanwu: Died in the conflagration of the Xie Palace.

Fengqin Prince Duanxuan: Beheaded. Body and head were scattered in the Fengqin Prince's Palace and the local market-place.

Shouqin Prince Duanming: Thrown down the Shouqin Palace well after being dismembered.

Eastern Duke Dajun: Died in battle with Peng soldiers. Descendants later erected an Eastern Duke Crypt.

Southern Duke Zhaoyou: Murdered by his personal bodyguard after surrendering to the Peng.

Northwestern Duke Dayu: After being drawn and quartered, his body parts were dumped into alcohol vats by local residents.

Southwestern Duke Daqing: Killed by a stray arrow while fleeing to the Yao Empire.

Northeastern Duke Dacheng: Committed suicide by swallowing gold.

Prime Minister Zou Ling: Killed personally by the Emperor of Peng while on his knees swearing allegiance to his new lord. Later generations cursed and spat on his name.

Former Prime Minister Feng Ao: Committed suicide by smashing his head against a wall. Considered a valiant minister of the Xie Empire.

Empress Dowager Madame Meng: Committed suicide by hanging.

Head of the Military Board Qiu Wen: Following the destruction of Xie, he spit up blood and died of anger and dejection.

Head of the Ceremonial Rites Board Yan Ziqing: He and his entire family swallowed poison to atone for national humiliation.

Commandant of the Palace Army Hai Zhong: Found dead in marketplace, cause unknown.

FIFTEEN

M Y XIE EMPIRE, MY BEAUTIFUL, DISASTER-PLAGUED Xie Empire, now no longer exists, after naturally and helplessly being incorporated into the map of the Peng Empire, thus fulfilling the dire predictions of many sages.

The name of the Xie capital was changed by the Peng rulers to Changzhou. During that spring, a vast array of large-scale construction projects by Peng craftsmen got under way. Strange-looking round buildings, archways, and temples were built. The thud of hammers and the choppy, hard-to-understand slangy speech of the Peng people resounded all over the capital; it was as if they were intent on erasing every trace of the Xie Empire. The residents of Changzhou, who had changed into the bulky, elaborate dress of the Peng, picked

their way through the ruins of their city, worn out and dispir-
ited. For them, a life of turbulence and instability would continue; whether the place was called Xie City or Changzhou, it
had always been their home, and in it they must live on, however prudently.

I wandered amid the ruins of the Xie Palace like an
orphaned spirit. The site had become a sort of Paradise for
Changzhou's residents, who scoured the rubble for valuable
objects. Many people spent the entire day picking through shattered eaves and shards of roof tiles, hoping to find a precious
item overlooked by the Peng people. There would be loud quar-
rels over a silver teapot with a crane-beak spout, usually ending
in fisticuffs, with others jumping into the fray. When the stout
victor left the ruins with his teapot, women and children would
pelt his fleeing figure with broken bricks. I once saw a boy
squatting on the ground, surrounded by broken tiles, studiously
digging in the ground for something. I went over and stood
behind him to quietly watch his labors. He looked to be about
twelve or thirteen. His face was filthy. Guardedly, he kept an eye
on me, probably out of a fear that I would simply take whatever
he found. So he quickly slipped off his jacket and used it to
cover up the things that lay at his feet.

I don't want anything of yours, not a thing, I said as I
reached out and rubbed his head, wanting him to believe in my
innocence by seeing my clean hands. What have you found after
all this digging?

A cricket jar, he said as he took a gilded clay jar out from under the seat of his pants. When he held it up, I saw at once that it was one of my favorite boyhood toys.

What else?

Birdcages. He lifted his shirt to show me a pair of fancy birdcages. They had been flattened by something heavy, but those too I recognized as cages that had once hung in Cultivation Hall. As a matter of fact, I recalled that on the day I left Cultivation Hall for the last time, the cages contained a pair of red-billed songbirds with green feathers.

I smiled and helped the boy cover up the cages. These were playthings for the fifth Emperor of Xie when he was a boy. They may be priceless, they may be worthless. You should keep them.

Who are you? the boy asked suspiciously as he looked up at me. Why aren't you digging?

I'm the one who hid those things, I replied softly.

Seventeen circus performers were buried in the Changzhou potter's field, where grain had once been stored. All the Xie grain had been plundered during the war, leaving behind only some straw mats and an array of straw roofs. It is where I personally buried Swallow, Jade Locket, and the other performers. I do not know who first used the grain storage site as a graveyard, but like the local burial parties I observed that day, I loaded a cart with the bodies of the seventeen itinerant circus performers, waited until the sun went down, and then sneaked the corpse-laden cart past the Peng sentries and followed others to the grain storage site. New grave mounds dotted the landscape, and I had to find available space where I could, so that the performers who had died so violently would have a little space of their own. Many of the other burial parties had completed their sad task and were sitting near the grave sites, drinking strong liquor to take the edge off the spring night chill. A curious fellow came over and asked, Why are you burying so many people? Were they family?

No, they were members of the Tightrope Emperor Traveling Circus. It was I who led them straight to the tips of Peng swords, and it is I who must put them safely into the ground.

You don't have to bury them deep, the man said after a brief silence. The rainy season is on its way and the bodies will decompose quickly. Besides, burying people like this is really only a way to soothe the conscience of the living. Burying people is hard work, and you need to know the tricks of the trade. Give me something to buy a bit of spirits and I'll help you bury them. Half an hour is all I'll need.

No, I'll do it myself. I refused the grave digger's offer.

There was no moon that night, I recall, throwing the grain storage site into inky darkness. Burial parties that had secretly finished their work left, until I was alone. I wasn't afraid at all. I worked as the sky got bluer and brighter and my hands turned bloody from wielding the spade—no more pain, just numbness. When the cock crowed three times I buried Swallow and Jade Locket together in the deepest and largest hole. By the time the last spadeful of wet earth covered Swallow's ashen face and the balancing log in Jade Locket's hands, I collapsed like a toppled wall, totally spent. Now there was no one to reproach me with a sad look in his eyes. The final break with my past had occurred. With Swallow dead, I was truly a man alone.

I lay down on Swallow and Jade Locket's grave and slept, a straw mat for a blanket and the grave mound as my pillow. I'd once said that I would never become one of those porters or beggars who lie down and sleep wherever they happen to find themselves, but that night I was just too tired, too sleepy. The first light of dawn found me sleeping more soundly than ever before in my life. The sky and I were so close that I had one dream after another about birds. All the birds I dreamed about were white as virgin snow, the sky I dreamed about was transparent and boundless. All the birds I dreamed about flew into that sky.

I dreamed of a new world.

Once again my backpack was empty, except for a dog-eared copy of *The Analects* and a coiled tightrope. The way I saw it, those two unrelated objects perfectly summarized my life.

In all the years that had passed, I'd had no interest in studying *The Analects*, but I kept the sagely tome along with my rope anyway. My feeling was, so long as I didn't end my life with this rope around my neck, I'd find the time one day to finish reading *The Analects*. I was reminded of the monk Juekong, who had left me so many years earlier. His simple yet extraordinary maxims, the superior intelligence and unqualified tolerance that showed on his face, all flashed into view like a divine light.

. . .

The last time I saw Lady Hui was in the Changzhou secondhand market. I could not tell if the way she looked—ratty hair, grimy face, muttering constantly—was a sign of madness or not. Sitting amid bustling crowds of bobbing heads, she looked like she truly belonged there. I saw she was trying to sell some colorful, finely trimmed slips of paper with poems written on them to passersby. Take a look, these are fine goods. She spoke rapidly in a hoarse voice. Authentic love poems written by the fifth Emperor of Xie, fine goods, buy them and you won't be sorry.

I watched her from a distance, not wanting to disturb her opportunity to earn a living. I was hoping that someone would stop and barter with her, but the passersby in that secondhand market appeared interested only in pots and pans and other kitchen tools, and no one so much as looked at the poetry slips in Lady Hui's hand. Maybe the people she accosted assumed that what she was offering was nothing but worthless junk.

It was a warm spring afternoon, and as I stood off in the distance watching Lady Hui on that street in the secondhand market, I caught the faint aroma of peppermint and orchids mixed with the fragrance of ink. The odors seemed to float above the street on that afternoon in the secondhand market, and I knew they could not have come from the poetry slips she was trying to sell, nor from the body of that ill-fated prostitute. No, they were the final memory of my early life.

That was also the last day I spent in the city where I was

born. On the next day, the Peng rulers opened up to the outside world after sealing the city off for many days, and I joined a line of salt porters on my way out of the city of sadness.

It was the nineteenth day of the third lunar month in the Yihai year.

SIXTEEN

I HAVE SPENT THE SECOND HALF of my life in Bitter Bamboo Monastery on Bitter Bamboo Mountain. It is a long way from the Peng Empire and a long way from the Xie Empire. In previous centuries it was a densely forested mountain under no one's control. Word had it that this otherworldly idyll was discovered by my childhood mentor, the monk Juekong, who arrived here eight years before me. He had planted a rice paddy and started a vegetable garden, and had spent three years slowly building the so-called Bitter Bamboo Monastery.

By the time I made my roundabout way to Bitter Bamboo Mountain, the monk Juekong had already passed from this realm. He left for me an empty mountain monastery and a weed-infested vegetable garden; four words were written on a wooden sign in the center of the vegetable garden—Emperor of the Patch—which would be praised by future generations. In the weeds I found a wolf-hair writing brush with which I had practiced calligraphy as a boy in the palace. All this indicated that Juekong had waited for me those eight years.

Later on, the Peng Empire went to war with the Chen and Di Empires. Their defeated soldiers made their way to Bitter Bamboo Mountain with their wives and children, and Bitter Bamboo Mountain gradually became a site of bustling activity. Late arrivals built houses at the foot of the mountain, and on clear mornings they have a clear view of Bitter Bamboo Monastery midway up the mountain. They can also see a strange monk standing on a rope strung between two pine trees, either walking rapidly or striking a one-legged crane pose.

That person is me. I walk my tightrope during the day and study at night. Over a period of many, many nights I have been studying *The Analects*. Sometimes I feel that this sagely book holds all the wisdom of the world; sometimes I don't get anything at all out of it.